the
RED '65

A novel of deceit and power play

Published by Brolga Publishing Pty Ltd
ABN 46 063 962 443
PO Box 12544
A'Beckett St
Melbourne, VIC, 8006
Australia

email: markzocchi@brolgapublishing.com.au

Copyright © 2016 Grant Peake

National Library of Australia
Cataloguing-in-Publication entry

Peake, Grant, author
The Red '65
ISBN: 9781925367157 (paperback)
Subjects: Missing persons--Investigation--Fiction.
A823.4

Printed in Australia
Cover design by Wanissa Somsuphangsri
Typesetting by Tara Wyllie

BE PUBLISHED

Publish through a successful publisher. National distribution, Macmillan & International distribution to the United Kingdom, North America. Sales Representation to South East Asia
Email: markzocchi@brolgapublishing.com.au

the RED '65

A novel of deceit and power play

GRANT PEAKE

RED '65

A novel of dream and power play

GRANT PEAKE

In memory of my loving and wonderful parents,
Lloyd and Ida, who taught me so much in life.

CHAPTER *one*

Detective Chief Inspector Martin Hislop (known to everyone as Marty) leaned back in his chair and studied the file he had just been given by his boss, Superintendent Charlie Solomon.

Hislop was 49 years old and had been in the police force since he was 19. An officer of great talent and skill, he had an uncanny way of extracting information from people with lightning dexterity, but lacked tact. Treading on toes to get to the bottom of things did not cross Hislop's overactive mind. Prone to be impatient and to act upon impulse, had landed Marty in deep water with his superiors over the years. This did not phase Marty at all – he had just told them to shove it, more or less! Yet for all his faults, he was a good cop who got the job done with a minimum amount of fuss.

Marty Hislop was single, but that didn't mean he hadn't had some fun with the ladies in his life. Once he had approached his late forties, the ladies had began to drop their interest in Marty, favouring the younger guys. They couldn't come to terms with the fact that Marty was dedicated to his job in the force, and they took second place.

What on earth does Charlie think I can do with a case that is over 40 years old? Marty thought. Nearing 50 years old, the case file contained only a few skimpy pages of handwritten notes.

He flipped through the flimsy, ageing pages and noticed a black and white photo of a young child at the back of the file. He turned the photograph over and saw on the back had been written in black ink: Billy Parsons on set Universal Studios Apr 9, '65 aged 7 years.

Marty gave a deep sigh and looked carefully at the photo of this kid who had just vanished without a trace, on July 21, 1965. He vaguely recalled his mother mentioning this Billy Parsons whenever she was reminding Marty and his kid sister, Marion, about the importance of never going anywhere with a stranger they did not know. "Beware, stranger danger." was the catch phrase uttered from his mother's lips. "Look what happened to young Billy Parsons, 7 years old, and vanished. Probably accepted a lift from a stranger and then disappeared into thin air!" said his mother with warning to her offspring.

When Charlie Solomon had knocked on Marty's door and asked him did he want to take on a real nutcracker of a case, Marty had no idea this would be it. Marty had thought it would be drug running along the southern California coast or a gun dealer found murdered or a brothel madam found bashed to death in her expensive Mercedes, or just anything else, but not this.

"Hell," Marty had exclaimed to Charlie Solomon, "you want me to investigate a cold case from years ago, when we have crime and corruption on our doorstep. Surely you must be crazy Charlie, what's the big idea anyway? This case is nearing 50 years ago, it should be put to bed, man!"

Superintendent Charlie Solomon, a man of large frame and a good listener, lifted his body in the chair facing Marty, and cleared his throat. Charlie had been with the Los Angeles Police Department for over 45 years, knew the system well, and its faults, but still felt he had something to give the service before retiring. A native of the deep south, from Alabama, he started cotton picking at 6 years of age. His hard working parents had slaved hard to get their only son into college, and eventually taken on by the police force. Charlie had known discrimination because of racial colour and had been overlooked for promotion in the early years, but he was diligent and determined to change the old order of things. The inspiring speech in '68 by his great mentor, Martin Luther King Jr., had spurred Charlie on to succeed and not give in to tyranny, deceit and most of all, racial prejudice. Today, he was at the pinnacle of his career and enjoyed the role, even if his loving wife, Thelma, was wanting Charlie to hang up his boots and call it a day.

Being accustomed to Marty's brisk manner, Charlie ignored the distinct reluctance from Marty's remark and knew he had to convince this man to investigate this poor kid's disappearance. Charlie responded to Marty's outburst with the usual tilting of his large egg shaped head to one side, smiling coyly, and said in his big booming, yet rich voice, "Yeah sure Marty, I agree, the case is out of date and what good can we do now to find this kid? If this kid is still alive, he would be in his fifties now. His face was splashed around the newspapers and on TV for days on end." With that, Charlie gave a short chuckle and continued on, "Plus the fact that the witnesses have most likely kicked the bucket or shifted camp. It's a tough one, I appreciate, but we must attempt to unravel some of the mystery surrounding this poor little mites fate, Marty".

Marty was silent but the expression on his rugged face was not one of joy by any means.

Charlie looked long at Marty before continuing on with his droll voice, "You see man, this case has been brought to our attention by the Australian Federal Police in Canberra, Australia. They have been approached by relatives of this Billy Parsons, to seek any answers regarding his disappearance. The parents are still alive, though apparently in their eighties and not in good health. Mr Parsons has terminal cancer and Mrs Parsons has the early signs of dementia. They have another son and two daughters, who with the assistance of their local Member of Parliament, contacted the Australian Federal Police recently to find out anything they could to put their parents mind at rest; especially Mr Parsons, who would like to know what happened to their young son. I know it is a huge long shot man, but we can only do our best. You are the ideal man for the task, Marty. No one else has the expertise and ability to get this case by the teeth and pull out the crap and deal with the facts. I will give you, and La Paz, all the support you will need. My only stipulation is that no one, and I repeat, no one, is to know what you are both doing. If word leaks out that we are reopening a cold case from over 40 friggen years ago, the press will have a field day, and I will have the hierarchy come down on me like a ton of bricks. We won't know what struck us man, so discretion is the key element to this. The case is sensitive, to say the least, regarding a very young child. Basically, we are just revisiting the case and checking witness statements. Anything you can dig up that will shed any light on the kid's disappearance, will be a bonus to solve this case. I know what your thinking, but we have to deal with what we can work with. Yeah, I know you will be banging your head against a wall of stone after all these years, but for the sake of the parents, I have agreed to reopen the case."

Charlie finished his words with an air of finality and gave Marty the "don't argue with me" look. Marty sniffed and looked away from Charlie. The office window, three floors up, gave Marty a view of the people below on the pavement going about their everyday lives. Automobiles and trucks surging along the distant freeway, a jet in the hazy sky above, coming in to land at the Los Angeles airport. All these people had a purpose and a reason to be living, breathing souls. He glanced back at the file now laying open on his dishevelled desk. This poor kid never made it to manhood, let alone become something in life.

Poor little guy, 7 years old, in a strange country and far from home, he must have felt lonely and frightened, but he just disappears like a cherry blossom vanishes when blown by the wind. This kid deserved to be known and have his soul put to rest, *if* he was dead. Now his elderly parents and siblings want some answers. *And answers they will have,* thought Marty. Emotions were running high in Hislop's heart. Not one to show his feelings, he had been touched by the photo of the boy, looking so innocent and yet the eyes told him that this soul wanted to be avenged, to be at peace.

He swallowed hard and fixed his gaze on Charlie Solomon and said, "Okay, you're on. La Paz and me, we will find out what happened to this kid. Even if he is dead, we will satisfy the family that we have left no stone unturned to get to the truth. Just one thing I don't understand boss, why was Billy by himself here and not accompanied by a parent? It seems strange to leave a very young kid alone in someone else's care, and such a long way from home? There does not seem to be any mention of that in the case notes, Charlie." Marty closed the file, placed his hands together and laid them on the yellowing manila folder containing next to nothing about this young Billy Parsons from Australia. Starring at Charlie Solomon, Marty awaited a response.

"Apparently from what we can gather now from his Aussie family," said Solomon, with a slight wave of his left hand, "the parents could not leave their farm in northern New South Wales. The father was involved with the farm and the wife had the other kids to look to. They lived in a remote part of the country, I understand. Money was scarce, and they had an acute labour shortage, so Billy departed on his own, with a woman chaperone provided from Universal Studios. A free passage was offered to a parent to accompany Billy, mainly Mrs Parsons, but she declined, and now possibly to her eternal regret. The file was in the archives, so I had to get it retrieved Marty. There is nothing else pertaining to the kid at all. No clothing or any personal belongings had been retained."

Charlie awaited Marty's reply.

Marty got up out of his chair, and said quickly to Charlie, "Well, I had better go through the file in more detail and get La Paz in, to brief him on the case. I think he is down at the DA's office but he should be back soon. I am not promising anything quickly boss, but we will tackle this head on and keep you informed".

Rising from his chair, Charlie Solomon reached over with his hand to shake Marty's and said, "I knew I could count on you Marty. Any help you need, just let me know. Oh, and by the way, I have to mention that Billy's elder brother, Andrew, attempted to have the case reopened about 20 years ago. He made the trip over here and made a special plea on behalf of his family, but met with a brick wall. Noel Dawson was the guy Andrew dealt with, I need say no more."

Charlie Solomon gave Marty Hislop a knowing look.

Marty comprehended immediately and said quickly, "Yeah, I understand perfectly. Senior Detective Noel Dawson is a real jerk, as though his shit doesn't stink!"

Marty had come up against Dawson before and sparks had flown between the two men. Dawson would have been very down putting to this Andrew Parsons and cast the request aside. So long as Dawson was receiving all the praise and credit for something he hadn't done, to advance his career prospects, that was all that mattered to this guy. Something like this missing kid would not have interested Dawson in the least. Ancient history to him; hardly any leads, no concrete evidence to go on. Too much work for Dawson. Terminate any further enquiries, would be Dawson's attitude. Totally different to Hislop, who enjoyed digging around a bit to get the exact facts.

Charlie Solomon ignored the comment from Hislop, but knew the statement was an accurate description of Dawson. Solomon left the room and Marty to his deep thoughts. Marty wandered over to the window again and tried to imagine being a scarred and bewildered 7 year old kid, leaving his family to go to another country, far from his familiar home. How would he have coped, he wondered? Yes, the family would get answers, but this was going to take time and a lot of planning.

Where was La Paz? Marty thought. He should have been be back by now. Marty had requested that La Paz report back to him as soon as he was back from the DA's office about this drug lord case they had been working on. La Paz was never one to get himself in a frenzy, took his time and plodded along, yet he got good results. Marty Hislop would not work with any person who was not up to the task, especially when working with him. Marty was straight to the point, minced no matters and did not put up with any bullshit. Getting annoyed and frustrated,Marty slammed down his pen on the desk with force. He wanted to get on with this new case and get things moving, but he needed La Paz, to tidy up the loose ends and piece together the facts, from what was provided. *That was shit all anyway*, thought Marty.

Suddenly the door opened and Detective Sergeant Miguel La Paz entered the room. A striking looking chap, nearing 40, with a good physique and a shock of wavy black hair. A native of Mexico, at 6 foot 3, he was much taller than Marty, but was happy to take the back seat, so to speak, when Marty was around. Marty Hislop was the action man, while La Paz was the thinker and organiser. Between the two men, they made a formidable team, and had worked together successfully for over 12 years.

"Where the hell have you been La Paz? I've been waiting for you for over half an hour and now you decide to come in! I have things to discuss with you and we need to work quick and fast. None of this lumbering along hoping that the next lead will come to us La Paz. What took you so long anyhow?" growled Marty.

La Paz, never one to take offence at Marty's gruff words, quietly said, "The DA was in a meeting when I arrived, so I had to wait, before I could ask him about the Henderson case. He reckons boss, that Henderson could go down for 20 years. Even if he squeals about the drug cartel based in Colombia, they have enough to sink him for a long time."

Before Marty could reply, La Paz went on to say with some

humour in his pleasant voice, "I saw the big boss in the corridor. Said he had just left seeing you about a new case. Says it will keep us busy and to keep quiet about it all, but you would explain the finer points to me boss."

With that, he looked knowingly at Marty and waited for the expected outburst. However, Marty realised he had been caught out and managed a smile from the corner of his mouth.

"Sit down La Paz. This one's a tough one. Missing kid from 1965. Aussie by birth, came to Universal Studios in March '65, just after his seventh birthday. Made three films and did a bit of TV ad stuff. On July 21 '65, he disappears while walking down North Beaumont in the Hollywood Hills. Some dame said she saw the kid, walking on the pavement, she thought, to the drug store on Roy Rogers Avenue. He used to go there for a cool pop! Never made it and just vanished from the face of the earth. Oh, sorry, thanks for going to the DA's office and yeah, let's hope that bastard goes down for a really long time."

With an air of closure, and satisfied that he had mentioned La Paz's visit to the DA's office, Marty flung the file over to La Paz. La Paz was used to this bullet point and not to be messed with, Hislop. La Paz had a calm temperament and had kept Hislop in tow on a number of occasions.

Marty Hislop was quick to shoot his mouth off and then have to back track to keep face. La Paz liked working with Marty Hislop. He knew his strengths and weaknesses, but he always admired the man for his honesty, sticking to the book but sometimes bending the rules to accommodate a case closure. The other guys always asked him how he could manage working for such a hard nut workaholic, but La Paz could see the other side of Marty Hislop. He had invited the bachelor Hislop home for a meal on a few evenings, with his wife and five children. Four daughters, ranging from 19 years to the youngest, who was 7. Jonas was in the middle, the only son. Hislop was a different man away from the office and loved to play baseball with the kids and eat Mexican food. La Paz's wife, Gloria was quite a beauty and also an excellent mother and cook. She worked part time two days a week at a beautician salon on Sunset Strip, cleaning the faces of the haggard makeover ladies, who could not remember which part of their body was real, fake or uplifted! Miguel and Gloria enjoyed the company of Marty Hislop and sensed his loneliness and need for an adopted family. They were happy to provide this.

Marty had taken Miguel and the 14 year old Jonas, on a fishing trip last autumn, up to a favourite fishing haunt of Hislop's in Washington State. They had stayed in a log cabin overlooking a crystal clear lake, with a roaring log fire. The lake had been a good source of excellent fishing and much fun and laughter amongst the three men. The bond between Marty Hislop and Miguel La Paz had grown deeper and Jonas thought that his "Uncle Marty" was the best yet at fly fishing! The trio had come home with a large esky full of fish and tales to tell the waiting Gloria and the girls.

La Paz began to read the scant case notes and Hislop stressed the need for complete secrecy, while they were tackling this case. La Paz nodded in comprehension and made some notes himself in his notepad.

"Boss", said La Paz with a question mark in his deep voice, "Why was the boy walking alone to the drug store and not with an adult? I know it was 1965, but even then kidnapping was prevalent. You would have thought that someone would have driven Billy to the store. It seemed a bit risky for a young kid, 7 years old, to be out alone."

"Yeah, I know", Marty was looking out the window again and turned around to face La Paz. The expression in Marty's face had altered to one of concern. He said in a lowered voice, "Would you allow your youngest, Maria, aged 7, to walk alone to the drug store to buy a cool pop La Paz? I think not!"

Marty's voice was raised now, "Yes, regardless of the difference in crime rates then to now, it does appear to be bloody thoughtless and irresponsible. See there in the notes that it wasn't the first time that the kid had walked alone to the drug store. Whoever was looking after the poor little guy needed their head knocked against a brick wall, common sense didn't exist! I think it's stated in the notes, the names of the couple who were looking after him; if you can call it that! Come on, let's get together now, band together and decide our course of action." Marty Hislop's reaction to this case that had been conveniently forgotten.

Yes, he pondered, *that was it. The case that was a bit too hard, so they shoved it under the carpet!.*A kid from another country – not important enough. Well not to Marty Hislop, no way. He was going to solve this one, for sure.

The pair sat for some time and decided who was going to research the file,that would be La Paz. A super sleuth on background information, he could filter facts from fiction and had some good contacts to boot. An expert with the computer, not one of Marty's strong points..

Marty's claim to success was in questioning people, asking the right questions and grasping a lead with a vice like grip. He followed up any clue and covered every angle. He did not give up without a fight.

The two men fell silent as they perused the notes, one sheet each at a time. La Paz was constantly making notes with his large handwriting. Hislop kept looking at the child's photo and wondered who had written the words on the reverse of the publicity shot.

Finally, after some time La Paz said he would check on the internet for any information that may exist on Billy's walk to nowhere. People put anything on the Internet these days. He wanted to also check background details on the witnesses, see if any were still alive and contact Universal Studios to arrange a meeting with their Media people and ask about Billy's contract. Someone from the period may still work there and remember the poor little kid.

La Paz shook his head, and looking over to Marty, said, "Gee Boss, hardly any witness statements, and what there is, gives us little to go on."

Marty agreed and replied, "Yeah, I know. See what you can

do. We may be able to speak to at least one of these people."

Hislop was keen to interview the main witness, Mrs Marjorie Femmer. She was the one who had seen Billy walking along North Beaumont on that fateful day. However, he knew they would need to check if Mrs Femmer was still alive and kicking, and where did she live now?

After a little assistance from faithful La Paz, they found out that she still resided at the same address in the Hollywood Hills. Hislop was out of the office before La Paz could turn his head to see his boss leave.

CHAPTER *two*

It was a cooler day as Hislop drove along the winding road leading up to the spacious, palatial mansions in the Hollywood Hills. He thought again of Billy Parsons. According to the case notes, there was nothing there to tell Hislop if Billy was unhappy or was he really enjoying himself, all that way from his family.

Eventually Marty located the home of Mrs Marjorie Femmer. Number 1768 North Beaumont was located in an older, yet quieter part of the district. Hislop had to slow down as the driveway sloped down from the main road. Hislop was hoping that she would be home. He had not phoned to warn Mrs Femmer of his visit. Hislop liked to catch people unawares, they often slipped up and gave themselves away. Spontaneity was Hislop's tool to break open hidden knowledge that otherwise lay nestled away with care or just completely dormant.

So, let's see what this dame has to say after all this time, thought Hislop, as he parked the unmarked car in the wide semi circular driveway.

The house was from the '50s, definitely. Stone feature front porch, fashionable from that era. The cement between the stones was crumbling in places. Wide windows, however the wooden frames were in need of a paint job to freshen the place up. The roof tiles looked tired, but for its age, the house was in average condition, on the outside anyway.

Someone is tending to the house, long time to be still living at the same address. This Mrs Femmer is probably getting on in years now. I wonder if there is a Mr Femmer? Marty thought.

The bungalow spread across the wide block and he noticed a below ground garage, probably under the lounge room, Marty assumed. That was typical for these homes too. The garden was mostly cacti, planted amongst small stone pebbles – another characteristic of homes from that period. Some of the cacti plants had seen better days. *Would be better if they were dug out,* thought Marty. There were light coloured pavers surrounding the cacti beds. Some of the cacti were in flower and had attracted the bees; who were busy humming away and collecting nectar.

Marty skipped up the two stairs on to the porch and pressed the doorbell. He was quite agile for his age, hair thinning a bit and going grey at the temples, but to look at, he was still a pleasant looking chap. Straightening his tie and wiping his shoes on each trouser leg, he waited for a response to the bell.

Shortly, the door was carefully opened by an elderly woman with dyed brunette hair. There was a tortoise shell hair comb pushing the hair up in the centre, something reminiscent of the '60s period. She wasn't young, could be late seventies or eighties even. *Hard to tell with all this makeup they wear these days*, Hislop thought. This woman's makeup was quite thick. She must scrape it off with a knife, it was certainly well applied. She was dressed in a brown slack suit that was well worn and definitely not from the chic boutiques of today's fashion houses. *From the '70s*, Marty reckoned. An orange and white scarf adorned her neck. The woman's lips were painted a vivid red and she wore gold bangles on her thin left arm. The face was pale, but the skin had been tended to. *Not unattractive, even for advanced years*, Marty mused. Her eyes were sunken and puffy bags were thinly disguised by makeup. The hands were shaking a little, Marty observed. An odour of perfume lingered about her, along with the smell of liquor.

Before the woman could speak, Marty got in first and introduced himself and asked if she was Mrs Marjorie Femmer.

"Yes, I am Mrs Marjorie Femmer." came the croaky and suspicious reply. The voice was quivering a little and she seemed on edge, almost frightened.

Strange, thought Marty. *Perhaps she did live on her own.*

Showing no sign of observing anything amiss, Marty explained the reason for his visit and requested if he might come in to go over the events of that day she saw Billy Parsons.

Mrs Femmer was now unwilling to open the door, and with almost hysteria in her voice replied, "I gave the police a statement about what I saw years ago, and I don't know anything else! I cannot help you, I'm sorry." Mrs Femmer attempted to close the door in Marty's face but he was too quick and placed his foot between the doorframe and the wood door. Mrs Femmer's body was slightly shaken and she seemed to become unbalanced. Hislop grabbed her by the right hand and steadied her. She was visibly shaking and teary.

"I think it may be better if I helped you inside Mrs Femmer, to sit down. I know this has probably come as a shock to you, but I just need to ask a few questions and then I will be on my way." said Marty gently. He was using his skills of diplomacy to gain access to the house and then he would strike.

Carefully, he guided the clearly distressed Mrs Femmer inside. Into a large lounge they slowly walked. The room was bright and airy and had a large window overlooking the front cacti garden. Mrs Femmer slumped down into a well worn sofa and just seemed to stare ahead into space. Her body was trembling and Hislop could detect that a sweat had broken out on the woman's forehead.

So, thought Marty. *Something to hide have we, be sure I shall get it out of you my dear, by any means.*

Marty's eyes were fixed on this woman who was trembling.

"Can I get you a drink Mrs Femmer?" was Marty's first draw card to get into this woman's mind and unlock the dark secrets that lurked there. Water was what Marty had in mind – but not Mrs Femmer.

"Yes, over there by the window. The drop down cabinet has whiskey." she managed to quiver out of the depths of her silent reverie. She pointed to the cabinet with an unsteady arthritic finger.

Marty noticed that she wore no wedding band but had rings on the right hand only. The jewellery appeared to be good quality with one ring having a large brilliant cut green stone, possibly an emerald Marty surmised.

Hastily, Marty walked to the old cabinet and poured Mrs Femmer a stiff whiskey. He walked back to the anxious looking woman and handed the glass to her. Mrs Femmer grabbed the drink and gulped the liquid down as though it was just water.

"Another, please," she blurted out with an audible burp.

Marty raised his eyebrows, without the woman seeing him and went back to the cabinet to pour another drink. This time he noticed that the cabinet was well stocked with mostly whiskey and some crème de menthe. There was also an opened bottle of sherry.

Well, well, thought Marty. *Mrs Marjorie Femmer likes a tipple, if ever anyone does!* Pacing back over to the hapless creature, who just seemed to be languishing amongst the many cushions, Marty handed the second drink to Mrs Femmer. She was fiddling with a thick gold chain around her scrawny neck. Once again, the fluid was washed down with a flourish. The effects of the whiskey had settled Mrs Femmer and Marty purposed to go ahead with his questions.

"There, is that better Mrs Femmer?" asked the inquisitive Marty

"Yes, thank you, much better. It was just the heat, it will pass." the woman gasped in reply. The head was lolling around a little bit but the hands were now settled.

Poor bitch, thought Marty.

The day was actually on the cool side, so Marty knew that the answer was just a lame cover up.

CHAPTER *three*

Marty sat down next to Mrs Femmer. With all the tact he could muster, which was difficult for him, he began to go over the statement that Mrs Femmer had given to the police on the day Billy Parsons had gone missing.

"Now, is there anything, any small detail, you can tell me about that day? We want to cover all aspects of the day, just in case we left some vital detail out. Did you see anyone else loitering around, a car or someone else on the street? Who knows, it may just help us find what actually happened to the boy." said Marty with a spreading of his arms. Marty made his voice sound very plausible and caring. He looked at the woman next to him, she was thinking a lot, Marty knew that.

Still starring ahead, Mrs Femmer started to unravel herself and commenced to talk like a person possessed. All the words came rolling out, perhaps this was a release of tension over many years. Or was it just the effect the drink had on Mrs Femmer? The voice was more composed and the woman was in control of her emotions now.

"I did not see anyone else that day, no car, or anything out of the ordinary." Mrs Femmer's high pitched voice continued on, "I knew Billy Parsons well Inspector. He came here often to play. I had bought some toys for him to play with. A toy car to ride around the yard on and a model plane to throw into the sky and a large red ball that we played with Billy, Max and I. There were some other things too, but he liked the little car. He raced around the place and pretended that he was driving on the freeway. Billy was lonely, Inspector. The couple he was billeted with were older and I don't think they had a real interest in Billy. I found him one day out the front, just wandering along the road. He was upset, so I brought him inside; gave him cookies and a soda. He wanted to stay the night with us, but my husband Max took him back to where Billy was staying. Over time, Billy was a regular visitor here. You see Inspector, Max and I could not have a family. Max had a rare blood type and having a family was out of the question. I begged Max to adopt but he wouldn't have it, so we just had to be satisfied being alone, until Billy came along. He was such a vivacious child, full of life. He missed his family but I think he was just too young to take it all in. The glamour of being made a fuss of at the studio and everyone telling him he was a handsome boy, which he was. The time Billy spent here was one of the happiest times of our lives. Perhaps more so for me, as Max was at work during the day. Of course, Billy had his contractual obligations with Universal Studios, but when he was not on set, Billy quite often came here. On weekends, we would take Billy out into the country. He loved going out with us, a picnic or a day at the beach. Naturally, I grew to love him but in my heart I knew I could never actually have

Billy as my own. He was someone else's boy and besides, Max would not allow us to get involved. After all, he was really the responsibility of the couple who Billy was staying with. I don't understand why they were chosen to look after him, they were an older couple and foreign. Billy must have felt very alone and cut off from any love. That is why he must have got out and started walking down the road and the rest is history, but it's just as though it was yesterday, Inspector. I used to take him with me when I went food shopping. He loved that, trying to push the shopping trolley or helping me with the groceries and having a ride in the car. I would take him to the drug store on Roy Rogers Avenue and buy him a cool pop or a spider drink. Billy was quite adventurous for his age and apparently had taken himself to the drug store before he came attached to us. He told us himself, how he walked down the steep path and went along the Avenue to the drug store with his pocket money to buy a cool pop. Billy was permitted a small allowance from his contract at Universal Studios, and I think he felt quite grown up with his own money. Quite honestly Inspector, I don't think that Billy was fed very well either, he was always hungry and said that he didn't get much to eat, poor little thing."

Mrs Femmer paused and seemed to reflect, then carried on, "Then came the day of his disappearance. I was coming home from a guild meeting at the Amateur Dramatic Society in Brentwood around 11 a.m. or just after, and as I was driving down our street, I passed Billy who was walking along the pavement. I waved to him and he waved back with a big smile. He was probably on his way to the drug store. He always walked on the other side of the road as the pathway down the valley was on that side. He only crossed the road if he was intending to come to our place. Unfortunately, by fate, I did not stop to offer him a lift down into town as I was wanting to get home to get my bowls for a ladies indoor bowling tournament, which I was running late for. The meeting at the guild had run over time and the bowls tournament was due to start at noon at the Hollywood Indoor Bowls arena. I now wish with all my heart that I had taken the time to bring him with me to the arena, or take him home with his beloved cool pop; and be late for the tournament. We didn't win anyway! It was very hot that day too, Inspector. Dear child, out in all that sun, no hat on his head. This has plagued me for all these years, and I blame myself for his disappearance, I really do." Mrs Femmer buried her face into her hands and wept bitterly. Her body shook with grief and sorrow.

Not what I expected, thought Marty with a deep sigh.

After a few minutes had passed, Marty asked in a questioning tone, "Can you remember what Billy was wearing that day, Mrs Femmer?"

"Well, I think I can, yes." came the lame reply. "He had on a blue shirt, from memory, and grey shorts and his sandals. That's about all I can recall, Inspector. I was driving, you see and I only waved and glanced at him fleetingly. I did not really take too much notice of what Billy had on." Mrs Femmer turned her gaze onto Marty with a look of despair.

"But you can remember that Billy wore no hat, Mrs Femmer." replied the enquiring Marty.

"Oh yes, I can remember that. It was a hot day, as I said previously, and I did think how hot the sun would have been on his head. Billy did have a white fabric hat with a wide green border, he sometimes wore it when he came to our place. He said that his mother had made it for him. But on that day he was not wearing the hat." came the rapid response from Mrs Femmer.

"Did you know the couple that Billy was staying with Mrs Femmer?' asked the inquisitive Marty.

"Not very well. They lived at number 1811, on the other side of the street. They have both since passed away, I understand. Vladimir Nijinski was from Russia or some other Balkan country, I'm not sure on that. His partner, Olga Serenova fancied herself as a leftover from the Russian Royal family. Delighted in telling everyone that she was a grand niece of Czar Nicholas of all the Russias, if you can believe that! I only met them on a few occasions briefly. They had been involved with, or worked at Universal Studios or some such thing. I don't know the full background. They were older than Max and I, and frankly appeared a little eccentric, I always thought. I do know that Olga's daughter lives in the house now. I think her name is Anna, but I could be wrong. I don't think that Anna was living there at the time. Anyway, they had the custody of Billy from the time he arrived in Hollywood, which was the

March of '65. How they could have not have loved him, I can't understand." said Mrs Femmer, looking down seriously and shaking her head. "I know we did ask Billy if he was being treated okay by the couple. He seemed to clam up and just shook his head and said, yes. Both Max and I had our doubts but there was little we could do. On one occasion, not long before Billy disappeared, we noticed some bruising on his arms and legs. When we asked him what had happened, Billy shrugged his shoulders and said that he had been naughty and was punished and had to stand in the corner cupboard, which was very dark. This incident had upset him a lot, so we did not press him for more answers. We just gave him love, Inspector. He craved for it, poor boy." was Mrs Femmer's answer. She gave Marty a pleading look of anxiousness tinged with helplessness.

Marty felt he was achieving something here, and decided to plug on, while the going was good.

"Tell me about this pathway that went down from North Beaumont onto Roy Rogers Avenue. Was it steep? How long would it take Billy to walk down the pathway, do you know, Mrs Femmer?" responded Marty, looking at this relic from a bygone age.

Marty had noticed that the furnishings, whilst well cared for, were also certainly outdated by today's standards. The straight lines of the '50s and '60s were apparent. The cushions on the sofa were looking a bit tattered in parts and the carpet was a bright orange with yellow flecks through it, and showed signs of going threadbare.

Mrs Femmer paused before she answered Marty. Obviously thinking about her answer, she finally said, "Well Inspector, I would say that it would take about five to seven minutes to walk down the pathway, but in Billy's case, it could have taken longer, being a much smaller person. I rarely used the pathway myself. It was fairly steep, especially coming up. There was a handrail for you to hold onto, but Billy might have been a bit short for that. I understand that the pathway was put there as a shortcut for pedestrians, rather than walk all the way to the end of North Beaumont and then have to backtrack along Roy Rogers Avenue. The pathway is not there anymore, it was all dug up some years ago. It wasn't safe at all."

"I see." came Marty's reply. Changing the subject now, he asked Mrs Femmer, "Do you live alone Mrs Femmer?" Marty assumed that Max was no longer alive, but he had to be sure. She might have a star boarder living here now, but Marty knew he was barking up the wrong tree with this lady.

Quietly, Mrs Femmer feebly said, "Yes, my husband Max died not long after Billy disappeared, the following year to be precise, 1966. Heart attack. He was only 53 but he smoked a lot and had a heart condition. But life goes on, so they say." Tears had welled up in the poor woman's eyes. Marty felt a bit of a prick asking the question, but he had to know.

"I gather your husband was at work the day of Billy's disappearance Mrs Femmer?" was Marty's next tackling point. Did he notice a slight reluctance before Mrs Femmer replied? There was something she was holding back on.

Marjorie Femmer rallied herself and said with a casual voice, "Yes Inspector, he was. He worked for Walt Disney you know. Max was an accomplished artist and the principal artist for Walt. His work was greatly appreciated by Walt Disney and his other work colleagues. Max loved to draw. Come with me, and I will show you his studio."

Marty got the impression that Mrs Femmer was trying to steer the conversation away from the day Billy disappeared. Especially in relation to her husband, Max Femmer.

He helped Mrs Femmer to her pigeon toe feet, encased in tapestry slippers and they both walked out of the lounge room and down a dim passage to a doorway at the end. Marty noticed that Mrs Femmer walked like a crab, favouring the right side. *Probably arthritis*, thought Marty.

Mrs Femmer opened the door with a key from around her skinny neck. She pushed open the pale blue wood door and went inside the room. She carefully walked over to the long windows and opened the drapes and did the same to another set on the other side of the large room.

Marty saw a door in the far corner of the long room. *I wonder where that door leads to,* Marty thought. *Could quite likely lead down to the garage I saw.*

It was just like walking into a time warp. There were some unfinished drawings on the desk, strewn with other completed works. Pencils and coloured crayons littered the desk. Some easels had cartoon character sketches in the process of being completed. A heavy crystal ash tray with an abundance of yellowing cigarette stubs lay on the desk. A lighter and two packets of Camel filters were randomly positioned next to them. There was a framed drawing of Pinocchio hanging on a pale yellow wall. In fact, there were cartoon drawings and sketches hung all over the walls. The room had a stale mustiness about it, as though it had never seen the light of day since Max Femmer had died.

Mrs Femmer noticed Marty looking at the framed drawing of a character that had an uncanny resemblance to Pinocchio, and said with some happiness in her voice, "That was one of Max's drawings for the 1937 film of Pinocchio. Walt thought it was wonderful. Walt adapted it into Pinnochio. He was a good boss to work for and encouraged Max to do some marvellous drawings. See that one over there of Bambi, and the one of Snow White next to it. Max also did the drawing of Red White, over there on the far wall. Walt Disney was going to incorporate the two characters into a film, but never got around to it. Max spent a lot of time in here Inspector, creating his work. Max was originally from Hungary, a Jew by birth, and had gone to live in Germany. His parents had shifted there for work reasons, his father was an artist for the German film industry. But alas, they had to flee Germany when the Nazi uprising began in 1933, and they came to America. Max got a job eventually with Walt Disney and the rest is history. Sadly, Max's life was cut short and I was left. We had some happy years together, and I have those memories. I can't get rid of his drawings, they mean so much to me and to Max's memory." Marjorie Femmer dropped her head and touched carefully a sketch laying on the desk.

Without thinking, Marty picked up a brass plaque sitting on the desk. The desk was quite long, one half was flat and the other half was on a slant, probably for Max to draw at. There was a stool placed at the slanted end of the desk and a ragged looking dark Brown rug, which Marty was now standing on. The plaque had the wording "Secundus Nilli" engraved on it in black Gothic lettering. Marty knew what the Latin words meant, it had been his high school's motto; "Second to none".

Max Femmer must have been very proud to have a motto like this to display. An ego to boot, no doubt, thought Marty.

There was a sharp intake of breath from the direction of Mrs Femmer, who ejaculated, "Put that down at once!" in a sharp command, glaring at Marty with a look of "How dare you!"

Marty placed the plaque back onto the dusty desk and apologised.

Mrs Femmer realised her manner had been brusque and quickly said in a quieter voice, "It's alright Inspector. It's just that Max would not like anything to be disturbed. He was very particular about his studio and did not like me entering the room. I think we had better leave."

The woman now appeared to be eager for Marty to leave the room, and was standing at the doorway with a gesture of her trembling hand. There was certainly a creepy feeling about this room, thought the intrepid Marty.

Why the sudden exit, and change in demeanour from this

lady? Interesting, there is more to this room than meets the eye, thought the observant Marty Hislop.

He had noticed that there were no photographs in the house, nothing on the walls or a table. That struck Marty as being acutely odd. If Marjorie was so devoted to her beloved Max, why wasn't there a photo somewhere? He also wondered how Mrs Femmer kept the place going, assuming that she didn't work at her age now – unless there was a private income. Marty would have La Paz check her finances out, wouldn't hurt.

"Just one last thing before I forget, Mrs Femmer. Would you by any chance have a photo of Billy? Perhaps on one of your outings with Billy, you took a snap of him?" suggested the expectant Marty.

"No, I do not have any photos of Billy. We were not photography minded, Inspector," was the quick and cool response from Mrs Femmer.

Yeah, sure lady. Pigs might fly too! I bet you have something, you thought too much of Billy, concluded Marty.

Marty decided he had better make his exit, he had got all he wanted for now. Mrs Femmer had been helpful to a point, but there was an underlying current. Marty detected that Mrs Femmer was concealing some vital information. But that could wait, give her time to think about it all.

Marty thanked Mrs Femmer for her time and said farewell – for the moment anyway.

CHAPTER *four*

Marty was walking to the car when his mobile sounded. He could see the call was from La Paz.

"Yeah, La Paz," was Marty's blunt response.

"Hi Boss, are you still in the vicinity of North Beaumont? You might like to hear this. There is a lady who lives at 1817 North Beaumont, called Peggy Cavallaro. She was living there when Billy Parsons went missing. Apparently she knew the couple where Billy was staying and is a wealth of information about the old days of Hollywood. I got this info from Universal Studios. Apparently the couple Billy Parsons was staying with are now deceased. Might still be worth talking to this lady, Boss," was La Paz's suggestion.

"Okay, will do. Good work, La Paz. I'm going to pay a visit to number 1811 North Beaumont right now. That is where Billy Parsons was staying. A daughter of the dame who looked after Billy, lives there now. Called Anna, according to Mrs Femmer. Didn't get the family name, assume it is Serenova, after her mother. So when I have done that, I will pay a visit to this Peggy Cavallaro. We can get together when I get back La Paz, bye for now," was Marty's parting comment.

So that was good, kill two birds with one stone, just doors apart too, thought Marty. As he got into the car he looked over to a window of the Femmer home and noticed that a curtain had been parted open but was now quickly closed. A figure had moved away from the window. *So, Mrs Femmer was having a looksee*, thought Marty as he chuckled to himself. *Something to hide, definitely.* Mrs Marjorie Femmer was a frail person really and the only comfort she had now, was her craving for drink.

Marty left the Femmer residence and drove out of the driveway. *Good idea that was, with the semi circular driveway. Easy to get out onto the street.* Up the street Marty went and slowed down to check street numbers. Number 1811 came up quicker than he imagined.

Pulling into the neglected driveway, he thought the whole scene before him was just like the house from the TV series *The Addams Family*. The large three storey wood home was in desperate need of repair. The paintwork had peeled off considerably and there were signs of rot in the timber. The grounds, whilst quite large, were overgrown with thorn bushes and clambering roses. A rust bucket Ford F250 stood languishing in a corner of the block under a makeshift carport.

Marty got out of the car and carefully negotiated his way up the path to the once black double front door. The entrance was littered with rubbish and weeds grew out of the crevices in the wood planks. Lifting the well worn brass knocker, it almost came off in his hand. Marty knocked with his hand instead and expected a grim faced butler to open the door and say in a deep flat voice, "Yes". Instead, the door creaked open to reveal a hag.

Well, she looks the part, thought Marty.

Her face was dirty and displayed a disdainful expression. She smelt of stale urine and nicotine and some other aroma. Marty could not place it, but he had smelt it before during his time with the force. The creature before him wore a long purple caftan with gold embroidery running through it. No shoes on the feet and a long thin cigar was stuck in the surly lips. Black lipstick had been smothered over the lips with very little care. Smoke billowed from the mouth like an inferno. The face was wrinkled, almost gnarled in places. She sported a large mole on the left cheek, which was sprouting black facial hairs. Her finger nails looked long and deadly. Leaning against the wood doorway and placing an arm on the thin waist, this weeping willow of sorts, eyed Marty through slit like eyes. The hair was long and dyed jet black. A silver coloured head band adorned the greasy hair.

Well, thought Marty, *what have we here? Certainly no advertisement for L'OREAL , 'you're worth it'!*

She looked like a vulgar, voluptuous vampire gone terribly wrong. Her eyes were cold and indifferent and her body language suggested something else.

Marty took the plunge, introducing himself and said he was looking for Anna Serenova.

"What for!" came the brittle reply. The voice was expressionless, yet deep. Marty noticed that some teeth were missing.

Marty explained briefly about the Parsons case and the information he had regarding the couple who Billy was staying with at that time.

"Hmmph. When was this, 1965? How would I know, can't be expected to remember that far back? I was probably at university, protesting about the Vietnam War. Pity the Viet Congs didn't win. At least North Korea has something to offer," sniffed this delightful female. "What's this got to do with me anyway?" said the dancing dolly with a sneer in her smoky voice. She folded her arms and stood in a menacing stance in the doorway giving Marty a fierce once over. Smoke oozed from the mouth like foul smelling steam.

Not getting anywhere, thought Marty. Instantly, Marty picked up on the smell he could not discern earlier. *Of course, it fits in. Let's get this hussy a bit rattled. Be straight to the point, man.*

Marty responded with a fierce tirade and said, "I assume you are Olga Serenova's daughter, Anna? And the date was July 21, 1965?" Marty moved forward like a gridiron player and pushed past the lacklustre creep with ease.

Entering the den of Aladdin's cave, Marty was confronted by a thin haze of smoke. Striding further into the filthy house, Marty tried to make out where the smoke was coming from. A room just down the hallway had a closed door – that was it.

Madam Butterfly scuttled behind Marty. "You can't go in there, someone is sleeping. Get out you pig!"

Marty was too quick for the "purple panther" and opened the door of the forbidden room. In the corner of the room, near a grimy window, was a day bed, veiled with a thick curtain. A table had the smoking apparatus sitting on it. Over hurried Marty, and flung back the curtain to reveal a hapless figure. A woman dressed in some flimsy silk gown clutched a hookah. The cheeks were sunken and the face gaunt. There was no recognition in the eyes of the woman. She was in an opium stance for sure – just a blank stare in a void. *Wretched creature,* thought Marty. A plant of marijuana stood on a plant stand by the window. Another table had a selection of "sweets", namely what looked like to be amphetamines.

The other wonder woman, he assumed to be Anna, began to claw at Marty and scream. "Leave us alone, you pig. You cops are all the same, bastards!" She spat in Marty's face and tried to slap him.

Marty grabbed her bony wrist firmly and said in a calm, yet no nonsense voice, "Get me all the information you have on Billy Parsons, or I'll have the pair of you locked up for possessing an illegal substance. I'm not joking sister, get it now. Don't tell me you don't know what I am talking about because I have first hand information about this joint! Now hop to it, Fairy Floss." Marty shouted at the stinking woman. He was playing a game here but the look of shock in Anna's fierce eyes were enough to know that he had struck a chord.

Marty's quick thinking worked. The partisan from hell raced out of the room. Marty followed, leaving the lifeless figure to its self-induced dream.

Back down the hallway to some clear light and fresh air

went Marty, if that was at all possible in this mausoleum. Anna had faded into the depths of this shady hovel. Without warning, a huge hulk appeared from out of the gloom and stood in Marty's way. *Well, finally,* thought Marty, *the butler has arrived!*

He must have been seven foot tall, massive biceps and thick shoulders plus a neck like an ox. Bare-chested, there was enough hair to weave a carpet and have some left over. His hair was long and hung down like ringlets over the hairy shoulders. Gold rings had been inserted into the nipples and an enormous chunky gold chain around the neck, rattled when he moved. Clad in torn leather trousers, steel capped patent leather black biker boots and a leather skull cap. Arm bands with pointed studs and a very large right eyebrow ring, completed the armoury. Enormous black studs were set in the ear lobes. The face was just like cement, with a shiny film covering the features that had been carved out with a chisel. The left eye was covered with a patch. A long scar was etched into the left cheek bone area, and a handlebar moustache, resembling cat's whiskers, adorned the upper lip. Cold venomous grey eyes surveyed Marty. An abundance of colourful tattoos covered the beefy arms. He wreaked of body odour and some other delightful smells. Presumably this guy liked that new men's eau de cologne by Chanel, called "Stink". Marty dubbed him "Pirate Pussy".

Brandishing a baseball bat in the right black gloved hand, Marty reckoned that Pirate Pussy was ready to play ball, but with Marty's head. There came a distinct grunting sound from this well attired baseball player. A twisted smile formed on the thick lips. The head drooped to one side, taking in the defenseless Marty. A sinister laugh came from the depths of this warlord. The gold chain clinked heavily as its owner lumbered along the passage. Swiftly the bat was being swung at Marty's head but Marty saw it in time and ducked. Pirate Pussy was not impressed! Marty endeavoured to position himself against the wall whilst Pirate Pussy ambled forward to strike again. He made a loud "Aagh" sound as the baseball bat was being flung around in the stale smog like passage. Out of the corner of Marty's eye, he could see Princess Loveliness. She was edging on Pirate Pussy saying, "Get the bastard, break his friggen neck, smash his head to bits!"

Lovely talk from such a demure lady, mused Marty. *Such a delight to bring home for the folks to meet!*

Both men eyed each other off, Marty knew Pirate Pussy had the upper hand. Silence now filled the moment. You could cut the air with a knife. There was a faint scuttling noise and Marty saw a large cockroach squeezing itself between the wood floorboards, just in case it was crushed to death by the boots of Pirate Pussy. Without warning, Marty's mobile began to ring, but Marty couldn't answer the call. He had more important things to tend to right now! The mobile rang out. Immediately, the mobile sounded again, and once more Marty had to let it ring out.

What seemed to be minutes, but in reality was only seconds,

ticked by. Marty continued to move along the wall but facing the incredible hulk before him, not game to take his eye off the playful weapon.Pirate Pussy raised the baseball bat to make a home delivery, when there was a deafening sound of voices and wood being broken, pandemonium broke the silence. Down the hallway charged four heavily reinforced figures, sporting bullet proof vests, protective head gear, assault rifles and batons. *Hell*, thought Marty, *cops!*

Cherry Blossom Apple Pie tried to make a run for it and fled further into the house with two boys in blue after her. Pirate Pussy made a swing at the police but a baton hit to the giant's knee, brought him down like a paper doll.

Marty heard the familiar voice of La Paz calling out, "You okay, Boss?"

"Yeah, no worries. Just a little ball game with our friend here, that's all. We had an audience, but she got a bit scarred and ran off." Marty hurriedly replied, getting his breath back.

Pirate Pussy was yelling "Latin" abuse at the top of his voice as he was taken out to the paddy wagon.

Before long, Anna, was rounded up, trying to grab a shot gun from a chest of drawers. Over powered, she put up a struggle and managed to scratch a deep gash in the face of one of the tactical response boys. The boys literally dragged her out by the hair, shouting and screaming like a real storm trooper.

"Dear thing, really," Marty recalled his mother using this expression when someone was down and out, or the subject of gossip. *This one was far from that*, thought Marty.

Seething with fury at being arrested, Anna was bundled into the black maria also. The other sleeping beauty, yet to be identified, was brought out and taken into custody.

"A good haul!" said the smiling Marty. Marty looked at La Paz and said with a question mark in his voice, "What made you guys burst in here? Did you have a tip off?"

La Paz answered, "When you told me you were going to number 1811 North Beaumont, I just thought I would do a background check on the joint. Came up as a red circle boss. That guy who was playing ball with you, is known as Thor. Calls himself "Thor the Viking" and has a list as long as your arm. His real name is John Ingmar Armitage. From Amish stock in Pennsylvania. Been inside before, GBH, drug dealing, robbery with violence, and get this, child pornography! There is a website called "1811" and it is a child pornography site. Heaps of photos of underage kids in compromising postures, some have just been taken at random. I got the boys together in case you ran into trouble with Thor. That was me phoning your mobile. When you didn't pick up after the second time, I gave the authority to break in. Boss, I wanna see if there is a computer or lap top somewhere. We might get something from it. I'll have a hunt around for any paperwork, photos that may link us to Billy Parsons."

Marty nodded, collecting himself from the baseball practice.

"So my playful boxing pal has something to write home about. The folks at home would love to hear about their son's exploits." giggled Marty.

La Paz went on, "This Anna Serenova, has been a noted political activist for many years. Been behind bars on a number of occasions. Organiser of protest marches and rallies, and has a connection to Ku Klux Klan members too. A known police hater, she has assaulted officers before. She was also a founding member of the Women in Purple brigade. You have heard of them, no doubt. A real nasty dame if ever there was one boss."

"Yes, the Women in Purple Brigade do ring a few alarm bells. They are usually behind any political unrest and spurn the law to a tee! Well, well. We may have hit the jackpot here La Paz. Thanks for dropping by, you saved my head from being belted off! Tell you what, you clean up here, get what you can, and I will head up to this Peggy Cavallaro's place at 1817. See what she has to say. I will catch up with you back at the office. Oh, don't go getting high on that hookah La Paz, okay. We have work to do!" said Marty with a laugh.

"Oh jeez boss, I was kinda looking forward to a having a puff, now you spoilt all the fun!" was the joking reaction from La Paz.

CHAPTER *five*

Leaving La Paz and the boys to go through the putrid house, Marty drove the couple of doors up to 1817 North Beaumont.

Quite a difference awaited Marty Hislop, as he pulled up outside the well kept grounds of number 1817 North Beaumont. A two-storey, Georgian style mansion, *Probably built back in the '20s* estimated Marty. The house was set back from the road and built on high ground, which gave a commanding view over the valley below. Splendid black wrought iron gates, with a gold crest inserted in the middle of each gate. The gates were open, so Marty drove in. The house was painted white with bright, sunny yellow shutters to complement. A circular driveway led up to the house, where Marty parked the car. Getting out, he could see that the gardens appeared well manicured and had an English garden format. Low box hedges surrounded a statue of Peter Pan blowing water from his flute. There was a colourful array of bedding flowers, deciduous shrubs and rhododendrons of varying colours were the backdrop. A silver birch graced one lawn area and a golden ash another lawn area. A bay window had a bed of blue hydrangeas planted. The bushes were in bloom, the enormous flower heads standing out like beacons.

Well planned out, someone likes to garden, Marty guessed.

He strolled up to the front portico and saw that the house was named, "Harpenden Lodge". The white, double front doors had a fanned arch in the top of each of them. These arches had been painted the same colour yellow as the shutters on the windows. The house had been rendered and painted a glistening white. The yellow of the shutters stood out, plus the vibrant shade of blue of the Hydrangea plants complemented the overall sight.

Marty pressed the bell and awaited.

Promptly, the door was opened by a fresh faced young woman in her early twenties. Dressed in a maid's uniform, she gave Marty a pleasant smile. "Yes, Sir?"

Displaying his police badge, Marty explained he wished to speak to Peggy Cavallaro. The maid looked taken back and asked Marty to step inside whilst she saw if Mrs Cavallaro was available. Marty handed the maid his police business card. The maid hurried off to deliver her message. Marty wandered from the entrance doors into a foyer and could see an immense wooden staircase leading up to the upper rooms. The staircase encompassed either wall and met in the middle, at the top of the landing. *Very impressive*, thought Marty. Expertly carved hand railings and banisters were a draw card to this piece of workmanship. The wood was a light shade, could have been oak. Marty was not sure. Gilt framed pictures hung on the walls, which seemed to have a brocade like wallpaper stuck on them. Up high on the pale green wall, there was a painting of a handsome and distinguished looking man at the very top of the stairs. Possibly this was Mr Cavallaro. The high ceiling in the middle of the foyer led the eye to behold a gorgeous chandelier, which was highlighted by sunlight streaming through a glass dome in the roof structure. The wide carpet piece Marty stood on was plush and he could see that it was an antique. *Someone's flaunted some dough around*, mused Marty. *Not bad, a maid and a gardener to boot as well!*

In the corner of the large foyer stood an antique grandfather clock. Marty had not seen one of these for years. His grandparents had a clock similar to this in their home in Boston, but that was years ago. *I wonder what ever happened to that clock*, thought Marty. His rambling thoughts were broken by the maid returning. She appeared more relaxed and asked Marty to follow her through to the drawing room. Down a wide passageway they walked. Marty noticed the place was well maintained inside too,

Arriving at a double set of carved wood doors, the maid opened a large, heavily carved door, and motioned for Marty to enter the room. Stepping into the room, was like stepping into a palace. The walls were pure white painted with gold leaf friezes. The furniture was in the French style you often see in those French chateaus. Tapestries hung on two walls, another wall had a massive gilt mirror and the other had a wide wood bookcase, filled with old books. Sunlight shone into the spacious room and a sofa table had silver ware placed on it. Marty realised this was the room he had seen with the bay window and the Hydrangeas planted beneath. *Wow*, thought Marty. From the average Femmer house, to the flea bitten wreck of 1811 and now into a palace – he had seen it all today.

Sitting on a three seater sofa was an elderly lady, advanced in years but no expense had been spared on clothes and makeup too. There was a walking stick next to her right side. *Her hair is that blue rinse set stuff*, Marty reminisced to himself. His grandmother had joined the set, it was popular some years ago, but had gone out of fashion now. Marty used to think that ladies with blue hair suffered with poor circulation. This lady still belonged to the blue rinse set obviously. The pale pink floral dress was well cut, and what appeared to be diamond earrings, were placed in the ear lobes. The stones shone in the daylight coming into the magnificent room. A sizeable sapphire ring was placed on the wedding finger. Her eyes were a soft blue but were intelligent and took in all that was going on around her. Sensible walking shoes, of a soft pearl shade, were on the delicate feet. This lady gave the aura of someone of some importance, oozing with grace and elegance.

Mrs Peggy Cavallaro spoke first, "Detective Chief Inspector Hislop, hello. How may I assist you? Please, do sit down." She indicated for Marty to be seated in an expensive looking chair opposite where she sat, in regal state. Her voice was definitely refined, and Marty detected English grass roots in the pedigree of this lady.

"Thank you, Mrs Cavallaro. I won't take too much of your

time." Marty gave the woman a flashing smile and seated himself in the large wingback armchair. Showing Mrs Cavallaro his police badge to confirm his identity, Marty sat back in the chair. Marty had already analysed Peggy Cavallaro as one who stood on social standards as the norm.

"Some tea or coffee, Chief Inspector?'

"Yes, thank you, that would be nice Mrs Cavallaro. Tea is fine with me." Marty got the idea that this lady would be a tea drinker rather than a coffee connoisseur. So he chose tea for this reason.

Mrs Cavallaro turned her head and said in a pleasant voice to the maid, who was still in the room, obviously awaiting instructions from her mistress, "Matilda, can you please arrange some tea for the Chief Inspector and myself, thank you".

"Very well Mrs Cavallaro", replied Matilda meekly, and floated out of the room to complete her quest. "Well Chief Inspector, this is a surprise, having a visit from the police. I don't often have such a pleasure," came the very plastic response.

Her eyes were surveying Marty's clothing, that were a bit dishevelled after playing ball with Pirate Pussy. He realised that his tie was not properly in place and his suit coat was rather crumpled. The tired looking white shirt had come out of his trousers and hung loosely in the front. Marty's hair needed a comb that was standing up at the back of his head. At least he had not noticed that – but Peggy Cavallaro had.

Oh shit, thought Marty. *To hell with it, she doesn't know the circumstances.* Marty ignored the "once over" look from Mrs Cavallaro and came straight to the point of his visit. Pleasantries annoyed Marty, they covered a multitude of sins, he always said.

"I am investigating the Billy Parsons case, you may remember the child who went missing in 1965? We want to recheck some details, and wondered if you can remember anything

from that day?" Without pausing, Marty spoke on, "Can you tell me anything about the day Billy went missing or the people he was staying with?" said Marty in a professional voice.

"You did give a statement at the time, saying that you did not see Billy Parsons, but a red Ford Mustang went past your home much later in the day. Can you elaborate on this please, Mrs Cavallaro?" Marty smiled sweetly at the shrewd woman opposite him. He could tell that this lady was not someone to be taken lightly. This proved to be a good opening question for Mrs Cavallaro.

"Oh yes, I do remember Billy Parsons, Chief Inspector." came the gushing reply.

Interrupting Mrs Cavallaro, Marty asked her to call him "Marty".

"Very well, um er Marty," she stumbled, not used to first names for senior police officers.

"Not that I knew Billy personally, you realise ... Marty." Mrs Cavallaro was having difficulty coming to terms with this first name bit.

Marty smiled within and looked expectantly at Mrs

Cavallaro for more words to flow. A slight hesitation, so Marty took the plunge.

"No, of course not, Mrs Cavallaro", was Marty's glowing answer. This proved to be the catalyst Mrs Cavallaro was waiting for and she surged forward with a more relaxed disposition. Perhaps she did not fancy herself as "mixing with the riff raff" of everyday living, let alone a child.

"I knew Billy was living with that foreign couple, at number 1811. Occasionally, I saw the child out walking alone. It worried me dreadfully, Chief Inspector, oh I mean, Marty. That poor boy, wondering along the street, unaccompanied. Anything could have happened to him, and it did, poor little soul." Mrs Cavallaro completed her sentence with a look of woe and clasped her thin hands together in mock remorse.

Marty didn't fall for this crap. *This dame couldn't care one bit!*

On she went, like a clock wound to capacity. "No, I did not see the child on the day he disappeared. Although, I did see the red car speed by my home, later in the day."

Giving Marty an expectant look, Mrs Cavallaro halted and eyed Marty in a penetrating manner. Her eyes were conveying a message; what it was, Marty could not tell.

CHAPTER six

"Let me explain myself." Mrs Cavallaro said in an air of supreme knowledge and authority. "As you are already aware, no doubt, um, Marty, someone did see Billy on that day, Mrs Marjorie Femmer. Lives at number 1768, but you would already know that. She apparently saw Billy walking along North Beaumont, and said that 'he was walking in the direction of the pathway that led down to Roy Rogers Avenue'. What intrigues me Chief Inspector is, how did she know this, it is only an assumption Chief Inspector? Heavens know why she did not stop and take Billy home or take him to her own home. It was a tragedy just waiting to happen, I say. We all knew that Mrs Femmer had a soft spot for Billy, it was common knowledge." She shot a very direct look at Marty. Mrs Cavallaro was waiting for Marty to make a comment but Marty chose not to and played dumb. So Mrs Cavallaro went on with her "la de da" voice.

"Billy spent considerable time at the Femmer residence and went on various outings with them, I understand." Mrs Cavallaro looked up as there was a knock at the door. "Enter," came the authoritative response from Mrs Cavallaro.

The door opened to reveal Matilda coming in with the tea. The grand dame stopped any further speech and waited patiently for Matilda to set the china tea pot, cups and saucers in their correct place. A plate of small decorated cup cakes and petite biscuits had also been provided. Once completed, Matilda asked Mrs Cavallaro if there was anything else.

"No, thank you Matilda. That will be all." replied the efficient Mrs Cavallaro.

Matilda departed from the room as silently as she had arrived.

"Shall I play mother, Inspector?" asked Mrs Cavallaro with a grin of very white false teeth. *Nothing natural about those dentures*, thought Marty. *Hell, even this lady's teeth are the most expensive in Hollywood!*

Pouring the tea into the gold and white, egg shell china cups, she leant over and passed the tea to Marty. Offering Marty the plate of delicacies, Marty chose to have a biscuit, to keep the pace going with Mrs Cavallaro's outpouring of vital information.

Truth be said, Marty was ravenous.

***

It was now late morning and Marty had an eventful day, so far.

Breakfast had been on the run, as Charlie Solomon wanted to meet with him early. The biscuit was not too sweet, *Better not reach for anything else to eat, it might put her off talking. She might think I'm a pig,* Marty reasoned to himself.

There was a faint, yet pleasant aroma, wafting into the room through an open window. *Must be from those Hydrangea bushes outside the windows*, thought Marty. His mother adored Hydrangeas, especially the Oakleaf variety, which Marty suspected were the species being grown here. As a youngster, his mother would scold Marty and his friends for breaking the flowers or the new shoots of her beloved Hydrangea plants. Not that he knew much about plants at all, but he recognised these plants for sure. Marty's parents had shifted some years ago to live in Vermont. Mrs Hislop had joined the local Hydrangea Society of Vermont, and was an active member. The perfume was not overpowering, you could almost say therapeutic to the senses. Their colour was almost surreal, an intangible shade of heavenly blue that darkened on the outside of the petals. The flower heads were immense. Quite a stunning display!

"Now where were we? Ah yes," said the informative Mrs Cavallaro. Cradling her tea cup and saucer in her lap, she spoke on, "The red car that Mrs Femmer drove around from daylight to dusk, and I might add with Billy in tow as well. Never out of it, the pair of them! Mr Femmer purchased the car for her not long before Billy came on the scene. Now what was the car again, yes, I recall. It was a Ford Mustang. All over red with white wall tyres. Thought she was the ace of spades, driving up and down North Beaumont all day long." Mrs Cavallaro ended at this juncture to sip her tea.

"Really!" said the interested Marty.

"As I said in my statement, many moons ago of course," chuckled Mrs Cavallaro, "I did see the car pass by here late in the afternoon, about a quarter to six. It was travelling at a heck of a pace too, I might add Chief Inspector – Marty – sorry, I forgot," finished Mrs Cavallaro with a apologetic gesture of her delicately shaped right hand.

Marty decided to throw a question at the "know it all" woman sitting before him.

"Can you be quite sure that it was definitely the red Mustang you saw? It must have been getting dark for you to see the car clearly." enquired Marty in a curious tone.

"I can assure you that I saw the red Mustang." The tone became brittle. "I was in the front garden. It was summer, and the sun had not set. I heard the vehicle coming up the street. I looked up and saw the car hurtle by like a flash of lightning. I unfortunately did not discern the driver, but it could only have been Mrs Femmer, it was her automobile, after all," retorted Mrs Cavallaro with a firmness to her ladylike voice. "I will prove it to you. Ever since I was 21, when my father gave me a diary, I have religiously kept a record of events. Now, if you will just pardon me for a moment, I will get the diary for 1965 from the bookcase." said the 'fastidious record keeper'.

Rising to her feet with the aid of the walking stick, Peggy Cavallaro walked over to the mahogany bookcase. Opening the glass doors, she selected a diary and brought it back to the sofa. Sitting down again, she flipped through the pages and got the date in question. Bringing the diary over to Marty, and holding it with one hand, she said with great pleasure, "There you are, told you so! It's all there, the date and time, as I stated before."

Marty saw the flamboyant style handwritten entry recording the time and the red Mustang "hurtling up" North Beaumont. Marty nodded his head in consent with Mrs Cavallaro.

This satisfied her dented ego! *Hmmmm*, considered Marty. *Was this woman correct in her statement or was there a subtle suggestion of placing Mrs Femmer in an awkward position? Yes, it could have been Marjorie Femmer at the wheel OR it could have been Max Femmer OR even someone else. It was feasible, after all. Max Femmer undoubtedly had an extra set of car keys and went out in the car himself. Or, was it another person altogether?* Marty had yet to find this out.

Marty took the bull by the horns, so to speak, and asked in his most charming speech, "Oh, do you think that Mrs Femmer would be out at that time, surely Mr Femmer would have been home by then? But, I guess you know more about the neighbours than I would Mrs Cavallaro."

This bait was taken by the wealthy woman who replied with relish in a sophisticated attitude, "Oh yes, it's quite possible that Marjorie Femmer could have been behind that steering wheel. You see," Mrs Cavallaro leaning forward in Marty's direction said quietly, "she was a law unto herself." Drawing her frame back into the comfortable sofa, Mrs Cavallaro gave Marty a wink with her right blue eye.

Marty raised his eyebrows and answered in a lowered tone, "Is that so, well I never!" Marty focused his attention on Mrs Cavallaro more intently. She loved this play on words and proceeded to reveal more secrets.

"You see Detective Chief Inspector, I know Marjorie Femmer better than anyone else in Hollywood. I know for a fact that Mrs Femmer was nothing more than a little gold digger when she arrived in town. Twelve years of age. Ran away from home and landed at Hal Roach Studios demanding work. Dear Mr Roach Senior, that is, not Junior, took her in and gave a roof over her head. Done herself up to look a right tart, could pass as being seventeen! Threw herself at any man that would have her. Late nights every night of the week. Loved to frolic with the men. Had to be escorted home, paralytic. Quite disgusting, no shame at all that woman," tutted Mrs Cavallaro. On she went like a steam roller out of control, "Poor Max rescued her from the gutter, and tried to make something of Marjorie. After some bit acting, Mr Roach gave her the role of leading lady in a film. Well, do you know how she repaid his generosity?" Mrs Cavallaro paused, her blue soulless eyes were piercing into Marty's face. "Got herself blind drunk onset. Loves the whiskey, always has! They could only make half the film before Marjorie was carried off in a drunken stupor. It did upset dear Mr Roach a lot. They had to sack her you know, yes, quite shameful the whole thing. Max thought the world of her, always buying Marjorie gifts."

Marty was aware that the "Mrs Femmer" had been dropped in favour of just "Marjorie". Mrs Cavallaro clearly did not approve of Mrs Marjorie Femmer, one little bit. "Black as she is painted", as his mother used to say. Marty wondered what part Peggy Cavallaro played in having Mrs Femmer dismissed from the studio. *Quite a big part!* Marty mused to himself.

Interrupting herself, Mrs Cavallaro said pleasantly, "More tea, Detective Chief Inspector?"

"Yes please, I will." replied Marty.

"Help yourself to a cake or biscuit too, don't be shy." Mrs Cavallaro grinned at Marty. Peggy Cavallaro was sizing up the man opposite her with some disapproval.

Brought up by the back of his pants, this one, thought Mrs Cavallaro as she gave Marty a "once over" examination.

CHAPTER seven

Having poured Marty another cup of the aromatic smelling tea, Mrs Cavallaro went on with her discourse.

"Then Max bought her that red Mustang. Raced all over the place in it. You could guarantee that she would be out gallivanting anywhere people could see her. Once Marjorie had Billy with her, there was no stopping her then. Telling the whole neighbourhood that Billy was her adopted son, dragging the little boy into the shopping mall, the gas station and the bowling alley she loved to frequent. Out from daylight to dusk, the pair of them." Mrs Cavallaro dropped her head and shook it with a look of contempt. On she went without pausing for breath, "Hardly ever had any food in the house, always forgetting groceries. Sugar or milk or meat to cook for dear Max. Quite disorganised. If it wasn't for Max, she wouldn't have a house to live in. A spendthrift, useless with money. Oh, yes, Max had his hands full with her, mark my words!" said the emphatic Mrs Cavallaro.

Marty began to feel a distinct dislike for this woman. Mrs Cavallaro liked to hold the floor and enjoyed an assembly of listeners, namely Marty on this opportunity.

"I was Mr Hal Roach Senior's personal secretary for many

years. He relied on me to arrange meetings, complete reports, discussing what the cast, producers and directors were up to. I had to keep him informed of everything, so I had to have eyes in the back of my head Detective Ch—Marty" completed Mrs Cavallaro with a superior raising of her well coiffeured head.

Yeah alright! Give us a break Peggy, Marty was thinking.

"You know, um, Marty," Mrs Cavallaro paused. "I think that Billy is alive." She gave Marty a knowledgeable look.

"What makes you think that, Mrs Cavallaro?" replied Marty with definite interest in his voice.

"You may not recall this, as this was before your time in the police force. There was a group based in Ohio, called the 'Mother Seekers'. It was operated by a group of women. They would take into their care any waif, stray or homeless child, and then arrange for these unfortunates to be placed in the homes of people, who could not have children or had been rejected adoption for some reason or another." Mrs Cavallaro took a deep breath this time and eyed Marty intently. "Its quite possible that Billy was picked up by this group. They were particularly active in California over a period of years. The authorities had the group disbanded a long time ago; but not before many children had just simply vanished! Now that is what I think really happened to Billy Parsons,"

Sitting back in the chair, Mrs Cavallaro gave Marty an autocratic stare of triumphal sovereignty. Her decision would prevail. *This is a lot to assume Mrs Cavallaro,* Marty's brain was ticking over.

Finally, he answered with, "We will check it out, it's a possibility. Thank you for your hospitality and help, Mrs Cavallaro. I really appreciate your assistance. Now I had best get back to the office."

He was going to ask her about the couple that Billy stayed with, but that would have taken on another marathon story. As both parties were dead, Marty decided to leave it, well for the time being anyway. Marty's ears were ringing by now and he was damned hungry!

Mrs Cavallaro positively beamed at Marty and said in a coy expression. "Oh Marty, an old lady like me, helping the police. I'm 98 you know, still got my marbles," she said in a bragging tone of voice.

You ain't bad for 98, I agree, exclaimed Marty to himself and smiling with wonder at the foible and vain woman.

As he walked out of the luxuriously furnished room, Marty saw a large glass vase displaying a bunch of the blue Hydrangeas, strategically positioned on an ormolu table against a wall.

Mrs Cavallaro followed Marty out of the drawing room and into the foyer.

With a wave of her right arm, she pointed to the painting at the top of the stairs, and said very proudly, "This was my husband, Chief Inspector. Antonio Cavallaro, but he was known as Tony. Wonderful man, I miss him so much. Passed away quite some years ago. He was a cartage contractor originally for Hal Roach Studios and then branched out into nationwide transport. You have probably heard of 'Wagon Wheels', that was my husband's business and now I am head of the company. There is a fleet of over 400 trucks travelling all over the country, even into Canada and Alaska!" Perusing Marty with a look of "see how important I am", Marty was searching the inner recesses of his mind. *I've never heard of it. Sounds like something out of the Wild West,* Marty thought.

Stifling a laugh, Marty answered with great care, "Yes, I have heard of the name, Mrs Cavallaro. They do a marvellous job!"

She gave a very false white flash of the perfect dentures embedded in her frivolous, yet intelligent, head.

Saying his farewell, Marty left Mrs Cavallaro behind to revel in her self-made importance. On his way to the car, he noticed a male chauffeur polishing a black stretch caddy and the gardener trimming the box hedges.

How the other half live! Marty shook his head.

CHAPTER *eight*

As he drove away and headed back to the LAPD, Marty could not help but reflect on the three women he had met today.

Firstly, Marjorie Femmer. He liked Mrs Femmer – even if she did have a drink problem. Marjorie Femmer knew love and gave it a hundred-fold to Billy, who returned his love for this lady. Max Femmer was too concerned about his sketches and drawings, to give much love to his wife. Marty didn't believe the story about Marjorie Femmer and her housekeeping. The other stuff about her acting failure was in the past, irrelevant gossip. "Black as she's painted" was Peggy Cavallaro's crowning achievement. Marty remembered a phrase his father used to recite – "Whilst you are being talked about, someone else is being left alone". This certainly applied to Peggy Cavallaro.

Then there was Anna Serenova – a lost soul, devoid of any feeling. Her upbringing must have been one of disrespect to others, especially law enforcement! Shown no love or care to other human beings, her nature had developed into bitter resentment for normality. Anna may know something that was imperative to Billy's disappearance. Marty might have a chat with her, see if anything slips out!

Finally, Mrs Peggy Cavallaro. Self appointed judge of

everyone, holding herself in the highest of esteem. Money was her "god". She had been blessed with a good financial provider, her late husband. Peggy Cavallaro did not know what it was to go without or display thoughtfulness to her fellow men and women. A thin veneer covered a woman who could be ruthless to the core. She was riding high, but Marty knew deep down that there was something being concealed. This may be the very "something" to bring Peggy Cavallaro to her knees.

Stopping to grab a takeaway to eat at the office, Marty knew there was still a long way to go, but some progress had been made. At least there was something to inform Charlie Solomon about. Marty was a man determined to achieve results. It was a basic instinct he had inherited from his mother, Eve. The training he had received in the police force had embedded this trait in Marty. Being single for so long had perhaps been something of a detriment to Marty. His mannerism was one of success at all cost, without regard for the feelings of others. Not that Marty thought he was sometimes harsh and straight to the point. On the contrary, Marty just had tunnel vision, and focused entirely on the end result. Complete dedication to his role was Marty's self imposed adherence to duty.

***

Marty was back in the office and walked in to find La Paz studying something on a laptop screen.

La Paz lifted his head up and said, "Oh hi, Boss. How did it all go with the Cavallaro woman?"

"Tell you all the info in a jiffy." Marty tucked into his food and ate ravenously. "You eaten La Paz?" Marty asked between mouthfuls of food.

"Yeah Boss, Gloria made some lunch for me today, tortilla. I've got the laptop we seized from the place we busted. Come and look at this, I warn you it's not a pretty picture Boss."

Marty realised that La Paz had found something on the child pornography as he strode over to view the screen.

"Oh God, these pics are from all over the world!" Taken aback Marty ran his hands over his face in disbelief as he looked at the multitude of files containing all manner of lurid images.

"Boss, I found this file tucked away in trash mail. Look at it!" exclaimed La Paz, peering up to Marty who was looking over his shoulder.

"See this file, open it up and hey presto what do you see Boss? Billy Parsons, and the dates of May and June 1965. These photos had been taken then and kept, and eventually uploaded onto the computer disc. Someone took these pics of the poor little guy over a period of time. But look at this, see this photo here. Who do you think this woman is, holding Billy on her lap? I bet you its Anna Serenova, in younger days. No wonder Billy wanted to get out of that shit hole he was staying at!" exclaimed the deeply annoyed La Paz.

Having kids of his own, La Paz tried not to think about this kid subjected to indecent interference. *Who took these pictures, the couple he was staying with? More than likely*, thought the horrified La Paz.

Marty agreed with La Paz that there was a resemblance of Anna to the woman in the photo. Naturally, the woman was younger, about 19 to 20 years old, but the likeness was remarkable. The mole was not quite clear, but it sure looked like Anna Serenova. Poor little Billy, stark naked being held by this creep! The hold on the child was one of restraint. This woman sported a short dress and was laughing at the camera with delight. Marty shook his head in disbelief. Some of the photos were black and white but some were coloured. Fortunately the photo of Billy with this woman was in colour.

"Whose laptop is this La Paz?" snapped Marty.

"It belongs to Armitage, or should I say "Thor". Password encrypted but I managed to break into it. Not nice, is it?" replied La Paz.

Marty grimaced and answered, "No, it ain't. We need to get these two together I think, and have a friendly discussion with Thor and Anna. We might get one of them to squeal if we apply enough pressure. I want a printout of that photo of Billy and the woman, to take to the interview, it will work a treat!" Marty said quickly, eager to have another meeting with his playground playmate, Pirate Pussy.

La Paz interjected saying, "Before we do that Boss, I will just bring you up to speed on my visit to Universal Studios.

Some interesting stuff I learnt."

"Okay, shoot La Paz. Let me have it, and then we'll go and see our fancy footed friends."

La Paz informed Marty that Billy Parsons came to Hollywood as the result of a talent scout on vacation in Australia in late 1964. Travelling around the countryside had led the chap to spot Billy Parsons with his mother, while she was shopping at the general store in the far north of New South Wales. After talking it over with the parents, it was agreed to sign Billy up for a five year contract with a further five year option. There were lucrative financial benefits offered to the family, with TV commercials being thrown in to pump up the child's earnings. As the parents were cash strapped, they allowed Billy to leave his home and take up the contract. This commenced in the March of 1965. Billy had made three films, mostly low budget films for the young kids market, and did a number of TV ads, by the time he disappeared on July 21, 1965.

By a stroke of good fortune, La Paz had been able to speak to someone who remembered the little guy. A cleaner, named Abel Harmer, who still worked at Universal Studios after all these years. He recalled vividly the "full of beans" Billy Parsons.

As La Paz completed his summary of the findings, Marty thought that was all. However, La Paz stalled before continuing.

"Boss, this guy then told me that he can recall Billy coming to the studio one day, not long before he disappeared, with red welts on his back. According to Abel, Billy was not himself and was distressed. He was hobbling along and when Abel asked what was wrong, Billy had burst into tears. As he picked the kid up to console him and sit him on a chair, Abel saw that the little guy's shirt was blood stained on the back in a few small areas. Billy seemed to be in pain, when Abel touched his back. Taking off the kid's shirt and singlet, Abel said he saw red welts on the lower back. These had bled and appeared to be caused from a leather strap or belt. Billy pleaded with Abel not to tell anyone. Abel did ask Billy how the welts had got there. Billy told him that he had been naughty, and had to be taught a lesson and then had to stand in a dark cupboard for a long time. The people Billy was living with had got angry with him about something. I got the guy to give a statement. Abel had always kept quiet because Billy had asked him to. Plus, the other fact was that Abel is black, and wondered if he might be accused of hitting Billy. So he kept his mouth shut. Seems a bit late now to tell us, should have done it when Billy went missing, but I can understand what the guy was thinking," said the saddened La Paz.

"Yeah, those days were tough on people like Abel Harmer. Who was going to believe him anyway?" remarked the curious Marty.

La Paz reminded Marty about his visit to Peggy Cavallaro.

"Oh yes, her. Very high brow and loaded with money. Knows all the goss but my hunch is that she knows more than she has told me or – " halted Marty looking sternly at La Paz with a raised finger, "she is hiding something that may incriminate her. I want you to check out the finances of Peggy Cavallaro including her transport business called Wagon Wheels. While you're at it, do the same for Marjorie Femmer. I would be interested to know how Marjorie Femmer can stay in the Hollywood Hills; she must have a private income to support her. Oh, and one other thing that comes to mind. I want you to check on a red Ford Mustang owned by Mrs Femmer in 1965. See if it is still in existence. I have a gut feeling that this red '65 holds an important key to this case, La Paz," finished the inquisitive Detective Chief Inspector.

Marty knew that he would have to ask Mrs Femmer about the Mustang. Why had she conveniently forgot to mention the vehicle? Having brought matters up to speed between the two men, they arranged their next modus operandi.

"Lets get these two lovebirds together in the same interview room and we will ask 'em about the Billy Parsons photos. One of them will break, I'm sure of it La Paz," came Marty's next statement.

CHAPTER *nine*

Having organised to get Anna and Thor together, the recording tape was running as the interview proceeded.

"Now, the laptop we seized this morning from your place belongs to you Thor. Some very interesting data on it too. Care to elaborate about it all?" was Marty first question fired at the couple.

Thor looked at both detectives with a "don't give a shit!" attitude. He responded with a harsh resonant voice and a blank stare, "No comment."

"How about you Anna," came Marty's next interrogation tactic, "what can you tell us about the images on the laptop?"

Anna's reply came swift, yet said with a sentiment of bitterness and a blank stare, "No comment."

Alright, play hard the pair of you and I will match you both, reasoned Marty to himself inwardly. The battle was on.

Marty minced no matters and came back sternly, "We located a file on the laptop, conveniently stored in the trash file. This file contains photos of Billy Parsons taken in May and June of 1965.

The photos are very compromising to say the least, especially this one taken on June 25, 1965." said the cunning Marty. With that Marty slid the photo of the woman holding Billy Parsons, in front of them both and locked his gaze on Anna Serenova. There was a cold stare from the vixen vampire as she returned Marty's look. Anna did not even attempt to cast her wicked eyes on the photo.

"Recognise someone in the photo?" asked Marty with an enquiring tone in his voice. He was waiting the reaction.

Thor did look at the photo and immediately he must have identified Anna as being the woman holding Billy. He turned his giant head in Anna's direction and said gruffly, "You told me to trash that file. How come you're in that photo? You said you knew nothing about it and it wasn't worth keeping. This is you, ain't it, you fuck-faced bitch!?"

Anna went wild with this accusation and replied hotly to Thor, "Keep you mouth shut you slimy, slobbering bastard. That's not me, how would I know who it is? I damn well wasn't there!" She was full of indignation and raised her dirty hand to strike Thor. La Paz told Anna to cool it in a menacing tone.

Anna swivelled her head around to face La Paz and addressed him with, "You shut yours, you filthy Mexican!" and promptly spat in the face of La Paz.

Marty reached over and took a firm hold of Anna's waving hand and slapped it down hard on the table.

"I will have you up for assaulting a police officer and being a party to child pornography, so help me sister," came Marty's defensive pledge to the vile Anna.

Anna delivered Marty a look of covert displeasure.

"So that was you in that photo. Your mother and that other bloke were behind all this weren't they? This kid was the one that went missing years ago, stayed at your joint. Photographed the kid whenever he went to the bathroom. You had him on your fucking knee you wretch, while that vodka swilling swine took pics. Made good dough out of it too, no doubt!" boomed Thor at Anna.

This was enough for the hateful Anna, who leapt at Thor like a lioness full of rage, and began etching her initials in Thor's cement like features. Thor moved back to avoid Anna's attack, and responded with a knuckle duster fist in her demented face. Blood gushed from the wound instantly. La Paz could see that the mole had been struck. He handed Anna his clean handkerchief to stop the flow of blood but the thankless woman threw it aside and got up from her chair. Throwing herself on Thor with all her strength, she screamed loudly and began hitting him with her fists and scratching Thor's ragged face. Anna's fists were like pistons pumping into the imposing physique of Thor. Blood streamed down her ragged features. Thor managed to deflect some of the blows as the two detectives got up and raced around to the other side of the table, restraining this despicable creature. Biting La Paz and Thor before being brought under control, with the aid of another police officer, who had been standing outside the door, the men breathed a sigh of relief. Seething with anger, Anna was handcuffed and marched from the room.

Thor was bleeding badly from Anna's physical frenzy. After some bandages were applied by the medics, Thor was given some time to himself. Marty was determined to get Thor to spill the beans on Anna. With Thor patched up, Marty wanted to complete the interview again. This time with Thor alone.

Entering the interview room again after an interval, Marty and La Paz recommenced their interview with Thor.

"Okay Big Boy," said a feisty Marty. "You better realise that Anna is going to jump ship and let you take the rap for this. So, what's it to be, huh?"

Thor was silent and seemed to be lost in contemplation.

La Paz took up the challenge and said to Thor, "You write down everything that you know about those images of Billy, every last detail and we promise to do a deal with you. Sure you go down for the other images on the laptop, but we're only interested in the Billy Parsons photos. Information from you and we give a reduced sentence, how about it Thor?" La Paz handed Thor a pad and pen in anticipation.

The giant man comprehended his predicament and gave a nod of his blood soaked bandaged head. "Okay, you win. But I'm no good at writing," Thor grunted.

"No worries," La Paz replied. "I can help, you shoot and I will write. But you have to sign this remember Thor." "Yeah, yeah. I know that copper." Thor grufly replied,

Marty elected to remain behind and hear what Thor had to say. His statement revealed that Vladimir Nijinski was originally a Russian ballerina with the Russian State Academy. Booze had been his downfall and he had been dropped from the academy. Then Nijinski moved to the States in 1949.

To make a living, he took up photography and resorted to pornography as it paid better than mainstream photography. He met Olga Serenova and they rented the house at 1811 North Beaumont. Nijinski was close to all the action in Hollywood and did very well. Later he specialised solely in child pornography and eventually had the good fortune of having Billy Parsons come to live with them. They both had secured some work at Universal Studios, but Thor noted he was not sure exactly what it was. Anna Serenova did go to the University of Chicago in the '60s and came home during term breaks. That's when Thor thinks the photograph was taken with Billy. Anna told Thor to load a computer disc she had given him, onto his laptop for safe keeping. When Thor asked her about the disc, Anna had told him it was some old photos of a young kid cousin that had stayed with her folks back in the '60s. The photos weren't important, just a bit of amateur fun with the camera. He did as he was instructed, as Anna did not have a computer. Some time later on, Thor had looked at the file and saw the name Billy Parsons. Thor had memories of the missing child and trashed the file; but never actually looked at the file contents! He had not asked Anna about the disc, in case she became angry. This did seem a bit of a lame excuse and poor reasoning on the behalf of Thor; thought the two detectives. However, they took into account that Thor was a pawn and easily influenced by the vivacious and smooth talking, evil Anna.

Both men believed his story. Thor's manifestation to the

nasty Anna about the photo of Billy and her had been enough to convince the police duo that Thor was innocent about the nature of the deleted file. The next piece of information Thor told the detectives was quite astounding.

"That rich dame who lives up there on cash hill, she won't be too happy about you cops spoiling her territory," concluded the deep sounding Thor, with a distinctive drawl.

La Paz glanced over to Marty and answered with a query in his Latin sounding voice, "What rich dame?"

"That rich bitch up at number 1817, who owns everything. All fancy and thinks her shit don't stink!" Thor replied rapidly.

Alarm bells rang in Marty's ears.

Thor could see that the two detectives were taken back. He continued on, "Calls herself Peggy Cavallo or somethin' like that."

"Do you mean Peggy Cavallaro?" came Marty's point blank question. Marty was glued to the spot, awaiting Thor's confirmation.

"Yeah, that's the name. So high brow and highfalutin, that dame. She owns number 1811, Anna just rents the joint off her. Her old lady and that Vladimir, they rented it, and then when they both snuffed it, Anna stayed on." Thor gave the detectives a definite look of self satisfaction, having told them something they did not know or anticipate.

As Marty was leaving the room, he looked back at Pirate Pussy, and said jokingly, "Oh and next time we meet, can you give me advance warning and I'll have some protective head gear on, okay?"

Pirate Pussy took the joke well and gave a ragged smile in return.

Leaving Thor to be dealt with by the duty officers, Marty and La Paz made their way back to the office.

CHAPTER *ten*

Sitting down his tall body in the chair, La Paz informed Marty that there were some other details he wanted to bring Marty up to date on.

"Okay shoot, La Paz. Hope its good pal; I want to check out this red Mustang real soon," came the hasty summons of Marty Hislop. He was eager to locate this automobile, and find out who was driving it.

"Max Femmer was never interviewed about the disappearance of Billy Parsons, mainly because he was at work that day. However, something told me to make some enquiries. I contacted Walt Disney Studios and asked about Max Femmer. They confirmed he worked there for a number of years until his death in 1966. His work was held in very high regard by all who worked with Femmer. I then asked the guy I was speaking with, if there was still anyone around who knew Femmer, or was friendly with him. He gave me a name of a Dirk van Zuutmeyer, who Femmer was very close with. He also worked at the studio but has since retired. By our good luck, this van Zuutmeyer is still alive and lives in West Hollywood. I phoned this guy, and he is willing to speak with me about Max Femmer. In my brief conversation with him, Mr van Zuutmeyer did say that Max Femmer had to leave work that day Billy went missing, some time after 11 a.m. There was a phone call from Mrs Femmer, sounding distressed about a fall she had. This could lead to something, I reckon. How about I go there tomorrow and see what he has to say, Boss?" said La Paz, pleased with this new knowledge for his superior.

"Great. That's good stuff, La Paz. So Max Femmer wasn't at work the full day, interesting." Marty was keen for La Paz to take this further. "Do it tomorrow. It's getting on now and I want the bank details for Peggy Cavallaro and Marjorie Femmer before you go home tonight, La Paz." said Marty, who felt like a coffee before doing any more. Going to get himself and La Paz a coffee, Marty was placing all the happenings of this eventful day into perspective. There was some light being shed on this case. Anna and Thor locked up and the revelation about number 1811 being owned by Peggy Cavallaro. The most significant, yet elusive piece of the jigsaw puzzle, was this red Ford Mustang. *Where was it now? Who had been driving it on that fatal evening? Was it in fact Max Femmer?* Marty was satisfied with the way things were shaping up. However, more work was needed to crack this case wide open.

***

Walking back to the office, Marty was still making a mental order of the facts they had unearthed. As he approached the office, Marty saw the figure of Charlie Solomon standing talking to La Paz.

"So the big boss has come to find out how us boys are going," mused Marty. Giving Charlie Solomon a nod and smile, Marty sat at his desk and indicated for Solomon to do the same. Marty could see from the face of Charlie, that trouble was brewing.

"What's up, Charlie?" said Marty, wondering what this was all about. Solomon's face was stern and serious and his speech was sharp.

"I had a phone call from the Commissioner just a few minutes ago. Your visit to Mrs Peggy Cavallaro did not go down too well. She lodged a stinging complaint about you." Solomon raised his hand at Marty, who was going to say something but instead sat bolt upright in his chair, and waited for the next words Solomon was about to say. "'Short on manners and very disorderly in his presentation. Total disregard for police rank, first name being preferred instead. Not what you would expect for a Detective Chief Inspector' were the words of the lady. Care to enlighten me Marty?" finished Solomon, turning his head to one side, and giving Marty a withering stare.

"Boss, that dame is a stuck-up bitch. So self-opinionated, got everyone under her neat little thumb. I know that she is withholding information, I can tell that! Yeah sure, I was a bit bedraggled, I admit, but I didn't think I was that crude with my approach to her," said Marty defensively.

"I just want the truth of the matter, Marty. No platitudes, just cold hard facts. Why were you looking like a garbage man?" said the impatient Solomon. Charlie Solomon didn't need complaints like this levelled at his officers. He prided himself that his staff were professional and courteous in their work ethics. Although, Solomon was more than aware that Marty was an exception to the rule.

Marty explained the morning's events and the baseball encounter with Thor. "Perhaps I was a little short with the woman, but gee boss, I had a job to do. I often ask people I interview to call me Marty. Is she frightened I might ask her something about her past? Because I tell you this much boss, that Peggy Cavallaro has a dark history. I have been a cop for a good many years, and I can discern that Mrs Cavallaro is not all she claims to be." Marty was angry in his response, and gave Solomon a challenging look.

"Alright Marty, point taken. But please, next time, go easy on this one. Mrs Cavallaro has connections in high places and she will make things very awkward for you. I don't want to have you taken off the case, man. I need you on this 100 percent with La Paz. Anyway, what have you both got so far?" came Charlie Solomon's more pleasant reply. He leaned forward in his chair with anticipation.

Marty was now acutely alert to the simple realisation that Peggy Cavallaro was trying to manipulate the powers that be, to have him removed from the case.

Well, she ain't goin' to get away with it! Marty laughed to himself. Debriefing Charlie Solomon on the case so far, satisfied the man.

"Well, progress has been made. I am impressed with you

both. Keep up the good work. You may crack this one yet!" Getting up from the chair, Solomon winked at Marty and said farewell to both officers, and left the room.

Marty was the first to say anything, "Bullshit! Short on manners and very disorderly in his presentation. Who does she think she is? Lady Muck, that's all!" Marty was disgusted and turned his head away for a moment to look out the window. La Paz went to speak, but thought it better left. He could tell from Marty's body language, that the man was very annoyed.

The afternoon traffic was building up on the freeway and there was a panic of commuters rushing to get buses, trains, taxis or to their parked cars, to hustle them out of the city and into the sprawling suburbs of LA. The weather looked threatening, possibly a thunderstorm approaching. Detective Chief Inspector Marty Hislop could see that his right hand man was busy, as always, following things through. *He's a great guy*, thought Marty. *I would be lost without him.* La Paz brought Marty out of his reverie.

"Boss, I forgot to tell you. That other woman in the house at number 1811, was a Leanne Fellstaff. She is a known user of opium and other barbiturates. A wonderful passport to paradise! Has a record for possession, but nothing serious. Fellstaff appears harmless and from what we can get out of her, knew nothing about Billy Parsons or the couple who lived at the place back then. The boys below will deal with her."

"Okay. Anything on those bank financials, Miguel La Paz?"

replied Marty, with a ring of humour in his voice. It was not very often that Marty addressed La Paz with his full name.

Miguel looked up quickly to his boss, a bit surprised. Stammering as he spoke, "Ah, ah … not yet boss. Still waiting for the bank statements to come through, shouldn't be long now. Will give them to you as soon as I receive them."

Marty got up from his chair and walked over to La Paz, and screwed his face up, and bent down to see what his comrade was doing. Marty should have been wearing his new spectacles for reading, but found it convenient to leave the glasses in the bureau top drawer at his apartment.

"What you doin' pal?" La Paz seemed a bit embarrassed and responded hurriedly.

"Boss, I thought you wanted those details about that red Mustang real soon. So I am checking it out with the traffic records. That way when you see Mrs Femmer tomorrow, you will have ammunition up your sleeve, if needed."

Marty wasn't one to reveal his emotions to his understudy officer, but on this rare occasion he decided to.

"My friend, pack up, you have done enough for one day. Saved my head from being slammed from here to kingdom come. And now doing his boss's work for him. Go home, there is a storm coming. Gloria and the kids are waiting! Come on," prompted Marty.

"Gee, thanks Boss. I think those details are here on that red '65 though." said the thankful and willing to please Detective Miguel La Paz.

"See boss, that rego on the Mustang was not renewed after January 1969. Never transferred to another name either. So the automobile could not have been sold. The licence has just lapsed I would say," said La Paz peering up at Marty.

"Yep, it sure looks like it. Mrs Marjorie Femmer certainly has some explaining to do tomorrow. Now hop it! You've done well," came Marty's final instruction to Miguel.

Miguel La Paz stated he would visit Dirk van Zuutmeyer tomorrow before coming into the office. Putting on his jacket and getting his lunch box, he said goodnight to Marty and left for home and his loving family.

Marty envied Miguel. A home to go to each night, with laughing kids and a devoted wife. Not that he was jealous of Miguel. He deserved his family and the bond they all shared. Marty had experienced their family union more than once, and felt a humbled man after being in their company.

After mulling over a few thoughts, mainly the visit to Marjorie Femmer, Marty decided to pack it in too.

CHAPTER *eleven*

Driving home, he called into a KFC outlet and got himself some Southern Fried country chicken with pineapple. Marty liked that.

At his upstairs apartment in busy Glendale, Marty relaxed and watched the ball game that had his favourite team playing. The almighty LA Rangers put up a powerful fight against the Pasadena Panthers, after leading for most of the game, but went down in the final ten minutes, 25 to 21.

Jeez, thought Marty. *They had them, and they let the bastards get away to win! Damn it!*

Feeling let down, his mind suddenly went back to the case. Fiddling with his third unfinished beer, Marty was not going to let some rich so-and-so interfere with this case. Those blue Hydrangeas came back to haunt him. What was it about those flowers; the colour or the lingering aroma he smelt whilst in the lavish room at the Cavallaro residence? Marty would like his mother to see those Hydrangeas. She would know the variety name. The plants were so lush and vigorous.

Falling asleep in front of the TV, Marty slept for some hours before waking in the early hours of the morning to hear rain falling outside. Thunder echoed in the heavens above and lightning flashed across the dark sky like a sword of silver. Rain was running down the window panes like silky gossamer threads in an unending stream of fast and furious activity. Outside was dark, bleak and threatening. *Foolish to be out in this type of weather*, thought Marty to himself.

Marty liked the rain. The heat could be trying. To tell the truth, Marty had always relished the heat of Los Angeles as a kid growing up in Woodland Hills. Surfing with his friends was a favourite past time in those far off high-spirited days, before heading off to college and finally university. As an older man now, Marty preferred the more temperate climatic conditions. His visits to upper Washington State to fish, had made him realise the cooler weather was his forte. Marty's father was a keen angler, and had taught his son just how to throw the line with one flick of the wrist, which hook to use for certain fish and how to gut and cook the catch on the river bank or by the ocean.

Marty relapsed into a heavy sleep and dreamt of blue Hydrangeas, red Mustangs and whiskey.

***

In the El Sereno home of the La Paz family, the evening had been one of congratulations and joy for the eldest daughter, Marisa, who had been successful in gaining an entry into the prestigious School of Fine Arts and Fashion at LA University.

Marisa had studied hard and gained excellent results against tough competition in the final examination. Now at 19 years of age, she was over the moon with happiness. Miguel and Gloria were equally overjoyed with their daughter's achievement. Her siblings, including the bashful Jonas, gave their big sister a kiss and hug to celebrate the news.

Miguel was a keen guitarist along with the budding Jonas. Both played a rousing Mexican rumba, while the ladies of the house danced around in harmonious rhythm to the catchy and jaunty melody. Their dinner had been one of Mexican favourites, flavoured with the usual red chillis, chicken fajita, Mexican rice and fried beans. Gloria had made a family favourite drink, cactus smoothie, topped with lime ice cream and pistachios.

The night was late finishing, after the family festivites. Some friends had also been asked to join them in rejoicing at Marisa's success. With the kids now in bed and the house quiet, Miguel La Paz lay in bed alongside his adored wife Gloria. He couldn't help think about Billy Parsons – so vulnerable and young, far removed from his loving family. Miguel thought about his kids, how would he cope without them here? Let alone to think of them living in a stranger's house faraway from familiar surroundings.

Gloria turned over and opened her black eyes, looking at Miguel with tenderness.

"Honey, what's the matter? You look all upset, what's wrong?" said Gloria as she raised herself up on the pillow.

Miguel turned his head to give Gloria his smile that never failed to melt Gloria's heart.

"I was just thinking about this kid, Billy Parsons, 7 years old. His life was so short and yet we don't even know what really happened to the poor little guy. No parents to hold him and tell him a bedtime story, cuddle him and tuck him into bed. Shown no comfort or love. I'm just so thankful that our kids are happy Gloria, and know they are loved, more than anything else in the world." Miguel felt a lump swell up in his throat and a wetness in his eyes. He snuggled up to Gloria, kissing her gently. She ran a hand over his hairy bare chest. Her caressing hand was soothing to Miguel.

"I know, Miguel. We are the happiest parents alive," whispered luscious Gloria, kissing the moist lips of her childhood sweetheart goodnight.

Slumber came upon them.

They did not hear the rain as it torrented down upon the earth – nor the thunder or lightning. Both were dreaming the sweetest of dreams about each other and their kids.

CHAPTER *twelve*

Morning came upon the city with a new freshness. Everything sparkled with the glistening of the raindrops. Rainbows appeared in the droplets like precious gems out of a jewellery box. The sky was radiant and renewed, as though an unknown artist had painted a new scene with painterly skill and wholesome imagination. The azure blue of the sky was peaceful and relaxing after the wild weather of the previous night.

Detective Chief Inspector Marty Hislop awoke to find himself still sitting in the living room holding the unfinished beer. The TV was still playing, albeit the morning sunrise show was screening – some crap about a transsexual wanting to become "hir". Originally born as a female, but fancied themselves as a male who dressed up as a female. Now, they were lobbying to become this new identity, and wanted pressure applied to the powers that be to recognise them.

Good luck with that one, thought Marty, stretching his stiff neck. *Before we know it, we will have goys and birls,* laughed Marty within.

After a bowl of cornflakes and black coffee with marmalade toast, Marty was ready to leave.

Oh shit, damnation! I have to wash. No I don't. Just a splash to the face and a quickie shave. A spray of deodorant, job done, was Marty's solution. Fixing up his loosened tie, wiping the black slip on business shoes and grabbing the crumpled suit jacket, Marty was out the door and down into the heavy commuter traffic, forging their way into the caverns of the city of Los Angeles.

Meanwhile, Detective Miguel La Paz made his way, with some traffic delay, to the address in West Hollywood of Dirk van Zuutmeyer. The apartment block was situated in a pleasant location. Landscaped sweeping lawns and colourful flower beds complemented the retirement complex where Dirk van Zuutmeyer lived. There were lockup garages for the residents and security gates to enter the village. Once La Paz had satisfied the gate keeper of his identity and appointment with Mr van Zuutmeyer via a intercom service, La Paz was allowed entry and parked the car in the visitors parking lot. Dirk van Zuutmeyer resided on the third floor.

Alighting from the lift, La Paz found where apartment number 311 was and pressed the bell. An elderly gentleman opened the green door and La Paz introduced himself.

Dirk van Zuutmeyer had an intelligent appearance, with dancing blue eyes and a long face. The nose was slightly crooked, perhaps the result of an injury or fight, La Paz could not tell. Wispy golden hair graced his head, but for his age, Dirk van Zuutmeyer looked remarkably fit and well.

La Paz had done a background check on the man before him,

gleaning that he was 90 years of age. The gentleman ushered La Paz into the unit with a warm welcome, and indicated for Miguel to take a seat. His stature was slightly stooped and he had a husky voice.

The room had a wonderful view over the gardens below and onto a distant golf course. La Paz liked golf, and guessed this was part of the facilities for the residents. Once formalities were over, La Paz commenced his questions.

"What can you tell me about the day Max Femmer left the office, after he received the phone call from Mrs Femmer?" began the enthusiastic La Paz.

Dirk thought a moment then started to speak in a slight European accent, possibly Dutch. "It would have been some time after 11 a.m., Max got a phone call. He seemed agitated with whoever it was and then went very quiet. The expression on his face told me something was definitely the matter. Max wasn't one to receive phone calls during work hours. He did not like to be interrupted from his work. Max put the receiver down, and just stared into space. I did ask him if everything was alright. Max mumbled that Marjorie had taken a fall and he would have to leave work straight away. Max also said that he may not return for the remainder of the day. I was his protégé, and Max asked me to take over and check the other workers were going along okay. Max liked to have his finger on the pulse, so to speak. Naturally, I assured him I would hold the fort. I did send my regards to Marjorie and hoped she was not too badly hurt. When Max came in the following day,

I asked how Marjorie was. Max seemed evasive, and passed it all off as a silly fall Marjorie had, but all was well now. I did not question Max again. He wasn't one you could enquire or pry into his life. I then learnt about the missing Billy Parsons, and Marjorie having seen the child in the morning. That was before her fall, I understand. The incident made headlines at the time Detective. Everyone was talking about it. Max did not utter a word to me, so I chose not to ask." Dirk folded his long, delicate hands in his lap and looked expectantly at La Paz. He began shuffling his large feet encased in brown moccasins.

"How well did you know Max Femmer, Mr van Zuutmeyer?' replied La Paz, sitting forward on the sofa. Dirk van Zuutmeyer informed La Paz, that both men had met at Walt Disney Studios. Max Femmer was already there when van Zuutmeyer came in 1954. He thought that Max had started there some time after 1936.

"Max Femmer was very considerate to me and gave me much encouragement and advice for my drawings. He could be downright rude, if the occasion arose. Prone to become angry if you did not perform your best, but on the whole, I did enjoy my time with him. I would have to say that Max was not one for making friends quickly. His manner was abrupt sometimes, and you had to know how to cope with Max's attitude. It was just him, but some of the other artists were put off by Max. Max and I were good friends outside work. I would often be asked for a lunch or dinner, as I was single. Marjorie was a good cook and a charming hostess. Both parties complimented each other. Marjorie adored Max, in fact worshipped him. Max had been her saving grace, when he had popped the question of marriage after a short romance. Marjorie was desperate for a child and when Max told her that he was impotent, it did come as a bombshell. She wanted Max to adopt, but he would not hear of it. I did try once to discuss the matter, on Marjorie's behalf. I thought that I may be able to talk to Max and persuade him to reconsider. It was the worst thing I could have done. He told me in no mean terms to mind my own business. What right did I have in probing into his private matters, and as I was a single man, how could I even think of raising the issue with him? I certainly learnt my lesson, I can tell you Detective! Eventually, Max got over it all and we remained firm friends until his untimely death. It was a real tragedy when Max died. We were all shocked. He had only just been to his doctor for a routine check up a week before he died. Max had a poor heart, and went regularly to his doctor in Beverly Hills. Max said the doctor was very happy with his health. He did take heart and blood pressure tablets, I believe. So when he collapsed at work and later passed away at the hospital, we were all so shocked. Marjorie was devastated with his sudden death and withdrew herself from people for a time. I visited her many times to see what I could do, offer advice and just be there as a support. Gradually, Marjorie recovered, and went back to indoor bowling, which she enjoyed. She was a member of the Amateur Dramatic Society of Brentwood for quite some years. That is about all I can say about my friendship with Max and Marjorie." Dirk said, awaiting a response from Miguel.

So, thought Miguel, *Max Femmer did not have a rare blood type after all. Mrs Femmer was telling a porky for sure!*

CHAPTER *thirteen*

Miguel noticed that Dirk's hands were fidgeting and realised that the man may be a smoker. There was a slightly smoky smell about the room.

Wishing to obtain as much information as possible, La Paz had an unexpected idea. Without pausing, La Paz launched another question, which did take the retired artist by surprise, "How well do you know a Mrs Peggy Cavallaro?"

Dirk sat up more in his chair, and replied cautiously, "Well, I do not know her very well at all. We were acquainted at some functions, but that was many years ago now." This was a bit too much for Dirk to contain himself and he hurriedly asked La Paz, "Would you mind if I smoked Detective? It's a failing of mine, I cannot break the habit. Started smoking as a boy during the war, for my nerves when I lived in Holland. I was on the run for a period from the Germans. Would you care to join me Detective?" Dirk looked earnestly at La Paz.

Miguel La Paz knew the best approach was to comply. This would make Dirk relax and open up more. Anything to keep the conversation flowing. La Paz hadn't smoked since marrying Gloria, but he still remembered the first smell of a lit cigarette. That lingering smoke as the flame burnt into the tobacco – so satisfying. With both men puffing away, the older man was visibly more at ease, Dirk van Zuutmeyer started to talk again without being prompted.

"Peggy Cavallaro married Tony Cavallaro, an Italian. Quite a nice chap, good at business. Did very well with the transport business, before that he was a private contractor. Mostly worked for Hal Roach Studios. When Peggy left working there, Tony went out on his own. They started up a business called Wagon Wheels, and it has been quite a success. I believe that Peggy runs the business now. They had no children to come into the business, or should I say, no living offspring remaining, to takeover the reins." As smoke poured out Dirk's nostrils, he shook his elongated head and appeared a trifle melancholy.

La Paz picked up on this immediately and his mind raced with possibilities. *What was this last comment about, "no living offspring remaining". Very interesting.*

Miguel La Paz answered Dirk, "Was there a child? Did something happen?" He waited with abated breath.

"Oh yes, there were twin girls. Marjorie knows about it all, she was still at Hal Roach Studios when it all took place. It all happened before I started working for Walt Disney. The twins drowned, I can't recall all the details. It all occurred some years prior to me starting at Walt Disney. I only heard it second hand. It was quite well talked about at the time apparently. Very terrible indeed." Dirk cast his blue eyes down and sighed. A cold shiver went down Dirk's spine. He had heard stories, not pleasant at all.

No, Dirk reasoned with himself. *I won't complicate matters by mentioning anything to the detective.* It was heresay, he could offer nothing to substantiate the statements he had overheard.

Miguel observed that Dirk was not entirely with him, and seemed to be mulling something over in his mind.

"Was there anything else you can tell me about the twins, Mr van Zuutmeyer?" asked Miguel, looking very intently at the older man.

Dirk recovered sufficiently to respond, "No nothing at all. As I said, it was before my time." He stubbed out his cigarette in the ornate coloured glass ashtray on the small table next to him. Dirk met Miguel's interrogating eyes, and managed a smile. Miguel realised there was nothing forthcoming, so decided to let the matter drop.

Now, the next important item was that red '65.

Miguel, using a very casual, yet tactical, approach, asked Dirk, "So what can you tell me about Billy? Did you ever meet the boy?"

Dirk lit another cigarette, before starting to answer the most crucial aspect of the interview.

"Yes, I met Billy on a number of occasions. All at the Femmer's house. Mostly on weekends, perhaps once or twice on a weekday. Marjorie would invite me home for dinner some evenings or on a weekend for a barbecue lunch. Being a bachelor has its advantages!" Dirk laughed with a throaty voice. "Billy was quite often there. A lovely child. Well-mannered and loved to talk to you. He literally adored Marjorie, and

Max as well. They lavished toys on Billy. Marjorie spent a lot of time with Billy, and Max was there on the weekends. They took him on outings and during the week, Marjorie had Billy with her when she was shopping or at the bowls or just wherever she was going. Billy loved to be out and about, a great explorer. That's how he first came into contact with the Femmer's. Marjorie found him one day out the front of their house, just slowly wandering along the street. Marjorie was worried that Billy could have been knocked by an automobile. So she invited Billy inside and their relationship blossomed from that. The red Mustang proved to be a hit with young Billy. He used to get so excited when Marjorie would tell him they were off somewhere." Dirk reminisced about those far off days, before tragedy struck and everything changed.

Miguel was pleased that the Mustang had come into the conversation. This would make it easier to delve a bit deeper.

"Yes, the Ford Mustangs were so popular back in the '60s. A good automobile, everyone loved them," said a zealous Miguel.

Dirk took the bait and replied ardently. "Yes, Max purchased the Mustang for Marjorie early that year. It was a vivid red with white wall tyres. The interior was the same colour scheme, quite eye catching! However, after Billy disappeared, Marjorie hardly ever drove the car. She didn't have the interest in life anymore. They sold the car some time later," ended Dirk, with an exhalation of smoke.

Miguel wanted to get some more information, so in an

unhurried tone he asked, "Oh, what a pity. Those cars are classics now. Did they sell the car after Max died or before?"

Dirk paused to consider the question. He thought this was a strange thing to ask. *What did it matter to the police when the car was sold?*

He was terse in his reply, "I do not remember when the Mustang was sold. Max bought Marjorie another automobile. It was a Plymouth Barracuda, a bit larger for her. Frankly Detective, I cannot see the relevance at all!"

Aware that he was plucking at straws and treading on thin ice, Miguel guided the conversation away diplomatically.

"Just one other thing, before I leave you. Did Mrs Femmer work at all? I gather that she didn't from what you are saying," said Miguel in his very pleasant Mexican accent.

"Oh no, Marjorie did not work. Anyway, Max would not have allowed it!" Dirk replied firmly.

Wow, thought Miguel. *Would not have allowed it – very strong words!*

"You see, when Max's parents died, he inherited a small fortune. They were Hungarian Jews and his father was an astute man, who had amassed a large amount of money. Then, when Max died, Marjorie came into funds from a life insurance policy that Max had. The crowning glory of the policy was that if Max passed away suddenly, before the age of 65, the benefit was doubled. Max had a policy for one million dollars, so the total payout amounted to two million dollars. Marjorie was a wealthy woman, Detective. No need to work again. It was a lot of money back in 1966, I can tell you that Inspector! Fortunately she had invested the money well." Dirk completed his words with a shake of his head once again.

Miguel was about to leave Dirk van Zuutmeyer, when he noticed that Dirk's appearance was troubled

"Is there something wrong sir, everything alright?" Miguel screwed up his face, peering at Dirk.

"I'm not sure if I should say this or not, mainly because I do not have any concrete evidence to support my statement," Dirk said, wanting some reassurance from Miguel.

"Anything is helpful to us Mr van Zuutmeyer. Remember, this all centres around Billy. I am sure you want to find the truth, the same as we do sir," came Miguel's calming yet positive answer.

"Yes, you are so right Detective. Billy deserves it. Now what I have to tell you is a bit long winded, but please be patient as I put all the facts together."

CHAPTER *fourteen*

Dirk looked appealingly at Miguel, who replied, "Take your time, I have all the time in the world Mr van Zuutmeyer."

Miguel's mind was racing, *What is this new startling revelation Dirk is going to tell me?*

"This all occurred sometime before Billy came on the scene. So it must have been no later than the fall of '64. I do recall that the autumn leaves were falling and the nights where drawing in a little. One day, Max left work before me, not by much, say 20 minutes. I was finishing a drawing and wanted to get it completed before starting a new project the following day. So I was later leaving work. On that particular day, I had my car in the garage. The owner had given me one of his courtesy cars to drive to work and return in the evening to collect my automobile. I had to drive down Sunset Strip and then turn right into Laminosa Lane, where the garage was. As I drove down the lane, I saw about 100 yards ahead of me, Max's car. It was parked alongside the wall of a florist wholesalers building. Max had a custom built 1962 Chevrolet Bel Air coupe. It was blue with a gold roof. There was a white flash down either side, along with white wall tyres. Max had it specially made to his specifications. I recognised the car instantly, and saw two people sitting in the front. One was a man and the other a woman. Naturally, I thought it was Max with Marjorie. As I drew closer, I decided to park my car and go over and say hello to Marjorie. I went to alight from my car, when I could see that it was Max with another woman. The pair were kissing passionately and were totally oblivious of me. Fortunately I had another car, otherwise Max may have spotted me. I was transfixed just watching them! I could not believe my eyes. You see Detective, the other woman was Peggy Cavallaro. No mistake, I know what I saw. I waited to see if they left. After about 10 minutes, Peggy Cavallaro left Max, blowing him a kiss, I might add. She then walked over to a car, parked close by, which I think was her own. It was a Cadillac Eldorado, pink with a white roof. You know the ones with the big fins from the late '50s and early '60s?"

La Paz nodded, and said, "Yeah, I know the car you mean."

Dirk rattled on, "I had a hat on and my sunglasses, so I think that helped to disguise my presence. I continued on my way down to the garage, leaving Max in his automobile. As a close friend, I never spoke of the matter to Max, and he certainly did not speak of this to me. Marjorie idolised Max, though Max could be difficult at times. He did not socialise with the other artists, preferred to keep to himself. I was really the only one who got to know him. Never liked anyone going into his studio at his home. I was never invited in. Max was stringent with Marjorie, but I suppose that is not a bad thing." Dirk's thoughts lingered momentarily, before speaking on. "The other matter that has always troubled me Detective, is that I had a feeling that Marjorie was being blackmailed." Dirk stopped to suck his fifth cigarette and gain some more chemical infusion to carry on talking.

Miguel was fascinated with this story Dirk had divulged, after such a length of time.

"Go on, what makes you think that Mrs Femmer was being blackmailed?" asked Miguel, sitting on the edge of the chair in eager anticipation.

"It was a statement that Marjorie let slip years ago, after Max passed away. It was regarding the fact that she was having to feed some else's nest to keep them happy. I did ask her what she meant. Marjorie quickly tried to cover up what she had said. Her reply was something along the lines 'that you're never finished where death is concerned'. After that, she changed the subject. I did not pry any more, but always felt that the inference was to her being blackmailed. I could very well be wrong Detective, but I am now telling you all this, after nearly 50 years." Dirk spread his hands open wide, clutching his beloved cigarette in his right hand.

"So you have never spoken of this to anyone else, the police included?" enquired Miguel.

"No never, sir. I did not come forward at the time when Billy went missing. Marjorie was devastated and I had my respect for Max to consider as well. They both always appeared to get on perfectly. They did not argue and there was not a shred of unpleasantness between the pair of them. Whether it was just a fling with Peggy Cavallaro, I will never know. Short of asking her!" Dirk chortled and smiled at Miguel with a yellow set of teeth.

"Just one last question, if I may. Do you still have contact with Mrs Femmer?" asked Miguel.

Dirk van Zuutmeyer replied without hesitation, "I have not seen Marjorie for around two years now. Since I gave up my driving licence, I don't get out so much. I have to rely on someone taking me. But, yes, I did see Marjorie on a regular basis. I would go to her place, and the next occasion, she would come to my apartment. I should give her a phone call and have a chat. Marjorie doesn't drive anymore either, so our only contact is with the phone."

Miguel La Paz ended his time with Dirk van Zuutmeyer, thanking him for his invaluable assistance. Dirk was pleased to be of some help, and felt a relief to be able to finally talk to the police about what he knew, and what he had surmised. Although, Dirk was loath to mention the talk that had circulated regarding the twins drowning .It had always haunted him, the gossip that had gone around the community. Was it true that Peggy Cavallaro had deliberately let her daughters wander off, to spite the nanny who had taken time off that day? There had been much speculation, even years after the event, but he did not wish to dwell on such a shocking thought. It was too horrible to imagine. It was better to let matters rest now.Dirk seated himself down again and his shaking hands lit another cancer stick.

CHAPTER *fifteen*

Miguel started to drive back to the police headquarters in Los Angeles. He was excited with the new information to reveal to his boss. He decided to phone Marty and fill him in with his findings.

"What's up, La Paz?"

La Paz told Marty about Max Femmer's impotence and his leaving work suddenly the day Billy Parsons disappeared, as well as the possibility of an affair between Max and Peggy Cavallaro and Dirk's reasoning that Marjorie Femmer was being blackmailed.

Marty whistled through the mobile to La Paz.

"Well, We have some good stuff here. An affair hey! I wonder what Peggy Cavallaro would say to that? She certainly wouldn't get all she bargained for with Max Femmer being impotent!" Marty was amused.

"Okay pal, I'm heading up to Marjorie Femmer soon. I am just going through the financials you requested. I will bring you up to speed when I get back from Marjorie Femmer. See ya back in HQ. Thanks for the update." La Paz ended his call to Marty.

In his mind was going over the discussion with Dirk van

Zuutmeyer. *What if Marjorie Femmer was being blackmailed? What for, and who was the blackmailer? Peggy Cavallaro, surely not*, he thought. *She had more to lose if it got out that she was having an affair behind Tony Cavallaro's back. From what the Boss had stated, Peggy Cavallaro was money-conscious and loved prestige. The sighting of Max Femmer in the arms of the Cavallaro was something! Had she found out something about Marjorie Femmer that only money could cover up? Or did this all have some connection to Billy Parsons? Yeah, that was it. Peggy Cavallaro was the one who said she saw the red Mustang being driven up North Beaumont around 5.45 p.m. on the day Billy went missing.* La Paz was thinking wildy. *What if it wasn't Mrs Femmer at all, but …no, no! Max Femmer drove that car, not Marjorie Femmer. But why so late in the day, after leaving work just after 11 a.m.? There are approximately 7 hours unaccounted for, 11 a.m. to 5.45 p.m.. Say 30 minutes to drive home from his work at the most. No peak hour traffic to contend with. Arrives home at no later than 11.30 a.m. BUT then does not reappear until 5.45 pm. Billy went missing some time after 11 a.m., if Marjorie Femmer's statement is correct. Yep, this needs further investigation. Talk with the Boss, he will be over the moon with this!*

La Paz sped along the freeway and into the city confines.

***

Meanwhile, Marty had gone into the office early to check

if those bank financials had arrived. He was rewarded with them on his desk as he arrived. Sergeant Robbie Clark had placed them on Marty's disorganised desk and was leaving the office, when Marty cruised in. Clark was a good cop who often helped out Marty Hislop and Miguel La Paz. La Paz had instructed Clark to leave the information on Marty's desk, when it all arrived.

"Hey Boss. Those statements and financial data have arrived. I just put them on your desk." Clark paused and waited for Marty to glance through the data.

"Thanks, Robbie. Gee that Peggy Cavallaro can write her name to a few mill, aye? Wouldn't mind a bit of her dough!" Marty said still flipping through the pages.

"Yeah, Boss! Well count me in on some of the dough too," said Clark jokingly, and left Marty to peruse the details.

The business of Wagon Wheels was posting good profits and on a personal note, Peggy Cavallaro, had sizeable balances in various accounts. There were a number of properties owned by her, including number 1811 North Beaumont.

But why let the place go to wrack and ruin? Marty thought to himself, *Surely she would want it looking better than the state it was in now. I guess if the rent was being paid, that's all that mattered.*

Marty then put his interest in the affairs of Marjorie Femmer. She was comfortable. Regular interest payments went into her account plus some share dividends. Something caught Marty's eye. There was a regular cash withdrawal of

$1000 every month. This was in addition to Mrs Femmer's other withdrawals for food, drink and other essentials, such as bills. Marty scanned through the statements and detected that this amount was regularly withdrawn over a long time span. Checking with his date block, he could determine that the $1000 was withdrawn on a four weekly cycle, and always on a Tuesday. *Why would Mrs Femmer be withdrawing such a large amount on a regular basis?* He cross checked the personal accounts of Peggy Cavallaro, but nothing for this amount had been deposited into the accounts. *Right,* thought Marty. *Now to tackle Mrs Femmer about the red '65, which she had conveniently forgot to tell us about. Was the person driving the Mustang, actually Mrs Femmer or someone else? Now it was a case of Mrs Femmer coming clean and stop telling porkies!*

CHAPTER *sixteen*

On his way up into the Hollywood Hills, Marty was planning his questions to ask Mrs Femmer.

The day was still basking in the morning warmth of the sun. The overnight rain had refreshed the atmosphere and the clouds were just little puffs of tissue wrapped in parcels of soft white lambs wool, passing by in the clear ethereal sky. Commuter traffic was minimal, as the majority of vehicles were travelling in the opposite direction. Up Hollywood Drive and into the quiet residential streets of the rich, famous and not so famous!

Carefully negotiating the sloping Femmer driveway, Marty brought the car to a halt. He could see a figure bending over a cacti bed next to the neighbour's stone fence; it was Marjorie Femmer. She turned to see who it was, and recognised Marty, giving a wave. With some effort, Mrs Femmer walked over to Marty. She had a large straw hat on with a red ribbon tied around the brim. Today she wore three quarter beige trousers, stone coloured sandals and a bright lime green short sleeved top. Mrs Femmer smiled at Marty, but it was a forced reaction. Marty could tell that she was uncomfortable with his return.

"Morning Mrs Femmer, great day for gardening isn't it?" grinned Marty.

"Yes, it is at that. The overnight rain has been wonderful. That bed," pointing to the cacti bed she had just come out from, "needs a bit of a tidy up. Some of the cacti flower at differing times, so it is nice to get the continued colour." Pretending to be in control of herself, Mrs Femmer pulled off her gardening gloves carefully and said with a casual air, "Anyway, Detective Chief Inspector, how can I help you?" Her voice was shaky and she avoided looking directly at Marty. Marjorie Femmer had known that Marty Hislop would return and had prepared herself for his return. She wasn't going to be fearful or intimidated. There was nothing to hide. *Why did it all have to be dug up again,* wailed Mrs Femmer within. *Haven't I been through enough already?*

The sun was just beginning to radiate its warming rays on the earth, and Marjorie Femmer felt a thin line of sweat developing on her wrinkled brow.

Detective Chief Inspector Marty Hislop could also feel the sun's rays on his head and moved himself into the shadow of the living room wall of the house.

"Damnation," muttered Marjorie Femmer under her breath. *I suppose he will want to go inside now and start firing questions at me. Well, he won't break me!* Marjorie told herself with total faith in her resilience.

Marty got the conversation going again with his first question, "Mrs Femmer, according to another person, you phoned your husband to come home on the day that Billy went missing. It is understood that you had a fall. Is that true Mrs Femmer?"

Marty was staring at Mrs Femmer with a fatalistic look, *I've got you now, my dear.*

Mrs Femmer defended herself vigorously with a steely response, "I cannot be asked to remember every detail of that day. It was so long ago. All I can say, as I said to you before, is that I saw Billy walking along the road. I waved to him and then came here and got ready to go to the bowling alley, and that was that!" Mrs Femmer folded her sinewy arms and positively glared back at Marty.

Marty smiled back in return and looking directly at his prey, and replied slowly, "Yes, you did tell me that story before, but I know differently. In fact, you haven't really answered the question I asked at all. I am sure that you can recall if you had a fall on that day or not. However, I shall leave you to consider that. Now let us move onto the red Ford Mustang. Let's talk about that shall we?"

Marty held his head up and peered very long and hard at the woman in front of him. Mrs Femmer would have loved to go inside into the cool of the house but she wanted to get rid of this nuisance. Well, he was doing his job, but making her nervous and bringing back unpleasant memories.

"What about the car?" came Mrs Femmer's curious response. *Think quick here, Marjorie. Don't let him get the better of you, stay calm and think clearly.* Mrs Femmer was plunged into a state of nervousness.

"How about we go inside and discuss this sitting down, Mrs Femmer. It will far more comfortable than standing out here in the sun", suggested Marty with a gesture of his hand toward the house. Marty knew that Marjorie Femmer was playing hard to get at but he had handled this situation before.

"Whatever you have to ask me, I am quite capable of answering here and now. No, we don't need to go inside! You know that I did have a red Ford Mustang. Max was a dear and purchased it for me in early '65. Yes, Billy went with me in the car, I have already informed you. I ... I c-can't see the need to ask me the same questions Detective Chief Inspector." Mrs Femmer was becoming rattled and impatient. She waved her arms in the air and shook her head.

Great, thought Marty. *The ole girl is on the back foot and tripping herself up.*

"Yes, it is a long time ago Mrs Femmer. However, your memory regarding the Mustang is quite vivid, whereas your recollection of the events of the day Billy disappeared are scant. Let me put it this way, Mrs Femmer. Sure, you did see Billy walking along your street BUT ..." Marty paused to make his point, "you did make a phone call to your husband regarding a fall you had. Mr Femmer comes home some time after 11 a.m., possibly closer to 11.30 a.m., which is the same time period, you say, you saw Billy Parsons walking along North Beaumont. Did he go to the drug store? There is only one answer for that Mrs Femmer, isn't there? He never made it, something happened. What was it Mrs Femmer?"

"How dare you try to say that I knew what happened to Billy!" Marjorie Femmer's voice held indignation yet there was a sign of wariness and definite fear.

"All right, you don't know. What happened to the red Mustang? Where is it now? Or do I have to get a search warrant, don't think I won't do it Mrs Femmer?" said Marty, parting his feet and placing his hands in front of him.

There was no reply from Mrs Femmer.

Think you idiot! What did you say last night to yourself, if he asked you this question? Mrs Femmer's mind was racing.

With remarkable poise, Mrs Femmer turned her head slightly and said in a tired tone, waving her right hand in the air, "Oh, the car was sold years ago detective. A young student bought it, 18 he was. Needed a car to go to university. I think his parents may have helped him financially. Nice boy he was too." She completed her sentence with a smile of subtle smugness. Mrs Femmer placed a hand on her hip and made eye contact with Marty.

"What was the name of the lad who bought the car?" Marty was not being fooled with this nonsense, he knew otherwise.

"For heavens sake Inspector, how can I recall his name? It was years ago and Max organised all that anyway. He dealt with the student, not me. I just signed some paper or another," Mrs Femmer gave a sigh and a look of annoyance. *How much longer do I have to endure this pest?*

"Just go, will you!" Marjorie Femmer could sense a sickening feeling coming over her. No, she would not give in. Her resolve was going to be steadfast, no matter what.

Marty noticed that Mrs Femmer was fading, but as she

was being difficult, he would too. He enjoyed seeing people squirm and shuffle their feet or whatever else they did to hide a multitude of sins. Marjorie Femmer was just another victim of this cool handed, yet hard-lined detective, Chief Inspector Marty Hislop.

"Bullshit!" was the rapid retort of Marty.

Mrs Femmer was clearly aghast with the one syllabul reply of Marty.

"You know what happened to the Mustang, don't try to pull the wool over my eyes lady. That car was registered until January '69 in your name, and then the licence lapsed. The Mustang was not sold." Marty's anger showed in his stony face.

"I - I ... d-don't know what ... you are talk - talking about," said Marjorie Femmer visibly shaking in her boots, so to speak! Her speech was garbled and she longed to sit down.

"I'll be back Mrs Femmer! Next time, I suggest you tell the truth. We are investigating a possible murder. I assume you want justice for Billy Parsons." Marty raised his finger at the hapless woman, and eyed her with a menacing gleam of his dark brown eyes.

Marty stormed back to the car and drove off spinning his tyres in the stone driveway, spurting stones into the air.

Almost fainting on the spot, Marjorie Femmer made her way back with some effort to the stone fronted porch of her home. Sitting on the porch step, she held her hands in her aching, swirling head and wept.

Marty was furious and drove like a man possessed back to the office.

Stupid bitch, why make it so hard for yourself? Just tell us where the car is or what happened to it, he thought. *Who are you covering for, probably Max Femmer? He can't tell us too much anyway, he's pushing up the daisies now! That search warrant will have to be implemented. Bloody hell, I forgot to ask her about the Cavallaro twins, that can wait.*

CHAPTER *seventeen*

Arriving back at LAPD, Marty got down to business with La Paz. Both men had a lot to put together and talk over theories, regarding the case of Billy Parsons. Marty relayed his conversation with Mrs Femmer, such as it was, to La Paz. Marty Hislop was still fuming, but gradually calming himself. It was no good becoming unravelled. There would be another time to break Mrs Femmer in telling the truth. He didn't want another complaint levelled against him. That would be the last straw! La Paz had checked out the 'Mother Seekers' group and found out that they were disbanded by the police in 1959. So they were struck off the list of possible involvement with Billy.

With Anna Serenova and Thor banged up, the suspects grew narrower. Dirk van Zuutmeyer was not considered a suspect. He had in fact been very open and helpful. Max Femmer was out of the picture, but if he had been alive, they knew he was entangled with this intricate web of deceit and lies. It now only left Peggy Cavallaro and Marjorie Femmer – unless there was another person or persons responsible for Billy's disappearance, unknown to the police. Otherwise it only left these ladies who could shed more light on the case. Neither were being helpful, both had first hand knowledge but were concealing a dark secret. Possibly many. Miguel and Marty bandied around ideas and went through the financials again of both women.

La Paz picked up on a payment that went into one of the personal accounts of Peggy Cavallaro. An amount of $10,000.00 was lodged every month from a company named "Rothenburg Investments". It had started over two years ago and had been deposited without fail. That was put on the list for investigation. La Paz agreed about the cash withdrawals of Marjorie Femmer, appearing suspicious. Blackmail was a certainty for sure. Who was the blackmailer? La Paz's assumption that Max Femmer was driving the Mustang, and not Marjorie Femmer, held credence. But where in the hell did he go? Max Femmer had left work just after 11 a.m., and yet he obviously must have been behind the wheel of the Mustang sometime later that day.

Marty's curiosity had also been kindled about the Cavallaro twins. This surely required some deeper sleuthing. It wasn't all that it seemed on the surface. After going over what information they had gleaned, both officers opted to have a break and go to the canteen for some lunch.

As they were eating ravenously, Marty said to La Paz,

"My hunch is that Marjorie Femmer knows a lot more, but is afraid of revealing anything. This could relate to the possible blackmail. When I go next time to visit her tomorrow, I want you to come also La Paz. I think with both of us there, she might crumble and give us the break we need to crack this case. I would give anything to know what is in that garage at the Femmer house. I would love to get a search warrant and check out that garage, but we need more evidence before doing that. We might even learn something concerning the Cavallaro twins too. I think I shall broach the subject with her. You know what I am going to do this arvo La Paz?" Marty was gulping down the last mouthful of a beef burger with all the trimmings.

"No Boss, what? You going fishing?" said La Paz with humour in his voice.

"No. I'm gonna go back to Peggy Cavallaro's palace and take a photo of those Hydrangea flowers. I've been dreaming about those damn flowers, can't get them out of my head. Mom would like to see them, she might know their name." Changing the subject, Marty said, "See who owns that company, called 'Rothenburg Investments'. Also, check out those automobiles of Max Femmer and Peggy Cavallaro, just to be sure. Dirk van Zuutmeyer was undoubtedly right, but I would like confirmation. And, just for the record – "

Marty was interrupted by La Paz who said knowingly, "See if Marjorie Femmer ever had a Plymouth Barracuda registered in her name!"

"Took the words right out of my mouth pal," said Marty as he got up and tapped La Paz on the shoulder. "I should not be long with Mother Superior, so I will come back here and see what you have been able to get, before packing up for the day. We are getting somewhere, but it is going to be a tough one, I just know it." ended Marty, giving La Paz a serious expression.

"Okay Boss, leave it to me. Yeah, I think we are making progress. At least we have some insight into the ladies from Dirk van Zuutmeyer. See you when you get back." La Paz rose from his chair and prepared to go back to the office.

CHAPTER *eighteen*

Driving back to the Hollywood Hills, Marty had his mind focused on the blue Hydrangeas. Those Hydrangea bushes were screaming to him about some tragedy – perhaps Billy Parsons. Or was it the Cavallaro girls?

The journey seemed to go relatively quick, and Marty was turning into the driveway of the immaculate grounds of Harpenden Lodge. The same gardener was busy with some roses in an arbour over the far side of the property. Marty had not seen the roses before, but they were in full bloom now. All white, draping over a trellis like a cascade of virgin lace. A stunning display. There was a statue of a goddess in the middle of the area. Some of the long rose stems were caressing the bosom and head of the naked goddess, with an attempt to hide her shame, but also crown her with utmost glory. Perhaps it was Aphrodite, the goddess of love.

The blue Hydrangeas were magnificent and Marty could not help but walk over to the bed and stand in awe of the giant flower heads. The soft petals fluttered in the light afternoon breeze and gently jostled the flower heads against each other.

Better get this over with, thought Marty. *Don't go hanging around the joint, you might even get arrested for loitering!*

Marty smiled at himself and paced over to the impressive front entrance.

Ringing the door bell, Marty awaited a response. Once again, Matilda opened the door, and seemed surprised to see Marty standing there again.

"Oh hello, did you wish to see Mrs Cavallaro? She is busy doing her exercises right now," said Matilda with a frown of concern.

Marty ignored this negative statement, and said happily, "Gee, I'm sorry its not a good time, but I just wanted to ask Mrs Cavallaro if I could take a couple of photos of the Hydrangeas, please." Marty replied in a boyish tone of bright amusement.

"The Hydrangeas, oh I see," stumbled out Matilda with unprepared astonishment. "I will have to go and ask Mrs Cavallaro. Would you like to step in and wait, I won't be long sir?" replied the meek, but genuinely perplexed Matilda.

"No, it's alright. I will wait here, thanks," responded Marty.

Just as the girl went to tell her message, Marty distinctly observed that Matilda's eyes were boring into Marty's face. There seemed to be an anxiousness, of wanting to say something, but not knowing how to go about it.

For a split second, Matilda was torn between reluctance or a longing desire to speak out about her dilemma. Her heart was struggling deeply within, yet she knew indecision was getting the better of her. Slowly she said in a soft tone, "Very well, I will come back shortly."

Marty stepped forward, and said in a quiet voice, "Was there something you wished to say, Matilda?"

"Oh no, sir. No, nothing …at all." Matilda recovered herself, but was very unsure. Her head dropped down, so as to avoid eye contact with Marty.

Marty waited, casting his mind back to his previous visit. Matilda just seemed an ordinary girl in service. Her large emerald green eyes were an attraction to the clear face, without the aid of makeup.

A nice figure, thought Marty. *Why was she shut up here working for Peggy Cavallaro?* Yes, she was a soulful girl and went about her duties with a solemn sense of loyalty to employer. Perhaps there was another side to Matilda. Marty continued to get lost in his thoughts. *Hmmm, I wonder what she wanted to say? Matilda was definitely trying to catch my attention, but was unable to continue. Was she frightened of Peggy Cavallaro? Yes, that was quite likely. A formidable woman to have as an employer, she could make things quite uncomfortable.*

Directly, Matilda came back looking a little flushed. Her cheeks were rosy red.

"Sorry to take a while. I will take you up to Mrs Cavallaro, if you follow me." Swiftly, Matilda departed from Marty's presence, leaving Marty standing with his mouth open catching flies.

Gee, that was quick, love! What's up with the great dame? Marty had a rough idea. Peggy Cavallaro was annoyed. The conversation that had transpired between maid and manager, were certainly not one of pleasantness.

Minutes before as Matilda hurried along up the grand staircase, she anticipated a frosty reception from Mrs Cavallaro. She did not appreciate being disturbed whilst doing her exercises. It was considered taboo! Knocking on the gym room door, Matilda waited with uneasy anticipation for the woman inside to bid her to enter. Finally, after what seemed to Matilda to be minutes, but were only some seconds, a raised voice was heard to say, "For heavens sake, who is it?"

Matilda opened the door and walked into the room, with her hands clasped firmly behind her back. They were shaking and her voice was unsettled.

"I'm v-very sorry to interrupt, Mrs Cavallaro, but the gentleman from the police …who was here the other day," a slight cough from Matilda, "would like to know if he could take some photos of the Hydrangeas." Matilda's were wide open with painful emotion, awaiting the impending outburst from Mrs Cavallaro.

Fleetingly Matilda wished she was with her lover, Ben Setter. He did not even know that she was here, at this overdressed mausoleum. Banished by her parents to come and live with Aunt Peggy, who she hardly knew. After all, she was only a family friend. Told to keep a low profile and do all she was asked, and expected to do, as a maid. Every night Matilda dreamt of her time with Ben, the lad from the Deep South, Tennessee, who she had the opportunity of meeting at an Equestrian event two years ago. It had been love at first sight for both of them. Ben was a mechanic from a small rural town but also an experienced horse handler. He had been chosen to come to the Kentucky gathering. A happy and genuine fellow, who was the salt of the earth. They both had an interest in horses and were nature lovers as well. Ben was 22 years old, and came from a family of five brothers and three sisters. Matilda, an only child, from her highbrow upbringing, longed to escape the endless matrimonial match making of her wealthy parents in New York. Financiers to the rich entrepreneurs, they had become prosperous and had a name to protect. Her father was a fifth generation Rothenburg. When the Rothenburg's discovered that Matilda had been secretly contacting Ben, after her time in Kentucky, the relationship was halted immediately, or risk disinheritance. However, as nature would have its last laugh, Matilda broke the horrifying news that she was pregnant to Ben. The shit hit the fan in the Rothenburg household. Ben was told never to have any contact with Matilda again. He was unsuitable and had no prospects whatsoever, by Mr Rothenburg.

"A total scum bag, who would tarnish the family name", roared Mr Rothenburg to his daughter, Matilda.

Matilda's child was whisked away when born. The grieving mother was never to hold her cherished new born, and forever had an emptiness in her heavy heart. Shortly after, Matilda was sent to this Aunt Peggy in California. Not that Matilda had ever had much contact with the Cavallaro woman in her life, but she knew that Aunt Peggy had business interests in Rothenburg Investments. Matilda was to be 'a personal assistant' to this woman she hardly knew. What a lie and joke that was! Matilda was just a maid or no better than a scullery maid. Endless tasks and errands to run for the rich woman, who exploited all who worked for her. Nasty and vindictive person, you never knew when she would strike next. Came on so charming, butter would not melt in her sour mouth! Outbursts of rage were quite common place. Matilda's parents were paying Aunt Peggy the enormous amount of $10,000 per month for her to stay with this demanding battleaxe. This had been going on for two years. When Aunt Peggy had been informed that Matilda had been in the family way to 'a downright low life fellow from the Deep South', and the family wanted it all kept hush hush. Peggy Cavallaro took matters into her own slimy slippery hands. Requesting the exorbitant sum of money to be paid each month to be kept quiet, the Rothenburgs were caught between a rock and a hard place. Peggy Cavallaro had a 20% stake in Rothenburg Investments. If she withdrew her capital, the company might flounder – plus the fact that the other investors were all well known to Peggy Cavallaro. If she squealed, the other parties might very well pull out as well, and leave the Rothenburgs with egg on their faces! So Matilda's parents had little choice but to comply with Peggy Cavallaro's terms.

Eccles the chauffeur, who had a past, had been a great help to Matilda. Giving advice and some comfort, that her natural father could never give. Whatever Eccles's past was, Matilda had not pried into. He was a tall man, nearing 50. Balding head with a fair complexion and very clear hazel eyes. His smile was quite refreshing after the insincere twitches from Peggy Cavallaro.

The gardener, a Mr Marsh, Matilda did not know his first name; was a very subdued man. She thought he may have been Italian or Greek origin, due to his swarthy complexion. Lived in a small cottage at the back of the property, but was rarely seen inside the dolls house, as Matilda called it. Mr Marsh kept very much to himself and was content to be working all day in the garden. Mr Marsh did an excellent job with the garden, at least that's what Matilda could say of the man. Occasionally, Mrs Cavallaro would lower herself to come and speak with Mr Marsh about the garden. Matilda could tell that there was a rift between the two, as Mr Marsh would often glare after the figure of Peggy Cavallaro, when she left his presence. Sometimes, Matilda could discern raised voices from the pair.

CHAPTER *nineteen*

Snapping herself out of her day dream, Matilda could hear the shrill articulated voice of Peggy Cavallaro saying to her, "Matilda, are you listening girl? Go and get the Detective Chief Inspector and bring him up to me. Now hurry up! I haven't got all day to entertain nuisance detectives. And I shouldn't have to be reminding you what to do either. Day dreaming again! You should be able to think for yourself girl. Now run along!" snapped the matriarch from hell.

The flustered and distressed Matilda literally ran down the passage and staircase to the waiting Marty. Arriving a little breathless, Matilda requested Marty to come up to where Mrs Cavallaro exercised her body with extreme diligence.Marty could see that Matilda was upset, and just followed the girl up the stairs and along the wide passage to the lair of Peggy Cavallaro.

Matilda waited for Marty to come to the gym room door and then opened the door cautiously and beckoned for Marty to go inside. She withdrew immediately and closed the door with extreme care.

Marty was greeted by the off beat soprano voice of Mrs Cavallaro singing, "All things bright and beautiful, all creatures great and small, all things wise and wonderful, the Lord God made them all." She was on the treadmill and pacing herself quite hastily. The lady of the lake had on black skin tight leggings with a bright pink cotton top. Around the head was a lilac sweat head band and pink and blue joggers adorned the little feet.

Well, well, thought Marty. *We like to look the full part when we exercise, by golly!* Marty decided to slowly walk over to "Peggy the Pacemaker".

As he did so, Peggy Cavallaro, noticed Marty out of the corner of her left eye. *Just look at those shoes of his, scuffed toes and in need of a damned good clean,* she thought. *Shirt not ironed properly, tie askew. Hair not combed, looks like a dishcloth. Dragged up by his pants, this one was!* She completed her rendition of the well known song. Coming to a halt on the treadmill, as the machine was switched off, Mrs Cavallaro lightly jumped off the platform and onto the parquetry flooring. Reaching for a fluffy peach coloured towel, Mrs Cavallaro wiped her dear little Pygmalion face. Giving Marty a sickly sweet smile, she said in a voice of lively importance, "Why Chief Inspector, how nice to see you again. I always perform my exercises in the afternoons. I love to show my appreciation of every good thing, with songs of praise. I am a devout Catholic. Do you attend church?" Giving Marty a look of wholesome disrespect and utter contempt in her soulless, empty eyes, Peggy Cavallaro awaited an answer to her put-you-on-the-spot question.

Marty, playing the same pattern, but in another way, answered very convincingly, "Oh yes, I regularly attend Vatican City parish church to have my sins forgiven." With a smile of nothingness and a voice so flat, you could sense the underlying current, Marty starred back at the woman who thought herself so pious.

Realising she had been challenged, Peggy Cavallaro placed the towel back on its rail and altered her manner, reverting back to the visit of this disdainful man standing in front of her,"Now, how can I assist you today?"

The gooing and gushing attempt did not fool the ever alert Marty.

Moments before Marty had entered the gym room, Peggy Cavallaro had been muttering to herself. *What an effrontery,* she thought.*To think that this man could show his face here again! I warned the Police Commissioner. Now this time I mean business. I won't have the man coming here ever again. Taking photos of Hydrangeas, absolute rubbish. He will be removed from the case. I will have this painful pest writing out parking tickets, before he can say Jack Robinson. By George I will!*

Marty followed the same game as Mrs Cavallaro and responded with a mocking joyfulness, "Yes, it's lovely to see you again Mrs Cavallaro." He continued his planned approach with, "I was in the area, and just wondered if I may take a few photos of the Hydrangea bed, out the front below the bay window. My mom would love to see them. She is a very keen Hydrangea grower. Always has been since I can remember.

The plants are a credit to you Mrs Cavallaro," ended Marty with a cheesy smile.

"Why, of course, Chief Inspector. Your mother likes Hydrangeas you say?" Mrs Cavallaro raised her head with some doubt to Marty's statement concerning his mother.

"Yes, Mom has been growing Hydrangeas since I was a young kid. Had to be careful not to throw my ball into the bushes and knock the flowers off! I was often scolded for that, me and my friends. Mom moved with Dad, to Vermont some years ago now. She is able to grow a lot more varieties, due to the cooller climate. But she would just adore your bushes, Mrs Cavallaro," concluded Marty with an over indulgent tone of voice.

Showing no emotion, Peggy Cavallaro said, "Vermont, you say. A much colder climate there. Why did they ever want to shift there for?" The woman was trying to catch Marty out.

Marty, sensing that a trap was about to be laid, ignored this and replied truthfully, "My kid sister and her husband had already moved there some years prior for work reasons, and they have four kids. In fact, there are seven grandies now, I think." Marty scratched his head. "So Mom and Dad made the move five years ago and have loved it ever since."

"Oh, how nice for your Mom and Dad. They would enjoy spoiling the grandchildren," replied Peggy Cavallaro, with as much lack of sincerity as anyone could imagine. Her mind was rampant with various thoughts. *Ridiculous thing to do. Vermont, humpf. Cold Atlantic gales, snow and sloshy ice, if you blink summer has passed you by. Very ignorant people, don't mix with the rest of the country. Closeted types. The Maritime States, they called themselves, those three states. Think they live in a world of their own! Difficult to Presidential canditates, can make them or break them. Yes, a foolish move indeed, they will regret it for sure!*

Conversation came to an end after Mrs Cavallaro's short reply.

Eyeing one another with as much dislike for each other as can be imagined, Marty broke the stalemate and said with eagerness to get these photos quickly and depart, "Well, if it's alright, I shall leave you and get these photos. Thanks again, Mrs Cavallaro."

"Oh, Chief Inspector, would you like to take a photo of me with the Hydrangeas, for your dear Mom of course," Peggy Cavallaro said in a condescending voice.

Heaven forbid! thought Marty. *No, I damn well don't.* The opposite response was the only option available with this woman.

"Yes, that would be great Mrs Cavallaro. After all, they are your Hydrangea bushes." Marty was cursing himself within. He had said the words with conviction, so hopefully Mrs Cavallaro had not perceived his unwilling intent to take her photo!

"Let me get myself changed Chief Inspector. It will be a privilege. Now you go downstairs and wait outside, I shan't be long," she said before giving Marty a tap on the arm with a well manicured hand.

Down the magnificent staircase Marty trudged. *Boy, why do I have to get this woman in a photo for? Just her pure vanity, that's all, man.* As Marty was about to cross the foyer and make towards the front door, Marty glimpsed Matilda, further down another corridor, coming towards him. She was carrying a large crystal vase with a variety of flowers arranged in it. Seeing Marty, Matilda slowed her walk and put the vase down on a side table in the oval foyer. She turned around to look at Marty.

Marty thought he had better explain what was going on and stopped his pace and said to Matilda, "Mrs Cavallaro will be down when she has changed. I am to wait outside and then I can take the photos." Marty awaited for the young girl's reaction. *Would she say anything now?*

"Very well, I shall see you out then sir." was all the distraught Matilda could utter. Her head was low and she certainly had been weeping. Matilda began walking to the front door to let Marty outside.

Marty heaved internally. *Poor thing, living in this place.* Instinctively, Marty took out one of his cards and grabbed a hand of Matilda's, and placed the business card firmly into her sweaty palm.

Saying nothing, but giving the girl a long look of concern, Marty left the house of deceit and lies.

Standing outside, he decided to walk around to the bay window, where the Hydrangea bushes were.

Yes, the display was extremely eye catching. Waiting for the "photographic princess" to make her debut for her photo shoot, Marty could see the gardener busy at work again. Dead heading some roses. *I bet that bloke thinks of Peggy Cavallaro, as he cuts off every dead rose head. Must be a pleasure for him!* Marty grinned to himself and shook his head.

After about a ten minute lapse, the front door opened and Mrs Cavallaro appeared dressed in long dusty pink, silk trousers that were intentionally baggy. A similar coloured loose fitting top matched the pants. Marty assumed she was dressed in her pyjamas. On her head was a hat containing a head band of artificial roses and lilies, once again of a light pink shade. For footwear, Mrs Cavallaro, had on a pair of open toe pale pink satin sandals. A long necklace of beaded pink glass hung around her neck. Pink stone earrings graced the perfectly shaped ear lobes of the dancing mannequin. Peggy Cavallaro was quite sprite as she scampered herself around to the "photographic pest". Garments flowing everywhere as she stood in front of Marty with an air of supreme expectancy. Marty could not help notice that Peggy Cavallaro had no walking stick. *Interesting, no stick hey! She didn't have it when on the treadmill either.*

Coming up to the detective with a fluttering of dangling beads dingling around her scrawny neck, Mrs Cavallaro said with an expression of coyness, "I must apologise for taking so long Chief Inspector. Now where would you like me to stand exactly?"

No where, lady. Just nick off! was what Marty wanted to say to her. Instead, he knew the game had to be played out to the end.

"Well, just stand to the side of the bushes here, yes that's it. Good, now when I say cheese, smile and I will do the rest."

Peggy Cavallaro positioned herself with great aplomb to the side of the Hydrangea bushes, giving her most lovely white smile, lips painted a bright pink and raising one arm up to touch her hat for effect. *She looks like Twinkle Toes. Gee, this dame loves herself,* chuckled Marty within. *You would think that she was auditioning for a part in "Gone with the Wind"!*

Thinking that one snap was sufficient with the face of Peggy Cavallaro, Marty was about to commence taking some shots of the flowers closeup. But Peggy Cavallaro hadn't finished yet!

"Oh, Chief Inspector. You must have one more of me, I will stand in the front of the bed with the Hydrangeas behind for background colour."

I don't need background colour, dearie. Piss off, will you! Marty would have loved to say this to her, but, once again had the manners to carry out the request of this wearisome, yet trivial woman, who thought her presence was foremost in people's minds.

Marty had the divine sensuous enjoyment of cutting off this dancing dolly's head, when taking the second snap with his mobile. Finally, Marty could go ahead and get the close up photos he really wanted, without the whole visit turning into a photo shoot with Peggy Cavallaro taking pride of place.

Vanity had worked its magic for the wealthy woman, who was happy that Marty would definitely give her some photographs of the afternoon's publicity shots.

Waving Marty off the property with a cheery disposition, her face altered to one of hardened mud once Marty's car had turned out onto North Beaumont.

CHAPTER *twenty*

Bustling inside the home, she made her way to the phone to render her disgust and fury to the Chief Constable. Her head was pounding with rage. Shouting at Matilda to run her a hot Radox bath, Peggy Cavallaro went about her mission like a true terrier.

Photos for his Mom, absolute rot. If this was true, Detective Chief Inspector Marty Hislop was wasting valuable police time. Supposed to be investigating the disappearance of that snotty nosed little scoundrel. No, Marty Hislop was a disgrace to the police force. Already he has blighted my neighbourhood, with that awful business at number 1811. Now I have to find suitable tenants for the place. Damn the man! Peggy Cavallaro was wild with anger. *I shall put a complete and final stop to this façade of nonsense, once and for all! As for having his sins forgiven every Sunday, that's an absolute abomination!* Peggy Cavallaro bellowed to herself.

Her hands were shaking with a fiery temper as she punched the direct phone number to the Police Commissioner at Los Angeles Police Department Head Quarters. The Chief Constable's ear was duly chewed off and a temporary form of deafness had taken over his left and right ears.

After her wildcat performance on the telephone, Peggy

Cavallaro's temper was still not appeased. *No, I cannot place any confidence in the poetic numbskull of a Police Commissioner. I will take matters into my own hands. Action must be taken now!*

Stomping outside, forgetting her hot Radox bath, Peggy Cavallaro made her way with haste to the cottage at the rear end of the enormous block. The stone block cottage was partially obscured by rambling roses, mainly Rosa Rambling Rector and Crepescule. Wonderful lingering perfumes wafted around the front wooden door, as the angry owner rapped her knuckles on the door with some impatience. Doing the "Toe Tapping Twang" as she waited for a response, Peggy Cavallaro was working out her next move.

Life to Peggy Cavallaro was like a chess board. You moved people where you wanted them to be. If you didn't want them at all, well you simply removed them from the board! Quite easy, really. Being the Queen, she didn't have to move, because no one had ever been able to checkmate her.

Eventually, after a few moments, the door was opened by the scowling face of the occupant. Peggy Cavallaro did not wait to be invited inside, she just barged in. The door was quietly closed, a curtain was drawn across the window.

The shadow watching the figure of Madam Cavallaro entering the cottage and the retreating nameless skull merchant closing the door, went unnoticed by both parties. The figure retreated into the leafy rose arbour and vanished from sight. If you happened to be a fly on the wall that summer afternoon, you may have been rather surprised by what took place in the cottage. All was not what one might expect. Emotions were running on high that afternoon, in many quarters.

But more of that later.

***

Marty Hislop travelled back to the LAPD to meet again with Miguel La Paz.

La Paz had done his homework, as always. Yes, Marjorie Femmer had once owned a Plymouth Barracuda registered in her name. It was licensed November 1965 and transferred ownership in February 1970. Peggy Cavallaro's Caddy and Max Femmer's Chevy Bel Air, were also correct too. So they knew that the details provided by Dirk van Zuutmeyer were accurate.

Miguel had also done some research on the Cavallaro twins – not much to go on there. Cause of death was given as accidental drowning, according to the official coronial enquiry. The girls were 17 months old, Ruth and Ada. Date of death was August 24, 1949. Time of death, approximately between the hours of 2 to 5 p.m. Both detectives were curious about the deaths of the twin girls. La Paz reasoned within himself to investigate their untimely deaths. A natural instinct as a father told him to fold away the thin veneer that had shrouded this tragedy for so many years.

"Do you think that Mrs Femmer could shed some light on the death of the Cavallaro twins Boss?" asked La Paz in a questioning tone.

Marty glanced across to his partner, and was about to remind La Paz that he had said the question would be put to Mrs Femmer, as discussed previously. However, Marty could detect that La Paz was troubled in mind. Instantly, Marty realised that this was a delicate matter to La Paz. Being a father, it was natural for La Paz to be keen to obtain any lead they could to vanquish the babes who had perished so prematurely.

"Yep, I think she could La Paz. I think it is worth our while to ask the question. She may have some information that could help. It does seem most extraordinary that a mother would allow her kids to wander off, unattended, and then drown. It's surprising what people can remember after a lapse in time. They suddenly recall some vital detail that is instrumental in solving a case. I promise to be diplomatic as well pal, okay?" laughed Marty, in an attempt to lighten up the atmosphere in the room.

La Paz smiled in response, but had a wistful look in his dark eyes. *Just as well I am going along with the Boss. I can steer the conversation in the right direction*, thought La Paz.

Then recalling what he wanted to talk to Marty about, La Paz said, "Boss, there is one thing I hadn't mentioned to you before. It was just a comment from Thor, regarding the couple who lived in number 1811," said La Paz, with a glint of hopefulness in his large black eyes.

"Yeah, go on, what is it?" said Marty, lifting his head up to face his second officer.

"Well, can you recall just as we were leaving the interview

with Thor, we were talking about number 1811 being owned by Peggy Cavallaro? Thor finished his sentence by saying that Anna took over renting the place, after her mother and that Vladimir bloke 'snuffed it,'" La Paz's gaze was alight with the last words he had uttered.

Marty replied, "Yep, I can remember that. So, what is the point I am missing here mate?"

La Paz leapt up from his chair and came over to stand in front of Marty. "Boss, it indicates to me that both parties died simultaneously. Not separate times, but both together. I could be entirely barking up the wrong tree, but I reckon that couple could have been removed from the scene conveniently. The reason being to ensure that neither person leaked any information out about Billy Parsons, especially the photos that were taken. What do you think?"

"You have a point there. But who would want them out of the way? Why wait so long too? Surely not Anna. Unless she was worried about her connection with Billy Parsons. Do you have another idea?" asked Marty, raising his head and puckering his brow.

"Yes, I do Boss. Peggy Cavallaro. She had a lot to lose. Reputation, vain glory and the risk that either one of these people could at anytime squeal. Perhaps they threatened to grass on her. I think there is more to it."

Following some more discussion, the pair were about to call it a day, when Charlie Solomon's figure loomed before them.

Oh shit, not again, thought Marty. He had been hoping that his visit to the Cavallaro dame had gone smoothly enough. Why, he even had the photos to prove it! Complete silence was the calling card of Charlie Solomon as he eased his large frame into the chair opposite Marty's disorganised desk.

"Okay, tell me. Peggy Cavallaro wants some more photos taken of her, is that it Boss?" Marty said with an impatient voice.

"What in the hell were you doing there taking photos of Hydrangeas, for your mom in Vermont? Are you crazy man? What's the big idea? You are apparently, according to my strict instructions," Solomon banged the desk with his fist, "checking into the case of Billy Parsons, who I might add, if you have forgotten, disappeared in 1965. What have these blasted Hydrangeas got to do with the case, huh? You had better have a good answer for me, 'cause I gotta report back to the Commissioner. And if I don't wring your neck before I speak to him, Mother Mary help me!" Solomon glared at Marty, steam almost pouring from his wide nostrils. His face was contorted with anger and with an element of confusion also.

Marty realised the situation Solomon was in, but Marty had a method in his madness. But would Charlie Solomon understand?

La Paz got up and said quietly, "I will pop out to get a coffee guys."

Without even turning around to look at La Paz, Solomon boomed out, "You will remain right here La Paz, until I am satisfied what you two are up to. Do I make myself clear gentlemen?"

La Paz raised his thick black eyebrows in the direction of Marty, and promptly sat down again.Marty had to explain himself.

"Boss, the reason I went to Mrs Cavallaro's home was to take some photos of the Hydrangeas for my mom to identify the variety. She has always been an avid Hydrangea grower. Since moving to Vermont, Mom's interest has become quite a hobby with her. When I saw these Hydrangea bushes at the home of Mrs Cavallaro, I couldn't help but think that Mom would love to see them. So I went to ask Mrs Cavallaro if I could take some photos, that's all. I'm going to speak with Mom tonight over Skype to let her see them." Marty spread out his right hand as he finished his explanation, and put his head on a side to face his disgruntled senior sitting opposite him.

"Don't give me that shit man. I won't buy it for a moment! Complete poppycock! There was a reason you went there, come on spit it out Marty. I'm not a complete fool ya know!" Solomon was moving forward in the chair. His features were distorted with fierce vexation.

Turning his head in the direction of La Paz, who was keeping a low presence in the room, for obvious reasons, Marty's eyes then pierced into the hot and belligerent face of Charlie Solomon.

"Okay, you win Charlie. As I have mentioned to La Paz, I personally believe that those Hydrangeas hold a key to the disappearance of Billy Parsons. Don't ask me why, 'cause I don't know the answer to that yet. But, those flowers have haunted my sleep for a couple of nights now. If my mom can identify the variety and when they were released to the gardening public, I might be in a position to explain further. In the meantime, please Charlie, have patience with La Paz and I. This is all a supposition we are working on together, Boss."

Charlie Solomon was silent for a few seconds, then sat back in the chair and put his head back backward. Breathing deeply into his lungs, his hands gripping the arm rests, Solomon spun around the swivel chair, and with a degree of acute alarm, said to La Paz, "Has he gone mad or what man?"

Miguel La Paz, taking the side of his immediate superior officer, replied in a sensitive, yet intelligent tone, "No, Sir. Detective Chief Inspector Marty Hislop is far from mad. We are following up a lead tomorrow regarding this aspect. When we do, you shall be the first to know the outcome."

Solomon, not fully aware of the recent developments, accepted the wise, but clever words of La Paz without further cross examination. The older man respected La Paz, so left the matter rest. Solomon turned back to Marty, and said with a lowered voice than previously, "Alright, but whatever this is, it had better be good men. I will talk to the Police Commissioner and appease him for now. Let's hope that the Cavallaro woman keeps her cool and does not take the matter even higher. Not that she can go any higher! Except for the press, but I doubt Peggy Cavallaro would want the media involved. Her privacy might be somewhat compromised."

Solomon nodded to Marty and La Paz and took his leave.

CHAPTER *twenty-one*

The air in the room was stale and close, and both detectives knew that they had to come up with the goods, or else!

Marty expressed his thanks to La Paz for coming to the rescue, when cornered by Charlie Solomon.

"No worries, at least what I said satisfied the big boss for the moment. Let's hope we can get some more gossip from Mrs Femmer tomorrow. She may let some important detail slip out unawares. Who knows, Boss."

Marty agreed and sat back in his chair, contemplating their method of approach with Marjorie Femmer. Perhaps he would talk it over with Mom. Run the facts by her, and get her slant on it. This was a woman's domain really, a missing child. How would his Mom have felt if it had been Marion or himself? Men did not always have the true understanding but a mother of a child always did.

The day was drawing to an end, not much more could be done until tomorrow. Marty showed La Paz the photos of the blue Hydrangeas, and the snaps of Dame Peggy Cavallaro. La Paz laughed out loud when he saw the headless figure of Peggy Cavallaro.

"I want Mom to see these flower heads and see if she knows

the variety name and how long ago they were released. Mom may not know, but she has contacts there in Vermont who may know the answer we are looking for. You see La Paz, I was just curious if those bushes were planted around the time that Billy Parsons went missing. Once again, I could be totally barking up the wrong tree. It's worth exploring this theory. Something tells me to delve deeper!" Marty felt the urge to go this far even if it was a long shot. Having discussed the method of approach with Marjorie Femmer for the next day, both men left for their respective abodes.

On the way to his car, La Paz said to himself, *I must get the boss to come over on the weekend. He looks wrung out. What with Charlie Solomon on his back and this dream he has been having regarding the Hydrangeas. Jonas will keep the Boss busy with some soccer skills and questions about fly fishing. Then we will have tacos and some family laughter, that will brighten up the Boss.*

***

That evening, Marty did feel weary but he was keen to hook up with his parents on Skype after his dinner was over – not that dinner was an elaborate affair at the best of times. A frozen meal, roast turkey with vegetables. A container of vanilla ice cream, a firm favourite. All washed down by a decent cold beer, or was it two? Now to contact Mom and get her to check out these Hydrangea bushes. Marty dialled his parent's Vermont home number.

Andrew and Eve Hislop, were already in bed when their phone awakened them from sleep.

"Now who in the devil could that be?" muttered Andrew Hislop, struggling up in the bed, switching on the bedside lamp and reaching for the cordless phone that was by the king size bed.

"Hel-lo," stammered Mr Hislop with a degree of uncertainty, wondering who it was at the other end. Marty's kid sister Marion, had arranged for her parents to have Skype especially to see Marty on the other side of the country. It had been wonderful to see and speak with their son. Marty who was always busy, rushing around with his work. Marty enjoyed the Skype sessions with his loving parents also. Not that he had been very punctual in using the system!

"Hi Dad, it's Marty. How are you?"

"Marty! It's so good to hear your voice son," came Mr Hislop's reply of joyfulness and surprise. Mrs Hislop had woken with the phone's incessant ringing and heard her husband talking to Marty.

"I'm good Dad, how's everyone your end? I know it's getting on, but I just wanted to ask Mom something, if that's alright Dad," said Marty in a considerate tone of voice.

"We're well son. Your Mom is here right beside me in bed, hang on and I will pass the phone to her. Bye pal," ended Mr Hislop. Handing the phone to his wife, Mrs Hislop, still excited to realise that Marty was on the phone, grabbed the phone from her husband.

"Marty. How good to hear from you! Are you alright son?

Are you eating well? You aren't working too hard are you? Is something the matter honey?" Mrs Hislop wanted to ask all kinds of questions but thought she had better stop and wait for Marty to answer her.

"Mom. I'm fine. Can you connect onto Skype right now? I want to show you some photos of some Hydrangeas I have taken. I want to know their name. Thought you would like to see them," Marty finished his sentence abruptly, waiting to hear his Mom's reply.

"Well, yes. We can go onto Skype now. If it's that important for me to see these Hydrangeas now. Your father and I are in bed Marty. Do you know the time here son?"

Marty had completely forgotten the time difference, and profusely apologised.

"Mom, I'm really sorry. I didn't think before I phoned. I can phone tomorrow if you would prefer Mom," came Marty's lame reply, with definite sorrow in his tone.

Idiot, you forgot the time difference! Marty screwed up his face at the thoughtlessness of waking his parents.

"No, it's alright Marty. Just give us a few minutes to get it all going and I should be with you. See you soon dear," ended Mrs Hislop, handing back the cordless phone to her yawning husband. Once seated at the laptop computer, with a woollen shawl around her shoulders, Mrs Hislop was able to speak and see Marty. Andrew Hislop pulled up a chair and joined in the conversation too. Mrs Hislop was very impressed with the photos of the Hydrangea bushes in their splendour. She had not seen the variety before, and agreed to find out their name. Marty did not show the photo of the headless Peggy Cavallaro! The President of the Vermont Hydrangea Society, a Professor Harold Gilbertson, he might know the name. A life long and dedicated pioneer in the cultivation of Hydrangeas, the Professor had introduced a few varieties himself onto the market.

The three had a good chin wag until Marty could fathom that his parents were tiring and bid farewell. Mrs Hislop promised to research the Hydrangeas and inform her detective son of their name. Marty slept better this night than he had since taking on the case. He even made it to his bed, collapsing onto it and happily snoring away the dead of night.

***

The new day dawned sunny and bright. The night had been tucked away and sunlight streamed down onto the ground. A heavy dew left glistening drops of clear effervescent beads dancing on the trees and grasses. The city had awakened and begun its routine of increasing traffic on freeways and link roads. Families scurried to their respective work places, colleges, schools, factories, offices, kindergartens or just simply, stayed at home. The heartbeat of industry whirled into action consuming the workers into a hive of activity and endless production.

CHAPTER *twenty-two*

Marty and Miguel were now on their way to talk to Mrs Femmer; not about the red '65, but regarding another matter. Hoping to acquire some more background information, that might assist in solving the riddle of the missing Billy Parsons.

Pressing the doorbell of the Femmer home, both detectives awaited a response. Marjorie Femmer had seen the car pull up in her driveway, as she was putting some ironing away in the chest of drawers. Looking at the electric clock in her front bedroom, she saw that the time was 9.27 a.m.

Oh no, not again! Two of them this time. So what do I owe the pleasure of having two detectives calling on me? Mrs Femmer could visibly see Marty in the passenger's seat, but the car was driven by another chap, who appeared to be taller. She watched the two men get out the car, and make their way to the front door. Knowing that her last encounter with Marty Hislop had been frosty, to say the least, Mrs Femmer shuddered to think what was in store this morning. Should she answer the door, or pretend that she was not home? *What to do*, thought Marjorie Femmer. Her hands were sweaty already and her heart beating ten to the dozen. She sat down on the bedroom chair and closed her eyes. The doorbell sounded. Still Marjorie

Femmer sat frigid, her body was unable to move. Her legs were like lead weights, incapable of movement. Marjorie's head was swaying backwards and forwards. The pit of her stomach was churning and her lips quivered like shaken leaves. *If only they would go away and just leave me alone.* The doorbell sounded again. The agony of the continued silence seemed eternity to Marjorie. The stillness in her bedroom was a haven from the world outside, and especially the two detectives who now stood at her front door.

Managing to keep her herself quiet without shouting or crying uncontrollably, Mrs Femmer remained seated, flinging her head back and breathing fast. Presently, Mrs Femmer could hear footsteps on the stones in the driveway. Car doors slammed, an engine roared into life and the car could be heard leaving the property. Tears streamed down her tired and forlorn face. The features were contorted with visual and mental pain. *So long ago, and yet it all seems like it happened just yesterday,* she thought. *The day that I wish had never been. If only the events of that day could be blotted out forever.* Marjorie Femmer was aware that she had to face what had transpired. No longer could she hide all she knew. She was at breaking point.

Trudging back to the kitchen, she took a headache tablet and washed it down with a good swig of morning whiskey.

***

La Paz drove the pair of them past the home of Peggy Cavallaro. Marty glanced over to the home and spotted the Police Commissioner's car parked in the circular driveway.

"Well, well, pal. Looks as though the big boss has been summonsed by Mirabella Fortunata. My last visit must have ruffled her feathers a bit too much I think!" Marty laughed loudly and turned to face La Paz.

Giving Marty a face of total misunderstanding, La Paz screwed up his face and replied, "Who is Mirabella-whatever-nata, Boss?"

Marty replied with a grin, "It's a name my mom used to give to a female who thinks she is a 'would be if she could be'!"

"Oh, I see." said La Paz turning his eyes off the road and towards Marty. La Paz was still uncertain of the full meaning of what his Boss had just explained to him.Sometimes he did not fully comprehend the English language. Some words sounded the same, but had a different meaning applied to them. Now this simile of words, this was different. Nevertheless, La Paz thought he had a grasp of what Marty had just said. Marty wanted to have a drive along Roy Rogers Avenue. Get a feel for the layout, which may have altered after such a length of time.

Pulling up outside a drug store, Marty guessed this could have been the same store that Billy Parsons had entered to buy his cool pops.The building was not new by any means. The shop frontage had been revamped, and was very presentable to attract the clientele of the vicinity. The windows up above the brightly coloured canopies, were wood framed and in desperate need of maintenance. Paint was peeling and the wood appeared to be rotten in parts.

Both men chose to check the perimeter around the drug store. La Paz said he would walk along the avenue and see if there was still any sign of the pathway leading up to North Beaumont. Marty chose to wander inside the store.

Wouldn't hurt, Marty thought. *You never know, someone might just still work here who was employed in the store in '65, or, may know of someone who did.*

CHAPTER *twenty-three*

The doors were the automatic opening type, and Marty walked in the store and fiddled with some sunglasses on a stand near the doors.

Within moments, a young woman was at Marty's side asking him, "Can I help you, or are you okay just browsing sir?"

The female was no more than 20 years old, but had an intelligent face and wore a face of plasted makeup, however this did not detract from her prettiness and genuine smile.

"Well, you may be able to help me," replied Marty, flashing his police badge in her face. The young woman raising her painted eyebrows, suddenly seemed to go quiet and looked sheepishly over to the counter on the opposite side of the store.

"Have I done something wrong, officer? Was it the way I parked this morning, I couldn't get past that green 4WD and had to park on an angle in the car lot? There wasn't enough space for me to manoeuvre my car." The expression of guilt was written over her honest face.

Marty endeavoured to reassure the woman by saying, "I'm not here about the way you parked your car. But, I would like to ask a few questions regarding a missing boy who frequented this drug store many years ago. You probably have not heard the name before, he was called Billy Parsons. He disappeared in 1965 without a trace. We understand that Billy came here. I assume that this is the only drugstore on Roy Rogers Avenue located directly below North Beaumont?" Marty, expecting the young lady would know nothing, was quite surprised when she replied, with a look of relief, "Yes, we are the only drug store along Roy Rogers Avenue. That name you just said, rings a bell. My gran used to work here back in those days. I'm sure she has mentioned that name before. Would you like to talk to her sir? Gran can tell you more than I could. My information is just secondhand, so to say. I can give her a ring and see if she is home. Gran only lives a couple of blocks away," offered the eager to please girl.

Marty had seen the name badge pinned to her white and blue tunic top, was Abby. "Thanks very much, Abby. That would be real helpful."

Abby showed Marty over to some chairs and said she would just explain what she was doing to her manager.

Shortly Abby was back, looking much more assured. No risk of a traffic infringement now! Phoning her grandmother on her mobile, Abby was able to ask if it was okay for Marty to come and talk to her. A short explanation for the reason was given by Abby to her grandmother. Gran, a Mrs Gwen Rushmere, was happy to see Marty and the address was provided for him to drive to in the next 15 minutes. Having thanked Abby, Marty waited outside for La Paz to return.

A few moments later La Paz came striding back in, saying

that he had asked a local man about the old pathway. The man had informed La Paz that it was closed off many years ago for safety reasons. Yes, it did exist back in '65 and allowed pedestrians to walk up to North Beaumont as a shortcut alternative.

"I did quiz him about Billy Parsons, but he didn't shift into the area until '78. How did you get on, Boss?"

Marty told Miguel that they were now going to talk with Mrs Gwen Rushmere, who was a former employee at the drug store.

As the men were belting up in the car, La Paz said, "Hey Boss. Look, a Mercury Cougar! Gee, it's in good condition too. Wow, I like the red and black combination. Nice chrome rims." La Paz was gawking like a kid at a new toy. Marty saw the car as well, parked on the other side of the Avenue. There was no one in the vehicle.

"Yeah, bud. I can recall when those cars were really hot stuff back in the late '60s and early '70s. Someone has cared for it, very nice." Marty also gaped at the car with interest.

CHAPTER *twenty-four*

Locating where the home of Gwen Rushmere was from their GPS, they drove away and focused on this new contact.

As the car turned into the driveway of 7117 East Drysdale Circuit, a woman came towards them from the verandah of the well kept Western Ranch Style home.

"Hello there," beamed the lady with a smile not unlike Abby from the drugstore.

Introductions over, Mrs Rushmere showed the two detectives into the house and got them both a lemon squash.

The day had become a trifle unsettled again, as though another storm was brewing. The breeze was warm and the birds were busy flying around, in preparation for something yet to come. Sitting comfortably in a large burgundy leather sofa, Mrs Rushmere sat cross legged and began her recollection of Billy Parsons.

"Why yes, I remember young Billy Parsons. Poor little mite, so lonely and wandering around all by himself. Came into the drug store quite often, as I can recall. Always bought a blue dolphin cool pop. That was his favourite flavour. It always left him with a blue tongue afterwards," giggled Mrs Rushmere. On she babbled, "He was a child film star wasn't he? Lovely face, so innocent and so, how should I say, alive. When I heard that Billy had gone missing, I was really upset. We all were in the store, most of us had spoken to him at various times. Its such a long time since it all happened. He was from Australia or New Zealand wasn't he?" finished Mrs Rushmere, looking earnestly at Marty and Miguel. Marty explained a few details to Mrs Rushmere, without revealing too much.

"Did Billy, from what you can remember, actually come into the drug store on the day he went missing?" asked Marty.

"No, he didn't. I was working that day. You see, I only worked four days a week at the drug store. Having a family to look to. I distinctly remember it was a Tuesday. Why I remember, is that it was my husband, Gerry's, birthday. The following day it was all on the TV and radio and all over the newspapers about Billy. Some lady had seen him apparently, I think she lived in North Beaumont from memory. After that, Billy just vanished into thin air. So terrible, and the agony for his dear parents." Mrs Rushmere was clearly a very friendly lady and just rattled on. Perhaps there was something that Mrs Rushmere had overlooked, this might just be a breakthrough for them.

"Is there anything, any small detail that you can recall, however minor, that might help us Mrs Rushmere? Did Billy ever talk about where he lived or anyone else he had contact with?" La Paz leaned forward and gave a look of appeal to the grandmother.

Mrs Rushmere blinked her large blue eyes, her mind was ticking over. "Well, come to think of it, there was a customer who came into the drug store later that day, and bought a blue dolphin cool pop. It wasn't a popular flavour with most kids, most of them liked raspberry or orange but this man insisted on a blue cool pop. I attended to him; he wasn't aware of the full name of the flavour. So I said, 'Oh, you mean the blue dolphin flavour, sir. How many do you want?' He just said the one would do, it was for his nephew. Most people would buy more than one cool pop, after all they were only 5 cents, even in those days. When I mentioned quite casually that his nephew would get a blue tongue, the man became agitated, and impatient with me. I was only doing my job you know, really, some people! Seemed to be in a rush I gathered, and left in a real hurry. Snatching the bag I had placed the cool pop into. In fact, I went to the window of the store to see if his nephew was in the car. The gent had parked fairly close to the store, and I could see quite well. But no, there wasn't anyone else in the car. It wasn't long before closing time, not long before 6 p.m. And I don't recall Billy ever mentioning anyone else. Hang on a minute!" Mrs Rushmere was thinking out loud. She raised her hand, in deep thought. "There was one time when Mr Marchant, the pharmacist who owned the drug store back then; he took Billy home one day in his car. It was nearing closing time, and Billy was still in the store talking to us all. He was such a character, but very polite as well. Rather than see Billy walk home alone, Mr Marchant said he would take Billy home. We all knew where he lived, at number 1811 North Beaumont, I mean. Billy had told us so many times," Mrs Rushmere giggled, and put her large puffy hand over her wide mouth. "It was getting a bit dark too. The following day, Mr Marchant did mention that when he dropped Billy off home, the people he was staying with were quite oblivious to the fact that Billy had been out. Not a care in the world, was what Mr Marchant said. You would think that kids grew on trees, he said. The chap who lived there, I don't his name, was drinking from a vodka bottle when he opened the front door. Mr Marchant did think that it did not seem to be a good environment for Billy to be living in. There was a woman also, dressed in some long gown and a tiara!" Mrs Rushmere exclaimed, raising her plucked eyebrows in amazement. "Seemed a strange setup if you asked me! Yes, it was such a shame when Billy went missing." Mrs Rushmere sat back and seemed satisfied with her account of the encounter with the man in the drug store.

"Had you seen the man who was in the drug store, before Mrs Rushmere, or the car even, in the area?" questioned Marty. He could smell that there was some light at the end of the long tunnel.

"No, I can't say that I had seen the man before. He was smoking and his hands were shaky, I did notice that. In fact," Mrs Rushmere said in a startled way, "the man was lighting another cigarette when he still hadn't finished the one he was smoking! Must have been a chain smoker, I would say. The car was a red Ford Mustang. Those cars were all the rage then!" exclaimed Mrs Rushmere. "Nice colour too. I like red and I remember thinking that the red paintwork and white wall tyres were very striking. He drove off like a maniac down the avenue, in the direction of North Beaumont. That's all I can remember gentlemen." Mrs Rushmere paused to reflect upon what she had just spoken, looking pleasantly at the two men opposite her.

Marty and La Paz were fired up now, a lucky break! Both men knew they were onto something here, but played it down.

"Could you describe the man you saw, Mrs Rushmere?" Marty breathed heavily, waiting to hear what the lady would reveal.

"Well, he wasn't that tall really. Probably 5 foot 6 or 7. Slim build, slightly stooped when he walked. Wore a dark felt hat. Had a distinct European accent, I would say at a guess. I did see a lovely ring he was wearing. It was an emerald stone. A wonderful shade of ivy green. Could have been a Colombian emerald, they say the best emeralds come from there, don't they? I like jewellery, and I particularly took notice of the ring. No, other than that, I can't be of much help I'm afraid. The old memory can't recall anything more." Mrs Rushmere gave a smile of defeat. After all, it was 50 years wasn't it?

"Mrs Rushmere, you have been superb in your recollection of the events of the day Billy went missing. Thank you again for your invaluable time," said La Paz as both men rose from the sofa to leave the helpful Mrs Rushmere.

Sitting in the Chevrolet car, both detectives were amazed with the information they had been told.

"Wow!" whistled La Paz. "Hey Boss, that could have been Max Femmer in the drug store, what do you think?"

"Yep pal, it surely does sound like it. So why would Max Femmer go and buy one blue dolphin cool pop, and be in such a hurry to get it? And so late in the day. Was Billy Parsons still alive then? Where was he taking it? The mystery deepens alright." Marty was starring straight ahead, thinking over all that had been told to them by Mrs Rushmere. *A very prospectful morning so far,* thought Marty.

La Paz quickly said to Marty, "Do you want to try Mrs Femmer again Boss?"

"Yes, I do bud. Let's hope she is home now."

Just as La Paz was about to reverse the car out of the Rushmere driveway, Mrs Rushmere came running across the lawn towards their car, waving her arms frantically. Sliding down the car's electric window, Marty poked his head out of the passenger's side to see what Mrs Rushmere wanted. Leaning breathlessly into the car, Mrs Rushmere was excited that she could remember another important detail.

"Oh, something has just come to mind about that man at the drug store. On his hat, there was a badge of some sort. It was a coloured one. The background was yellow and was like the sun or a group of stars. Then below that, written in black lettering was an unusual name that I had never seen before. There were two words. The first one was like the word 'second' and the next word was quite different, started with an 'n'. I can't be absolutely positive about the second word. He was moving his head of course, so it was difficult to read. Sorry, I'm not much help am I?" Looking a bit downhearted, Mrs Rushmere stopped herself and waited for a response from the detectives.

Marty, knowing that the lady had put the final clue into its place for them, stated phonetically for the benefit of Mrs Rushmere, "Were the words, 'Secundus Nilli'?"

"Well yes, now that you say it like that, it certainly does sound like the words that I saw on the gent's hat that day. Do you know what the words mean? I had often wondered what those words meant," asked the inquisitive Mrs Rushmere.

Marty explained the meaning "Second to none".

"Well, I never. Fancy getting around with that on your hat. Must have fancied himself a bit!" laughed Mrs Rushmere, shaking her dyed blonde hair everywhere over her face.

Waving the detective goodbye, Mrs Rushmere wandered back to her living room to consider the events of that day when Billy Parsons had become an overnight household word.

CHAPTER *twenty-five*

"So that seals it then, Boss. Max Femmer was definitely driving that red Mustang that evening. Why does he drive to the drug store to buy only one cool pop? He's in a hell of a hurry to get this cool pop too." La Paz took his eyes off the road to see if Marty agreed with his words.

"I agree with what you say pal. Femmer was desperate to get that cool pop, hell or high water! It also indicates that there is a distinct possibility that Billy Parsons was still alive around 6 p.m. So what occurred after that? That's the burning question we have to find the answer to," said Marty in answer to his second officer.

Driving back to Marjorie Femmer's residence, Marty was hopeful that the woman was home now. He would play the game carefully with her, especially in light of their previous meeting.

Arriving back at 1768 North Beaumont, the two detectives once again stood waiting at the door for it to be opened. Marjorie Femmer was still in the kitchen, when the doorbell sounded.

Oh no, just as I had suspected. Back here again. I will have to answer the door this time. I just cannot ignore them. They will keep coming back until I do, reasoned the ailing Mrs Femmer. Her legs were stiff from sitting, but Mrs Femmer managed to muster sufficient strength to shuffle to the door and open it. Anyone looking at Mrs Femmer would come to the conclusion that she was a dying duck in a thunderstorm!

Marty gave a very meaningful hello and introduced Miguel La Paz. Marty asked Mrs Femmer if they could come inside. Before Marjorie Femmer could begin to reply, Marty got in first and said that he wasn't going to ask her anything about the red Mustang, but wanted to discuss another matter, that required her assistance.Mrs Femmer was puzzled at this statement, but complied and showed the two men into the living room.With all three persons seated, Marty could see that Mrs Femmer was visibly on edge with their presence. In fact, she had the appearance of a sick cow!

Well, to hang it all! I have to ask her about this matter. She will just have to cope, that's all! I have a job to do, said Marty inwardly.

Beginning his chosen words, Marty commenced, "Seeing that my last visit met with unhelpfulness, on your part; I am giving you the chance to redeem yourself. We wish to know about the Cavallaro twins, what can you tell us?"

With both sets of eyes upon her, Mrs Femmer was taken back with Marty's question.

"The Cavallaro twins! Well, it was such a long time ago. A terrible thing, both girls drowning like that." Marjorie

Femmer was piecing together the details, after so many years. She looked at both detectives with some amazement. *Why are they asking me about the Cavallaro twins? That was years ago, long before Billy came into our lives.* She was stunned, her mind overwhelmed with the question asked of her.

"What can you, personally, tell us Mrs Femmer. You worked at Hal Roach Studios with Peggy Cavallaro, when it all happened. You must have had first hand information regarding the tragedy. I know it is years ago, but with your recollection, can you tell us anything?" Marty was pleading with Mrs Femmer, but using his skills diplomatically to get the woman to relax and throw some light onto this dark calamity.

"Take your time Mrs Femmer, there is no rush." added La Paz.

Lifting her drooped head up, and giving La Paz a look of comprehension, Mrs Femmer began to open up. Sighing deeply, Mrs Femmer gave both detectives a brief once over, and with a voice of deep emotion said, "It was a shock when we were told at the studio that the Cavallaro twins had drowned. I think it was in the summer of '49, if I am not mistaken."

"You are spot on there Mrs Femmer," replied Miguel La Paz, in a friendly tone. Gathering her thoughts together, Mrs Femmer opened up more.

"Apparently from what I can understand, and this I must stress, came from others at the studio, not directly from Peggy Cavallaro. To put you in the picture a little better, I must explain myself further. I was never one of her favourite people. I admit I was a harem skarem as a teenager, but that is all history. In my defence, I can only say that any child who had the upbringing of mine, would also go off the rails. My parents divorced when I was 6. Mother was an alcoholic and went from man to man. My father moved away and I lost all contact with him. There were no other children besides me. I was shunted around from one relative to another, even into some awful foster homes for a while. My mother didn't care for me, I was a piece of excess baggage she would rather leave behind! So I ran away when I was 12 and came to California, from Wyoming. Started a new life, but it wasn't easy gentlemen! You no doubt have been told some stories regarding my behaviour. My failed attempt at becoming a leading lady in films. Well, the truth is that my coffee was drugged, and I just fell listlessly around the place like a drunken sailor. Everyone assumed I was drunk and I was fired. I always felt that the coffee was purposely drugged. I had no proof but I had my suspicions."

Marty was in no doubt that probably Peggy Cavallaro had a hand in the doping of the coffee. Mrs Femmer stopped temporarily to contemplate her next words, "Not long before I left the studio for good and met up with Max, the Cavallaro girls drowned. They were around 18 months old. They were found by the nanny, returning from her day off, late in the afternoon. She had been given the day off. It was a Saturday. The cook had also been given the afternoon off. The butler was sick in hospital, with some gastric complaint and Tony Cavallaro was in Italy. He had left a few days before to attend his mother's funeral. So the only people in the home were

Peggy and the two girls, Ada and Ruth. Tony had brought them one day some months prior, to the studio, to show them off." Mrs Femmer was smiling, but more to herself than to the policemen sitting with her. Her thoughts were reminiscing when she had seen the two lovely faces of the chubby little girls. "Tony idolised the girls and was so proud of them. I am sorry to say that Peggy was not a mother who displayed much feeling to the girls. Always busy with her work. She only had a few days off work after their birth, and was back at the studio. Everyone thought that she was going to have longer time away, but no not Peggy! Anyway, apparently on the day of the tragedy, lunch had been prepared in advance by the cook. Peggy and the girls had their lunch, and then Peggy went to the study to complete some work or whatever, for the studio. Thought she was indispensable! It seems that the study French doors were open, and Peggy was so consumed with her work, that she did not notice the girls wander outside. There was an ornamental pond not far from the study, in the elaborate gardens. Well, it seems the girls must have fallen in together and both were found hours later by the nanny. Peggy had lost all conception of time and quite forgot to check the girls' whereabouts. I can't help but think how could any mother do this? The doctor who examined the dear little girls, said they died between 2 p.m. and 6 p.m. Now this is the startling aspect of the horrible event. The girls were buried without waiting for Tony to return from Italy. He wasn't even told! Peggy said it was better not to have him come home, as Tony was already grieving his mother's death. Tony was completely gutted. I have never seen a man so distraught with grief. Those girls were his life and suddenly he came home to an empty home, except for Peggy of course." Mrs Femmer was teary and stopped to dab her eyes with a tissue from her trouser pocket. Her voice was croaky, but the words kept flowing, "The other thing that was most unusual, was that the girls were buried at Lawnwood Cemetary. Now that is over the other side of the valley, miles away from this area. They could have been buried at Woodlawn Hills Cemetary. It was a private service, no one was allowed. The day after the funeral, Peggy was back at work. Mr Roach offered Peggy some time away, but she declined his offer. I understand that she said it was better to be busy than to sit around moping. I know I couldn't have been that strong if I had just buried a child, let alone two!" Mrs Femmer looked at both men with genuine sorrow and concern, yet they could perceive that she was still mystified about the whole affair.

CHAPTER *twenty-six*

Silence filled the room, the sort of silence that mankind longs for, yet has destroyed through his own thoughtlessness. Each person was reflecting on the account given by its descriptor, Marjorie Femmer.

"You do realise, gentlemen, that this all happened at number 1811?" Mrs Femmer looked enquiringly at Marty and then Miguel.

"No, we were not aware of that Mrs Femmer," replied Marty, screwing up his face, and glancing over to his second in command.

"Yes, you see, the Cavallaro's bought number 1811 back in the late '30s, and then when number 1817 came on the market, they purchased that and rented out 1811. The first house had a wonderful garden. Peggy was a keen gardener. There was even a tennis court and a swimming pool. All long gone now of course. The place has fallen into disrepair over the years. I think that the ornamental pond has been filled in too. It was a drawcard in its heyday. They had lavish parties, especially when Tony got the business going so well. He was an astute businessman, but very honest as well. He had a very good reputation, and was thought highly of by Mr Roach. Everyone liked Tony, a very jovial and kind man." Mrs Femmer halted now and ended her rendition of the Cavallaro background.

Yes, thought Marty. *I am sure that Tony was better liked than his wife, Peggy!*

"So that was when the foreign couple started to rent the home, after the Cavallaro's shifted out? Do you think they wanted to leave because of the memory of the girls?" asked La Paz, intently focusing his eyes on Mrs Femmer.

Mrs Femmer raised her painted eyebrows, and looked ahead of her. Then turning her head to La Paz, Mrs Femmer said with some consideration in her voice, "Yes, the foreign couple took up the lease of the property. But in answer to your last question; to be quite frank with you, Tony had cherished memories at 1811, but no, not Peggy. Once number 1817 was on the market, Peggy was all out to get the house. It had belonged to Charles O'Brien, an actor from the silent era originally and had made the transition to the talkies. He had the house built, and the grounds landscaped. He was a bachelor, and kept to himself mostly. Then he died, and the house came on the market. Peggy was after the prestige of the grand house, and wanted to flaunt their wealth. I just don't know why she had a family. I know for a certainty that Tony badly wanted children. Coming from a large Italian family, he naturally wanted offspring. He was over the moon when the girls were born, but Peggy was always preoccupied with her work for the studio. I did feel for him, poor man." Mrs Femmer cast her head down and dabbed her nose.

Realising that there was no further details for Mrs Femmer to say, Marty gave Miguel a nod to indicate that they would leave. Closing the front door behind her, Marjorie Femmer breathed a huge sigh of relief.

She walked slowly back to the living room and over to the drinks cabinet. Pouring herself a large whiskey, she sculled it down and poured another one. How refreshing this liquid was. Just the tonic she needed after her time with the policemen again!

Would they be back? Probably, to ask me about the Mustang. Keep yourself strong girl! Don't let 'em get on top of you, mused Mrs Femmer.

CHAPTER *twenty-seven*

No one had seen the same red and black 1968 Mercury Cougar that had been parked just further down North Beaumont. Neither detective noticed the automobile, as their car turned down North Beaumont, and went in the opposite direction. With sufficient view to see the two men leave Marjorie Femmer's residence, the eyes saw enough to know what that visit was probably all about. The person started the 351 Cleveland V8 motor. The engine purred into life and the car did a u turn and went back up North Beaumont. The day had been profitable all round, for many!

The chance meeting with Mrs Rushmere, and Marjorie Femmer's honest account of the Cavallaro twins; had shed some renewed light on the case that had commenced on a dark note.

That late afternoon, Marty Hislop sprawled out on his living room sofa. He delighted in putting up his feet on occasions to watch the TV. However, this time Marty had his laptop with him. Eventually, Marty was connected onto Skype and speaking with his parents in Vermont. Not wanting to inconvenience his parents, like he had done previously, Marty had come home early to organise himself for the conversation with mom and dad.

Marty was impatient and strongly desirious to know if his Mom had anything to tell him about the Hydrangea flowers. Broaching the subject first hand, Marty asked his mother, "Did you have any success to identify the Hydrangea flowers Mom?" Marty was watching his mother's face with keen interest.

"Yes, Marty. I have had Professor Gilbertson look at the photos you sent. He is President of the Vermont Hydrangea Society. Very well renowned with his study and cultivation of the Hydrangea species too. Now, I must explain all that he told me." Referring to some notes in front of her, Mrs Hislop began to tell Marty about the Hydrangeas. "That particular variety is know as 'Blue Lagoon'. It was introduced to the West Coast of America, in 1963. Bred specifically for the warmer climates, it wasn't much of a success. The plants often suffered from a magnesium deficiency and gradually wilted and then died. I don't remember growing it myself when we were living on the West Coast. According to Professor Gilbertson, they found that high doseages of animal manure or bonemeal assisted the plant to recover sufficiently. The Professor did remark that these plants appeared to be very healthy, and obviously had the right soil and location to do so well. This variety does have a soft perfume and is now hard to come by, mainly due to its delicacy to survive." Mrs Hislop waited for Marty to comment.

"Gee, thanks Mom. That is real helpful. Please thank the

Professor for me too. This is invaluable knowledge, and will help a lot with the case I am working on." Marty smiled back to his mom. Mrs Hislop, who had a good sense of intuition, was not entirely convinced that Marty was telling her everything. Not that he should, she understood that. His work was sensitive and not for all and sundry to know. Deciding to press her son for some insight into Marty's interest in Hydrangeas, Mrs Hislop asked him, "What is the sudden infatuation you have for these Hydrangeas Marty? I admit they are a beautiful specimen, but how do they link to the case you are working on?" Mrs Hislop's eyes narrowed a little, her face showing some uncertainty and doubt.

Marty tried to ignore his mother's question and said evasively,

"Oh, I just happened to notice these plants outside this house, and thought you would like to see them. So I took the photos for you, that's all Mom."

Knowing her son was deliberately avoiding eye contact with her, Mrs Hislop probed deeper and replied in a firm voice, that only Mrs Hislop used when someone like Marty was not being straight with her, "I don't altogether believe you son. You would hardly take the time to photograph Hydrangeas unless there was an ulterior motive behind it. Do these Hydrangeas have some relevance to the case Marty? You could have just said so yourself son." Fixing her eyes onto Marty's face, Mrs Hislop awaited her son's answer.

Marty was cornered. His mother was not one to be fooled

or taken for granted. Mrs Hislop had always known when her son was lying or not being entirely truthful with her. Like the time when Marty was 16 during summer holidays. Trying to tell his mom that he wasn't hungry when it was lunch. Staying up in the retreat watching TV, Marty told his mother. Mrs Hislop smelt a rat immediately. "Marty not hungry, no way! What was keeping him up there!" On further investigation, it was found out that the girl from next door was up there with him. Laying on beanbags canoodling. Snuck the pretty and petite 15 year old Brionny upstairs without his mother noticing. Marty was not a good liar when it came to his mother, you could count on that!

"Well yeah, they may do Mom. I'm not sure exactly, but I have this hunch that may be correct." replied Marty with a meek expression.

"You did seem to take more of an interest, when I said that the variety was introduced in 1963. Is there some connection to that time period Marty?" Mrs Hislop was not giving up!

"No, not really, but there may be Mom. I am just covering all options." Marty answered quickly, hoping to satisfy his mother's curiosity. It didn't work in Marty's favour.

"Marty, it's either one thing or the other. You must have some idea if that Hydrangea variety has any bearing on the case. You are talking in riddles, trying to get me off the scent aren't you?" Mrs Hislop replied impatiently.

At this juncture, Mr Hislop touched his wife's arm in an attempt to calm her down. Taking no attention of her husband's disapproval, another tactic was employed. Mrs Hislop came straight to the point, "Marty, just what is this case you are working on son? Is it an older case, not solved or something like that?"

Marty crumbled under the pressure of his mother's insistence, knowing he could not deter or dupe her any longer. Shaking his head in defeat, Marty said quietly, "Can you remember Billy Parsons, the young kid who disappeared back in 1965?"

Both Marty's parents nodded their heads.

"I am revisiting the case at my bosses's request. The family want closure. The parents are both unwell. You recall that Billy was from Australia?"

"Yes, I can recollect that missing boy. Why, he was so young, how old was he Marty?" quizzed Mr Hislop, taking an interest in what his son had just made known to them. With this, Marty explained to his parents the case background, including the red '65 Ford Mustang owned once by Marjorie Femmer.

"So, do you think that Mrs Femmer still owns this car Marty? Or, she knows where it is," beamed Mrs Hislop.

"Yeah Mom, I do. I think that the car is still around somewhere. We think that the licence has just lapsed, never been renewed. There is a garage at Mrs Femmer's house, it could be in there. I have to pay her another visit and see if I can break her into talking. She is withholding information, I can smell it!" Marty responded, moving forward on the sofa.

"Marty, go easy on Mrs Femmer." came the retort from Mrs Hislop.

"What for Mom? I have tried to be reasonable with Mrs Femmer, and I just get the runaround from her. I must admit that she was helpful the other day when I took La Paz with me. But I need to get the truth Mom. Perhaps I am going about it the wrong way." Marty sat back, with a helpless look on his face.

Mrs Hislop peered into her son's confused face via the computer screen. "Marty, from what you have just told us, it seems to me, that Mrs Femmer still holds a great sense of guilt regarding Billy's disappearance. Whatever it was that happened to the child, Mrs Femmer holds herself solely responsible. She is grieving unmercifully within. If that was me, who had lost Marion or you, so young, I would have retained something that belonged to either of you. A toy, or an item of clothing, a book you liked to be read from, or something that related to you. I don't believe for one minute that Mrs Femmer hasn't got something there that was part of Billy's time with them. Marjorie Femmer is a woman who loved dearly, and was devoted not only to her husband, but also very much to the child she could never have, that being Billy Parsons. Her love was indefinable, without limitation or reserve. For these past 50 years, Mrs Femmer has crucified herself. If only she had stopped to get Billy into the car, or did she actually do this, and something else occurred? Why did Mr Femmer come home and was seen hours later, in the red Mustang? Yes, it was his wife's car, but there must have been a reason why Mr Femmer chose to drive the car in the early evening." Mrs Hislop stopped to consider her thoughts. *Yes, Marjorie Femmer needed to be understood and above all, handled caringly. Marty's approach would have been brash.* Mrs Hislop resumed her words of motherly advice, "Mrs Femmer has been subjected to a divided loyalty, one to her husband, and the other to Billy. You see Marty, the fullness of our heart is expressed in our eyes, in our touch, in what we write, in what we say, in the way we walk, the way we receive, the way we need. That is the fullness of our heart expressing itself in many different methods.Tread carefully with Mrs Femmer. Let her open her heart to you. Don't come on heavy. After all my son, Marjorie Femmer requires closure too. It was her that enjoyed idyllic days of happiness with Billy, and suddenly that was extinguished. The light had gone out of her life, not to be seen again. I do feel for her Marty, and I hope, and trust, that in time, you will too." Mrs Hislop moved her head to one side, and gave her son a moment to digest her words.

Marty could feel tears well up in his eyes. Yes, he had been straight to the point with Mrs Femmer. Perhaps if he had handled her with more thought, Mrs Femmer may have been more amenable to his questions. Marty was a humbled man.

"Yep, you are so right Mom. I have been too hard on her. I haven't made any allowance for her feelings. She was deeply attached to Billy, and the loss of his joy, has made her withdraw into a shell. Those thoughts from long ago, are too cruel to be reminded of again. I will be far more caring when I visit her again. Thanks Mom for your help to open my eyes to Mrs

Femmer's needs, not mine, just to get the case solved."

Mrs Hislop, not wanting to openly hurt her son, answered with a loving voice, "I am only trying to see the facts you have presented, from both angles Marty. With your expertise, and the assistance of La Paz, I know that you both will succeed to close this case."

"Yeah, we will. Thanks for the encouraging words." Marty's features relaxed, as he gave his Mom a smile of sincere gratitude. Mr Hislop tapped his wife on the arm and then hugged her. Both parent hugged each other with genuine affection. Mrs Hislop wanted to remind Marty about another matter that was dear to her heart.

"Marty, please dear, promise that you can make some time to come and see us all. It's been three years now, since we have seen you. It's all very well seeing you on Skype, but to actually be with you in person, would be marvellous. You will try and come won't you Marty?" pleaded Mrs Hislop.

Marty could do little else, but succumb to his mother's plea. "Alright, I will promise to come over and see you all. I just wanna get this case behind me, and then I shall see about taking some leave I am overdue for," came Marty's honest reply.

Finally after saying their farewells, the family dispersed their separate ways.

Marty just sat staring into space, thinking about the way in which to tactfully speak to Marjorie Femmer. Coming to a definite decision, Marty opted to watch some TV and chill out for the night. Cracking open some beer, Marty had a more clear perspective and open mind. He was at peace with himself.

Before talking with his mom, Marty was so uncertain of many things regarding this case, but now matters had taken a new direction. Yes, he knew the way to do this. He would discuss it all with La Paz tomorrow.

The TV had on a James Bond movie from 1969, "*On Her Majesty's Secret Service*" which featured a red coloured Mercury Cougar convertible with a black vinyl roof. Marty liked these muscle cars and was glued to the set watching the car race in icy Switzerland, as James Bond and Diana Rigg escaped the clutches of Madam Irma Bunt and her illustrious gang of thugs.

The film finished late and Marty was exhausted; he flopped into bed. He was out to it almost immediately, snoring away with a contented smile on his face.

CHAPTER *twenty-eight*

The day dawned crystal clear, the sky was bright as the sun's rays penetrated onto the earth. The moon still hung out like a pearlescent disc in the azure loveliness of the heavens above.

Marty woke with renewed vigour, and with it came a sense of purpose to utilise skills he knew had not been used before. One was definitely tact, and the others were diplomacy and understanding of human nature.

Meeting Miguel at the office, Marty went through their proposed visit to Mrs Femmer. Miguel La Paz observed a distinct change in Marty's manner. The Boss appeared to be happier and the cloud that had shrouded his complexion for some days, seemed to have dispersed overnight.

What has happened? La Paz thought to himself as he typed in the name of Vladimir Nijinsky. *Bingo!*

Vladimir Pietrov Nijinsky and Olga Maria Nishka Romanov-Andrejevich Serenova both died together in an automobile accident on July 25, 1978. La Paz was in business. *An automobile accident, very interesting,* thought La Paz.

Checking out the report of the accident, La Paz found out that the incident occurred at around 11 p.m. The car lost control and left the road, careered down an enbankment and smashed into rocks, exploding on impact. Both occupants were killed instantly. The accident took place on the upper stretch of Hollywood Hills Rise. The odd aspect was that the 1975 Oldsmobile Cutlass Supreme, was travelling up the road, and not down. The car had smashed through a safety barrier. There were no witnesses to the accident. Some items were able to be salvaged from the wreckage. Miguel La Paz informed Marty of this information

"What's the matter La Paz, something bugging you?" said Marty, eyeing La Paz carefully.

La Paz sat back in his chair and cracked his knuckles, before responding to Marty's question, "It just doesn't seem right, that's all Boss. Sure, it sounds like an ordinary road fatality but, and hear me through on this. What if both parties were deliberately removed from the scene? Say they were going to drop the bundle about something. Something that was important enough to be covered up by having these two knocked off. You may think I'm crazy, but you can understand a car going off the edge on a dark night coming down, but this car was travelling up the road. Without reason, the car leaves the road, crashing through the barrier and plummets down into rocks. Yet, according to the report, the speedo showed the car was only travelling at 37 mph when the accident happened. The boys managed to salvage some bits from the car, fortunately the speedo was one. No pal, it doesn't wear with me. I reckon there must have been another car travelling in the opposite direction or something distracted the driver, who lost control. Now from what the report states, the driver was Olga Serenova. The bodies were partially burnt in the explosion, but forensics could identify the bodies from dental records and their respective doctor's notes. No alcohol was found in Olga's system, only with Nijinsky. We know he was a drinker, which explains why Olga was driving that night. Now, we have to ask the question, what were they doing at that time of night? They were obviously going somewhere. They were travelling away from where they lived. Perhaps we could try asking the daughter? She might just know something. I will wear a face mask to protect me too," laughed La Paz, moving his chair back with his long legs.

Marty did not answer immediately, but was digesting what Miguel had just said, "You could be right La Paz. Perhaps there was a reason more sinister than what it looks on the surface. As you say, why so late in the night? And, they must have been going somewhere. They weren't just driving around aimlessly just for the fun of it. Could they have been meeting someone? Or were they called out by someone, and that party had the opportunity to engineer a perfect car accident? Yeah, I do think it is worthwhile following up. Take Clark with you, and give the lovely Anna a go, and see what she may tell you. Whether she was still living at 1811 North Beaumont or elsewhere. May as well try. Don't hold out for too much from her though. Oh, watch the fingernails, and yes, wear that facemask. Better get one for Clark too bud!" Marty grinned with amusement.

La Paz was quick to reply, "But Boss, we can't involve anyone else on this case. I thought the big boss said to keep it all under wraps."

Marty knew La Paz was right, but decided to break the rules, so to speak, and answered La Paz, "Clark is alright. He is a quick learner and keeps things to himself. He will be okay. Only inform him of the vital pointers before you interview Anna."

"Alright Boss, whatever you say. I will go now and get this over with."

Marty knew that La Paz was probably not going to enjoy seeing the ungracious Anna once again, but it had to be done.

CHAPTER *twenty-nine*

La Paz took Sergeant Robbie Clark with him to talk to Anna Serenova about the car accident. Clark was brought up to speed regarding the accident report, and the anomalies that La Paz had reason to question Anna regarding. La Paz was careful not to say too much to Clark regarding other details of the case, but enough to keep Clark in the picture.

Arranging for the inmate to be taken to an interview room, the officers awaited Anna's arrival. The door opened, and in waltzed the heavenly Anna. Sneering at both men, she plonked herself down on the chair. Accompanying her was a solicitor, whom did not seem at all comfortable with Anna's presence. Fiddling with his pen, Byron Nebushki, tried not to look at Anna. Keeping his gaze down on the pad in front of him, Nebushki had definitely been henpecked by Anna. The fear of God was with him! La Paz commenced the interview with a question about the accident that killed Anna's mother and her partner.

"Anna, can you tell us why your mother and her partner were out that night so late, on the night of their automobile accident? Were they meeting someone in particular, do you know?"

Anna just glared at La Paz.

"What in the hell do you wanna know for? It's years since that accident, and you have the nerve to ask questions now? Get lost, I don't have to answer anything you bastard!" She leant forward and hissed the words in the face of La Paz. A look of distinct pleasure crowned her craggy face. The breath stunk of nicotine and the body odour was extremely repugnant, to say the least!

Well, thought La Paz, *that is a good start! Now the next angle of approach.*

Before La Paz could say anything more, Sergeant Clark piped up and said quite firmly to Anna's brittle words, "The automobile was travelling up Hollywood Hills Rise. So, the question remains, how can the automobile career off the road, smashing through a safety barrier, when only travelling at 37 mph? It would have been a different matter, if the car was going downhill, but it wasn't.

Visibility was good and the weather was dry. It was a warm summer's night. We are wondering if the driver's attention was distracted or was there an oncoming car, that may have swerved into their path? After all Anna, your input could have an impact on solving this mystery," finished Clark, with a voice of definite credibility.

Surprisingly, Anna blinked in Clark's direction and replied in a more composed tone, "But what has the accident got to do with me, so many years later? I can't see it man. What's the drill here? I can understand what you are saying about the car.

It does make sense. I was at home that night. I can remember that my mother answered a phone call late in the night. They both told me that they were going to meet someone. Not to wait up, as they may be late back. They didn't say who it was or where they were going to. Mom was agitated, and sort of unsettled. They sometimes did go out at night. I wasn't always home myself, but on this particular night, I was. In fact, I hadn't long been home from a political rally in New Jersey. The plane was delayed, and I got into LAX later than expected. I got a taxi, and just crashed on the living room sofa. I was dog tired. I remember waking to hear the phone ringing. It was Mom that answered the call. Shortly after, they both said they had to go out. That would have been some time after 10.30 p.m. There wasn't anything unusual about them going out at night, as they had done it before. Mom said she would drive, as Vladi had been drinking. He was hardly ever sober, the sex crazed bastard!"

Clark had broken the ice with Anna, who had opened up some information that was previously unknown.

La Paz endeavoured to ask a question regarding the photos of Billy Parsons, found on Thor's laptop. "Did anyone else know about those photos of Billy Parsons, besides yourself and Vladimir Nijinsky?" La Paz waited with some hope that Anna may respond favourably, but the opposite reaction resulted.

"What's it got to do with you, you Mexican rat? Crawled over the border with ya family strapped to ya back. Millions of you, roaming the country. Getting all the jobs, taking us over. Expecting all the welfare handouts and feeding you all with chilli soup! Get back to where you came from. We don't need the likes of you lording it over us ordinary citizens." Spitting the words out like a venomous rattlesnake in full attack, Anna turned her greasy head and grabbed the startled solicitor, Nebushki, by the arm and screeched at him to give her a cigarette. Complying with Anna's request, lest she punch his lights out, and we wouldn't want that would we, Nebushki meekly proffered a crumpled packet of Camel filters to the nasty and bitter, Anna. She snatched the packet from his nicotine-stained hand, and hurriedly took out two smokes and shoved them into her wretched mouth. Making a noise like a female panther, before she looms upon her prey, Anna glared at the shaky Nebushki for a light. He fumbled for his cigarette lighter and tried to ignite it, but his large clumsy hands were not functioning very well at all. Nervous as a frightened fawn, Nebushki attempted three times to light the fags in the twisted mouth of the spiteful Anna.

Losing patience with the man, Anna seized the lighter and with outstretched hands, lit the two cigarettes simultaneously. Puffing wildly, she blew the horrid smoke over towards La Paz.

"That better now, Anna?" said Clark, with a definite smirk on is face.

"Heck yeah, man. All I need now is a bottle of Absinthe, and I would be in seventh heaven." Anna gave a lusty, yet chesty, raucous laugh. She moved her slim frame in the chair, away from La Paz, who clearly wasn't in her good books at all.

Without prompting, Anna just carried on as though nothing had happened, and looking at Clark, answered La Paz's question.

"Yep, there was only one other person who knew about those photos. Now that you mention it, they could have arranged that accident. I wouldn't put it past them either." Anna drew heavily on both cigarettes, ash tumbling onto the table.

"Who might that be?" asked Clark, looking at La Paz with some intent.

"That stuck up bitch, Peggy Cavallaro of course! She was the one who commissioned Nijinsky to take the photos of Billy. When Billy wandered into her property one day, she decided that the kid would make a good subject for that creep Nijinsky. He was always looking for some excuse to take lurid photos, and sell them to one of those gossip mags, to make some quick dough. Peggy Cavallaro suggested that he take the photos, and do one of me also. She said that her connections would pay big dollars for them. Now that was the trap that Peggy Cavallaro set for us. The idiot Nijinsky went about taking the photos of Billy, and of course I was involved too. Mom told me it was going to bring in good money. So I just did what they wanted. When Peggy Cavallaro got the photos, the bitch told Nijinsky that if ever any one of us broke our silence about the photos, she would inform the cops, and deny all knowledge of the conversation between the air-headed Nijinsky and her. The cops would believe her more than us. The treacherous woman gave Nijinsky a hundred bucks to satisfy him. Oooh, I'd love to smack her teeth down her throat! Peggy Cavallaro had no intention of giving the photos to a magazine for publication. Those photos were her insurance. We were caught. Mom had been late a few times paying the rent, and we were told we would be out on our necks if things didn't improve. The stupid boozer, did have extra copies ran off, which my Mom kept. It was those photos that I later put onto the disc, then lumbering jackass Thor put the disc onto his laptop." Blazing smoke with great content, she concluded her lengthy account of the pornographic photos. Anna omitted to add anything about Thor's statement that it was her who told him to put the disc onto his laptop.

This aside, it was all very gradually being pieced together. The jigsaw was finally beginning to make sense. La Paz thought he might be able to ask a question, without being shot down!

Clearing his throat, he faced onto the seedy and smelly Anna, and said with caution, "What makes you think that Peggy Cavallaro had anything to do with the automobile accident involving your Mom and Nijinsky, Anna?" He hoped an answer would be forthcoming but once again a very negative response occurred.

Anna's head swivelled around to directly face La Paz. With a voice that almost was at screaming pitch, she said, "And what's that got to do with you, chilli chops? I am quite happy talking to this other copper here. What's the matter, got ya nose out of joint 'cause an officer of lower rank is askin' all the questions, and getting all the answers? Fuck off, and go back to your cactus ranch and piss yourself! And take your tribe of smutty offspring with you!"

Anna leant right across the desk to sneer in a leering pose at the visibly offended La Paz. Saliva dribbled from her mouth. La Paz clenched his fists in extreme anger. Clark saw this and nudged the foot of La Paz with his shoe.

Nebushki piped up and said in a stammering high pitched foreign accent, "Aaanna, that is no vay to speak to the polllice. They are only trying to get ...get all the facts to doooo their job."

Anna's face became hostile and she was venting rage. Without warning, Anna slapped the unshaven, chubby face of the hapless Nebushki. His head was jolted back in total surprise. The man was stunned and touched his face to ensure it was all in place! Surprisingly, Nebushki reached into his shabby suit jacket and pulled out another packet of Camel filters, and lit a cigarette with jittery hands. Blowing smoke into the already stale smelling room, he appeared to be whimpering to himself. *Poor guy*, thought Clark.

La Paz leapt to his feet, and standing up, put his long arms on the desk, and gave Anna a reply to this horrid outburst of utter maliciousness.

"You listen here, sleazy slut! I came into this country the proper way. No illegal immigrant stuff. My wife and my five kids. Sure there are plenty of Mexicans out there who are not accounted for. But I'm telling you," La Paz pointed his finger straight into the face of the speechless Anna, raising his disturbed voice, "that I don't appreciate your attitude to me.

I'm here to serve the people of the United States of America, I took an oath lady, and I intend to honour it. But I don't need the likes of you shoving shit into my face, cos you got nothing betta to do. Every citizen deserves a chance in life. This is now considered a murder investigation. Do you want juctice to be served, to find out the real reason why your mom and partner were killed?" La Paz was becoming uncontrollably hot headed, very unusual for this man. "And, I might add, you were a party to the photos taken of Billy Parsons. If you had any decency in you at all, you would have had nothing to do with those photos. However, seeing you thought more of making a quick dollar, instead of considering the exposure of this poor kid to the camera of Nijinsky, you went along with it. You are just as rotten as he is! I'll make sure that you go away for a long time, and don't think I don't mean what I say!"

La Paz was absolutely furious, and stood in a menacing stance. It took him all his strength from not wanting to hit her right across the snarling, ugly face. These words had a profound effect on the horrible Anna.

She even smiled and rolled her head back, saying, "Well, well Detective Sergeant. We do have a voice of a man after all! I am impressed!" She sat back and gave La Paz the once over, blowing acrid smoke into the hazy and hot room.

Cooling down, La Paz seated his tall frame back onto the chair. Recovering himself, La Paz, said with a no nonsense tone to his voice, "Now, answer the question that I asked before."

CHAPTER *thirty*

Pausing slightly, Anna lit another two cigarettes, puffed smoke across the table, and decided to give up some more information.

"Because that woman is capable of anything, that's why. For a while, there was this villainous creature, an Italian guy, that lived in one half of number 1811. Initially, we only had one half of the house, and this other guy had the other half. Boy, you wouldn't want to get on the wrong side of him! You'd get a bullet or a knife in the back, sure as look at you! Calls himself Eric Marsh, but his real name is Enrico Marchetti. Supposed to be some distant cousin of Tony Cavallaro's. Came over from Italy when quite young. He was only in his late teens. Had some connection to the Mafia in Sicily, but was quickly smuggled out to live in the States. Has a record back there, as long as your arm. I know, because I did some background research on him. He is bad news, I tell you guys. Nothing he doesn't know, and informs snobby madam Cavallaro. I went to bed with a baseball bat under my bed each night. He used to roam the grounds of the house like a fox. Watching any movement we made. Mom was petrified to go outside at night when he lived there. Mom had a cat, called Nickolas, named after Czar Nickolas of course. One morning when she went outside to give Nickolas his cat food, there's the cat. All strung up in four pieces hanging on the clothes line. Head was severed, the legs pulled off and intestines all over the lawn. That really upset Mom big time! I will say that Vladi did approach this beast about what had happened. What this guy does is not answer you. He just stands with a permanent smile on his face. Enrico told Madam Highbrow, who then had the audacity to threaten us with eviction for accusing this monster of killing the cat! Eventually, Peggy Cavallaro got him shifted up to their palace on the hill, and he was living in a gardener's cottage on the estate. The only thing this Enrico had a flair at, was gardening. He did all the gardening at number 1811, then at number 1817. I reckon 100 percent, that he would have carried out the accident. Naturally Madam Cavallaro would have instigated the job. I have always had my suspicions, but to save my throat from being slashed, I kept quiet. And don't think for one moment that Tony Cavallaro was any angel either. He did some shonky deals to feather his own pockets, I can tell ya that much. Vladi told me that Big Boy Tony was a crooked swine. Came over all gooey and gushy, got you into his confidence, and then he would strike like a lion, ripping every ounce of flesh from off ya bones. Vladi said once that he had been ripped off by Tony Cavallaro. I don't have any real proof, only heresay. Madam Perfection is the mastermind behind all the goings on. Big Boy Tony was the money whiz. So between the pair, they had it made. Then along came Enrico

Marchetti, who was a trump card in their crown. Want any one knocked off, get Marchetti to do it! Cheap labour but an effective result." Shrugging her bony shoulders, Anna paused to suck the cigarettes like a lolly stick. "I don't have anything to do with Peggy Cavallaro. I pay my rent online direct into an account, and that's it. I never see her, and what's more, I don't want to either." Puffing on the now almost extinguished cigarettes, Anna gave a rare toothless smile and flicked ash onto the table.

La Paz made notes of these details and then with a stern expression said to Anna, "What do you know about the Cavallaro girls?"

"The twin girls that died in mysterious circumstances? Yeah, I heard about that from Mom. She reckoned that Peggy Cavallaro deliberately allowed the girls to wander off and drown. She isn't a mother's bootlace!" Anna's face was one of disgust.

Look who's talking, thought La Paz.,

"There was this ornamental pond on the property, and that's where they drowned. How can you just forget that two infants are in your care, especially as their mother, and allow them to wander away and drown; without checking to see if they are okay? Mom said they were buried warm. Well, practically anyway. No sooner were they dead, and they were six foot under! Tony Cavallaro was in Italy for some funeral or another. Poor devil came back to find out his daughters had died. My mom always maintained that Marchetti had a hand in it all.

There were no witnesses to it. She could be right, but I guess we will never know." Stubbing out her pair of spent cigarettes, she pulled out another two fags and lit up puffing away and belching out thick smoke like a factory chimney – minus the carbon emissions of course.

Byron Nebushki was in a hopeless state of repair. Hands fidgeting continually, one grasping and smoking Camel filters, one after the other, and the other was groping aimlessly for a bottle of non-existent vodka. His saving grace was not to be found in this room!

The detectives decided to terminate the interview. A lot had been gained from the somewhat difficult conversation with Anna.

As Anna went to leave the room, she asked the two detectives, "Will you let me know if you find anything out about the accident? I would really like to know, that's all."

La Paz softened a little and replied, "Yeah, sure thing, we will keep you informed."

Anna nodded her head and swept from the room, followed by the useless Nebushki.

Upon their return to the room where Marty was still working, La Paz briefed his boss regarding the possibility that someone had caused the car accident, plus the new man on the block, to them anyway, being Enrico Marchetti.Sergeant Clark was relatively quiet, letting La Paz do the talking. Clark had no intention of saying a word regarding the scene in the interview room. Clark had deep respect for La Paz, and understood why the man had become unravelled. He excused himself from the room and resumed his duties. Making a short phone call, Clark left the office to follow up a lead.Marty was very pleased with the new facts, and asked La Paz to do a check on this character Marchetti

CHAPTER *thirty-one*

Forty minutes later, another event was about to unfold, but with disastrous consequences.

Following the visit of Miguel La Paz to Dirk van Zuutmeyer, the elderly man phoned Marjorie Femmer. She was very pleased to hear Dirk on the other end of the phone. Mrs Femmer asked Dirk to come for lunch on this particular day. Dirk had come by taxi, arriving early, at Mrs Femmer's request. She wanted to take him on a tour of the new cacti bed she had planted. Some of the cacti were flowering well, and Mrs Femmer wished to show Dirk her handiwork.

After showing Dirk around the front garden, the pair had lunch inside. Both had a lot to catch up on, and naturally the visit from the police regarding Billy Parsons, was discussed over the tasteful lunch Marjorie Femmer had prepared.

A red and black Mercury Cougar came to a stop some 200 yards away from the Femmer home. This was the chance that they were waiting for. Fate had worked in their favour! The information provided had been very useful. The dark and unfeeling eyes could see the couple walking around the front cacti garden. With the aid of binoculars, all could be viewed. This person only had to wait for the exact moment, to carry out the deed that was necessary to silence exposure for good.

Patience and persistence were virtues of this nameless entity. As time marched on, the moment arrived when the snake in the grass could strike.

Mrs Femmer had phoned for a taxi to collect Dirk, and the couple emerged from the house to stand on the front porch. Giving Dirk a big hug of affection, they began to move towards the couple of steps leading onto the gravel driveway.

The weapon was raised, loaded ready to go. Silencer equipped rifle, poised by its owner, waiting for the law of accuracy to be placed into this person's deathly hands. The finger was ready to pull the trigger. Excellent, the moment had now come. Exit victim now!

Just as the intended target was within the desired position, Mrs Femmer had the sun's rays blind her vision.

"Oh Dirk. I'm sorry, I will have to move, the sun is a bit strong and is in my eyes. I haven't got my hat with me."

The bullet had been released into the air, moving at lightning speed towards its unknowing victim.

Dirk van Zuutmeyer stepped aside for Marjorie Femmer to move. He stepped one pace too close to be within the firing line of the deathly instrument to inflict bodily harm of immense magnitude. Dirk van Zuutmeyer never knew the object that smashed his brains out of his head. Falling instantly, the limp body fell against the totally surprised Mrs Femmer. She fell also with Dirk, blood and brain tissue splattered all over her white top and pale green slacks. Their bodies were felled like trees in the forest that had just been cut down. Dirk's lifeless body slumped onto Mrs Femmer and pushed her back against the stone fronted porch. A stunned Marjorie Femmer lost her footing and crumpled to the ground. All was silent.

The deadly assassin was not pleased with the outcome.

A curse was uttered. The weapon was placed quickly under a blanket sitting on the front passenger's seat. The Mercury Cougar made a screeching turn and sped up North Beaumont.

A taxi was heading in the direction of 1768 North Beaumont, and the taxi driver saw the speeding red and black older model car travelling in the opposite direction. The scene which greeted the taxi driver was not pleasant.

No fare from this call out!

CHAPTER *thirty-two*

After a lengthy talk regarding the interview with Anna Serenova, Marty and La Paz had a burger each in the canteen. This new lead on Marchetti gave the case renewed impetus, and Marty was eager to wrap this up quick. Surely the car accident was definitely staged to wipe out Anna's mother and partner.

Now they must find this red '65 Mustang. This was crucial, as Marty always felt that the car was still at the Femmer home. It all rested now with Mrs Femmer, but breaking her was not going to be pleasant. A warrant for the search of the automobile maybe the only option, but time would tell.

La Paz drove the journey to the Femmer home, and as their car travelled closer to 1768 North Beaumont, a police cordon was in place a couple of blocks from the address. The detectives were informed that there had been a shooting at 1768 North Beaumont. One man dead and a lady injured. A taxi driver had found the pair on the front porch, no more than an hour ago. No, the officer could not provide any names as yet. Permitted access to the vicinity, Marty was going over the case rapidly in his confused mind.

La Paz cruised up North Beaumont as fast as the car would allow. Neighbours lined the street and TV camera crews swarmed the pavements, trying to get shots of the crime scene. A helicopter flew overhead, taking zoom shots of the scene.

Marty was annoyed with himself. *I should have seen this coming. Idiot!*

The ambulance was about to leave the home, when the detectives arrived. La Paz hurried out of the car to view the body. Instantly, La Paz recognised the body to be that of Dirk van Zuutmeyer. His head on the left side had a massive gaping wound. The poor guy did not suffer. Death was final the moment the bullet entered the head.

La Paz was sickened with what he saw. He had liked the gentleman and enjoyed speaking with him. Now this!

La Paz spoke to the body of Dirk, and said in a choking manner, "We will get the bastard who has done this. Rest now man." Some tears streamed down the face of Miguel La Paz, as he moved away from the ambulance.

Speaking to the taxi driver who had been asked to wait behind for questioning, La Paz asked the small statured man if he had seen anyone as he drove into the Femmer home. The driver was a Stan Lowrensrich, who worked for Red Cabs of West Hollywood. Without any reluctance, Lowrensrich told La Paz of the older model red and black Mercury Cougar that was speeding up North Beaumont. No, he could not say if the car had been at the Femmer house, nor did he notice the registration. The only thing he did see, was that the driver had dark glasses and possibly wore a hoodie or a beanie. La Paz instantly thought of the same car they had seen in the vicinity of the drug store on Roy Rogers Avenue. No coincidence here. This had to be the same vehicle. This was a car that was recognisable!

Meanwhile, Marty was with Marjorie Femmer inside the house. She had regained her consciousness, but was terribly upset. Two paramedics hovered around the lady, observing her condition should it change. Refusing to go to the hospital for observation, Mrs Femmer lay on the living room sofa. Stunned and horrified at the realisation of the shocking events that had taken the life of a close, long standing friend, Mrs Femmer openly wept. Cradling her aching head in her long arthritic fingers, the woman was deeply disturbed. Marty tried to offer words of comfort but was not very successful. He indicated for La Paz, when the detective entered the room, to see if he may be able to pacify Marjorie Femmer. *After all,* thought Marty, *La Paz has more experience at this than me! He has four daughters and a wife to deal with every day.*

Finally, after some soothing words from Miguel La Paz, Mrs Femmer rallied a little. Her wailing lessened, and the body began to relax. Marty went over to the drinks cabinet, and poured a large glass of whiskey for Mrs Femmer. Taking it over to the lady, he handed it to her. The liquid was swallowed in a rush, followed by a series of hiccups. One of the paramedics raised his bushy eyebrows at Marty.

"That did the trick," he said in a slow, deep voice.

Raising herself on her own volition, La Paz adjusted some cushions behind her back, making Mrs Femmer more comfortable.

"Are you sure that you don't wish to go the hospital, Mrs Femmer? You may have injured your back or hurt your head," asked a concerned Marty.

"No definitely not. I will be alright. I'm just bruised, that's all. Such a terrible shock! Poor, dear Dirk. We had such a wonderful time catching up. He did so enjoy the salmon fishcakes I made. Now, he's gone. How fragile life is Inspector." Mrs Femmer's contorted face told a story of tragic circumstances. Perhaps more than most people could imagine.

Marty knew that there was going to be some more tears and anguish, so suggested to the paramedics to leave.

Watching the two paramedics pack away their gear and leave the room, Marty decided to call over a lady police officer, who was standing in the corner of the lounge room. "Before we question Mrs Femmer, do you think that you could help her change out of the blood stained clothes and freshen up a bit? The forensic boys will no doubt want the clothes for analysis."

CHAPTER *thirty-three*

After about twenty minutes had elapsed, Mrs Femmer reappeared in fresh clothes, looking more alert and ready to speak to the detectives. Carefully seating herself again on the sofa, Mrs Femmer gave a smile and said quietly, "Alright gentlemen, ask what you want. I will endeavour to answer your questions."

Marty commenced by saying, "Did you see or hear anything Mrs Femmer, just prior to the shooting?" Marty was playing this carefully. He recalled his mother's advice, tact and understanding. "Take your time, we have all the time in the world, don't we Detective Inspector La Paz?" catching the attention of his second officer.

"Yes, Mrs Femmer. Anything you can tell us, no matter how insignificant, it may help us find who has done this," replied a caring La Paz.

Mrs Femmer managed a brief smile, and said in a tired voice, "Oh, I know who is responsible for this, gentlemen. I am not a complete fool. I was the intended victim, but fate has worked mysteriously, and taken Dirk instead." Pausing before she went on, Mrs Femmer clasped her hands together, closed her eyes and laid her head back against the cushions.

Reopening her hazel eyes, she shook her head and said, "We were talking, Dirk and I, on the front porch. I had phoned for a taxi, to collect Dirk. We had just come out of the house. I can remember saying to Dirk, that the sun was getting in my eyes, and I would have to move. He stepped to the side, to allow me to pass him, and the next thing, Dirk was falling against me. Everything happened so quick, there was no warning. I heard nothing. But that was the idea, to strike when I was in visual range. This was planned out to the last detail, but alas the wrong person has suffered the fatal price."

Both detectives looked at each other with comprehension of the words of Mrs Femmer. A deadly assasin, sniper attack. But this had gone very wrong!

Marty took up the opening statement of Mrs Femmer.

"So, you have a rough idea who is responsible, Mrs Femmer?" said the ever alert Marty Hislop. His mind was on fire.

Mrs Femmer looked at Marty very attentively, and replied, "No, I do not have a rough idea. I know, for sure, who is behind this. Peggy Cavallaro. She wouldn't get her pretty little hands soiled, so she was got someone to do her dirty work for her. I don't know who that might be, but you can bet your bottom dollar, that this is the work of Peggy Cavallaro." Marjorie Femmer was adamant on that score!

"What make's you think that it is her? Why does she want you out of the way, Mrs Femmer?" questioned La Paz. It was La Paz who decided to take the plunge and ask the million dollar question. "This all has something to do with the red

Mustang and Billy Parsons, doesn't it, Mrs Femmer?" He stared into the face of the now frightened woman.

Her body shivering, Mrs Femmer answered in a feeble voice, "Y-yes." No further words came from her quivering lips.

"You were being blackmailed by Peggy Cavallaro, weren't you?" La Paz waited in expectation of an affirmative response to this question.

"How did you know? Has she told you? No, of course Peggy wouldn't be fool enough to tell you that. What made you suspect that I was being blackmailed?" asked Mrs Femmer in an incredulous voice. She was looking at both men with a look of amazement.

La Paz, hesitating, replied carefully, "Dirk van Zuutmeyer suspected that you were being blackmailed. He even told me himself when I interviewed the gentleman." La Paz tactfully did not mention the $1000 cash withdrawals every fourth Tuesday, from Mrs Femmer's account. It could upset her, and that would finish their relationship with Mrs Femmer. Marty took over the method of offensive operation. They had to get Mrs Femmer to unlock memories that had haunted her for 50 years.

"Is there anything else that you wish to tell us Mrs Femmer?" said Marty, facing the woman's eyes with a direct stare.

Flinging her head back, Mrs Femmer's features were etched with mental pain. Tears trickled down her ragged face. Marjorie Femmer's mind was filled with violent sorrow and hopeless regret. *Why can't it all go away? I have tried all these years to bear my guilt, but I can't go on any longer. I would be better off dead!* She gave a howling sound, like an animal in deep distress.

"It was me that killed Billy Parsons. I accidently drove the car over him." Mrs Femmer just placed her head into her hands and leant over, uncontrollable weeping and gasps of agonised breaths left her frail body. The two men were stunned with this revelation.

Marty tried to take in the confession, but there was a niggling doubt in the background. *What else can we get out of Mrs Femmer,* he thought. *I don't believe that she killed Billy. We may have to come back, poor thing!*

Mrs Femmer appeared inconsolable. La Paz was doing his duty, and displaying empathy to this woman who had held a dark secret all these years.

Mrs Femmer gathered her emotions, and carried on, looking ahead of her, as though she was living that day all over again.

"Yes, I saw Billy walking down the street. I stopped the car, and called out to him to come and get in. Billy told me he was on his way to get a cool pop. The day was getting hot. I told him that I had a cool pop in the freezer at home. When we got home, which was only a few minutes later, I got Billy the cool pop. I went to get ready for my bowling tournament. I decided to take Billy with me. He knew the car was in the garage, and he went and got the toy car that he drove around the house. He only used it outside. I was in a hurry. I did tell Billy that I was going to reverse the car out of the garage, and to be careful."

Mrs Femmer, was attempting to control herself, and spoke on, "As I was reversing the Mustang, I heard an almighty scream. It was Billy." Mrs Femmer put her hands over her ears, reliving that awful moment all over again. "I braked the car, and raced around to the back of the car. There he was, pinned under the back wheel of the passenger's side. His legs were caught in the toy car. I tried so hard to move him. I managed to get one leg partially out of the toy car, but I couldn't do anymore. Billy had gone quiet. I thought he was dead. I cradled his head in my hands. He opened his eyes, looking at me with such love and trust. I was helpless. I called out for help. No one heard me of course. I was distraught! I thought if I moved the car forward, I would inflict further injury. The wheel had already gone over the little car and of course crushed Billy's legs. I ran to the neighbour next door, Mr Belcher, but he was out. He was retired, and I thought he could assist me. I went back to Billy. He seemed to be going unconscious. I ran inside and got a blanket to wrap Billy in. It was difficult, trying to get under the rear of the car. I just knew I had to work fast. Then I raced inside to phone the ambulance. In my haste, I dialled 911, but I couldn't get the words out. I panicked and hung up, and phoned Max. I told him what had happened, and he said that he would come home straight away. As soon as Max arrived, he took one look at Billy, and said that he required medical help. Max said he would take him to the hospital. Max very carefully moved the car forward a fraction, so as not to harm Billy any further. Then a lot of blood started to gush out. It must have come from his legs. It was so hard to see where the wound was. Gathering Billy up in his arms, Max took Billy inside and placed him on the rug in his studio. That was the rug you stood on Detective Inspector, when you came into the studio that day. I was worried that you might see the blood stains. I was never able to get all the stains washed out. Max didn't want me to throw it out. Then, Max took me by the shoulders, and said that I had to forget that this had ever happened. Billy never came to our home that day; if I was asked. I was hysterical, and said that I wanted to come to the hospital. Max would not hear of it. He became angry, and slapped me across the face. I fell across the desk, with the force! I was temporarily unable to function, every bone in my body screamed with pain. Max rolled Billy up into the blanket again, and left by the stairs, that lead down to the garage. He drove off in the Mustang and sped like lightning up North Beaumont. I waited and waited. Time just marched on. I was beside myself. No word from Max. I phoned the Good Samaritan Hospital in North Hollywood, but they told me no child had been admitted with leg injuries. Then I wondered if Max had taken Billy to the children's hospital, down at Pacific Glades. Once again, no Billy. What was I to do, but just wait? I couldn't tell anyone. To pass the time, I washed the rug, as best I could. Naturally, I cleaned the driveway with bleach to get the blood stains removed. I tried to eat but that was impossible. I felt sick with grief and worry. Evening came, and still no Max. Finally, just after 7.30 p.m., Max arrived home.

He was very aloof to me and clearly upset. He only told me that Billy was in safe hands, I was not to mention this to anyone at all. I asked and begged him to tell me if Billy was okay. He said that was all I needed to know. Max never spoke of Billy from that day on. It was as though Billy had never existed! I obeyed his wishes, but my heart was empty. The light had been taken out of me, and I was full of darkness and despair. I could tell that Billy had died. It was all my fault. Max covered for me. I had to pay the price of silence. Not knowing, hurt so much. If only I had been with Billy, when he died. Why did he drive his little car into the path of the Mustang? Why didn't I get him into the automobile before I reversed? There were so many unanswered questions." Mrs Femmer had relived the horror of that fateful day. She hung her head down in abject shame.

CHAPTER *thirty-four*

Her mind was awash with complex thoughts. The blackmail that followed shortly after Max passed away. The rattles on the back door handle at night. The shadow that slipped over her front bedroom window, in the full moon. Pieces of shattered glass on the front porch one morning. Unexplained faulty electric wiring, causing loss of power. The unseen face behind her back when out. The feeling of being watched and preyed upon, yes, it had all gone on for years.

Now it was time to relinquish her thoughts. She could no longer face herself in the mirror. Living with the death of her beloved Billy. The only way out was certain sleep, a slumber that she had not tasted since the day Billy died. La Paz discerned that Mrs Femmer was deep in thought. He held her dithery hands. They were ice cold, as cold as the mind that had inflicted this sentence of guilt on Marjorie Femmer.

"Why was Peggy Cavallaro blackmailing you, Mrs Femmer?' asked La Paz.

Mrs Femmer, who was still very much in contemplation, gave the question some thought before answering, "Because, Peggy Cavallaro knew that I had killed Billy. She told me so. How she knew, I don't really know for sure. The blackmail commenced only after Max's death. It started off with a small amount, but gradually increased over the years. I always have a feeling that I am being watched or even followed at times. I often have strange things happening. The back door rattling at night. Scraping noises at the bedroom window, once again, at night. Loss of power. Broken glass was splattered over the front porch one morning. When I am out, I have occasionally seen someone following me, then suddenly disappear. I don't know who it is. This has gone on for years and years. I got used to it, but it does give me the creeps at times. If Peggy Cavallaro is behind all this, then she has got someone to do it for her. It is all related, I know. I am not mistaken!" Mrs Femmer ended her words with an air of firmness, yet she was very emotional. The detectives were taking all this new information into their minds.

Could this "someone" be Enrico Marchetti? La Paz thought to himself.

***

Peggy Cavallaro had just arrived home, driven by Eccles the chauffeur, in her shining black Cadillac limousine. She had been to a meeting to secure a new transport contract. By good fortune, Peggy Cavallaro had obtained the contract, but only by a fractional sum of money. Another company, Canadian Pacific Transport, had also been vying for the contract too. They had been very fierce in their bid to add this contract to their already extensive network of transport routes. However, with a little persuasion, on behalf of the charming Peggy

Cavallaro, with some good connections to speak for her, the ageing transport monarch, had taken off quite a feist.This new contract gave her transport company the exclusive rights to the Canadian territories and the west coast, taking in the lucrative Vancouver area.

"What a marvellous acquisition!" exclaimed the wealthy woman to Eccles, as she stepped into the car to be driven to her exclusive hideaway. "Now don't forget that you must drive Matilda to her regular place this afternoon, will you Eccles?" came the shrill voice of the pixie look alike, Peggy Cavallaro.

"No, I haven't forgotten Mrs Cavallaro. I shall be ready to take Matilda," replied a wearisome and partially annoyed, John Eccles. *Always dishing out instructions, it is just as though I was some kid who has to be reminded of everything*, thought the down-and-out Eccles.

Turning into the driveway of Harpenden Lodge, Eccles looked at the car clock, and his mind began to plan. As Mrs Cavallaro alighted from the spotless limo, Eccles gave the woman a hardened face, as she walked away from the vehicle. Boasting all the way home about this new contract, "that only she had made possible". Eccles was thinking how totally consumed Mrs Cavallaro was with herself, and the company. Little thought was given to the feelings of others. He was aware of the helpless Matilda, and her predicament. Or was she, something could be done. *Why put it off any more? Act now*, thought Eccles. He went inside the mansion and searched for Matilda.

CHAPTER *thirty-five*

Back at 1768 North Beaumont, Marjorie Femmer had composed herself. The weight of all these years had been a burden not many people could take with them. Now was the time to release the truth. Mrs Femmer was struggling to her feet, aided by La Paz.

"I want to take you to the studio" she said.

Helping the lady down the passage was slow and laborious, however Mrs Femmer was showing great determination not to give in. Taking the key from around her neck, she opened the studio door, and turned on the fluorescent lights. The smell was one of mustiness, stale smoke and dust. Shuffling over to the desk, her hand touched a hidden drawer under the desk top. There was something in her hands.

Before delivering the item to Marty, Mrs Femmer took a deep breath and said with a peaceful disposition, "These are the keys to the Mustang. You will find the car below, in the garage. You can access through that door at the back of the studio." She pointed to the door; Marty remembered seeing the door the last time he was here. "That will take you down to the below ground garage. The Mustang is still there. It has never been used since the day Billy was killed. I did not drive the car again, and Max never spoke of the Mustang again. We made up a story that the car was sold to a university student. That was mainly for the benefit of Dirk." Lowering her head, Mrs Femmer placed the keys into the outstretched hand of Marty.

At last, now we can view this Mustang, thought the excited Marty. *Will there be any evidence to tell us exactly what happened?*

"Thankyou Mrs Femmer," was all that Marty could utter. What else could he say? Words were not enough to sooth this woman's feelings.

"I will go back to the living room, gentlemen. Don't worry, I shall be okay. It's just that I can't bear to see the car again. Too many sad memories." With her face appearing to be at peace and cautious steps, Mrs Femmer left the study.

Making their way downstairs, the detectives opened the garage door using the set of keys. It was a bit difficult, fiddling with the keys, but La Paz had the patience to persevere, and he was successful choosing the key to open the door, to what they had wanted to see for some days. La Paz fumbled around for a light switch, and was rewarded with a bump on the wall. Feeling around with his hand, La Paz pressed the switch down. Presto, the globe was still working! Their eyes gradually became accustomed to the murky gloom before them.

The light that shone from the old globe was dim, to say the least. The garage area was very dusty. No one had been down here for years. It was a large and deep garage, enough space for four cars. The area extended under a large area of the home. Marty made a whistle sound through his teeth.

"Gee, this is huge! That must be the red '65 Mustang over there in the corner," Marty exclaimed to La Paz.

Some shelving was on the opposite wall, crammed with tools and other paraphernalia. Both men strode over to the object covered by a canvas car cover.

"This will be it for sure. Careful La Paz, this dust is thick!" muttered Marty.

They gradually removed the dusty red and white canvass car cover. It must have been made expressly for the car, same colour scheme as the automobile.

Then, the red '65 Mustang was clearly seen. Having been under cover all these years, the paintwork was in remarkable condition. The tyres were deflated, but that was normal.

Walking to the back of the car, La Paz opened the boot. The original Ford factory trunk cover was still to be seen. However, La Paz noticed some dark inky stains, mottled through the cover.

He bent down to have a closer inspection.Marty was still in awe, standing at the driver's door.

"Fling me those keys, La Paz. I wanna take a look inside."

Before Marty could open up the car, La Paz called out to Marty, "Hey Boss, take a look at this will you? I think these are bloodstains, if I am not mistaken."

Marty agreed with La Paz, the stains did have the appearance of very dried blood. On further inspection, they also came across some stains on the driver's floor mat. Marty gave a knowing glance to La Paz, and said in a serious tone, "Billy Parsons was definitely in that trunk. Max Femmer must have got some blood on his shoes and carried it into the car. There could even be blood stains on the garage floor. Now we have to determine if the blood matches Billy Parsons."

La Paz replied simultaneously, "I will get onto the Aussie Feds, and see if there is any record of Billy's blood type. I will also check with Universal Studios, in case they may have the blood type in their archives. Boss, this is coming together nicely now. I still don't think that Mrs Femmer actually killed Billy Parsons, do you? He was probably still alive when put into the Mustang. That is why Femmer stopped to get that cool pop. Billy must have been alive, although badly injured. A lot of blood must have been lost, poor kid!"

"No, I don't think that Mrs Femmer killed Billy. The kid was still alive, as you say, but injured. He must have died some time later. Perhaps after the time that Gwen Rushmere sold the cool pop to Max Femmer. Which was around 5.45 to 6 p.m. That was obviously the car that Peggy Cavallaro saw hurtling up North Beaumont. But, where in the dickens was Max Femmer going to? The trail seems to go cold after that time period." Marty was in a reflective mood. His mind was pondering over a few possibilities; one of these was quite possible. La Paz was quick to mention to Marty about the red and black Mercury Cougar, seen by the taxi driver. The fact that it could be the same car that they had both remarked on just the other day in Roy Rogers Avenue. Marty was all ears on this and agreed that it must be the same automobile.

Forensics were called in to examine the red '65 Mustang, from one end to the other. The garage was also given a thorough search for any clues too. There was nothing more that the detectives could do at the Femmer home.

Checking with Mrs Femmer that she would be alright to leave for the night, her affirmation to the men was firm and strong. Mrs Femmer was now showing far more confidence in herself than she had shown before. Marty gave Mrs Femmer his card for urgent contact, should she need to. With great insistence on Marty's part, he told Mrs Femmer that two policemen would be posted at her home during the night. Mrs Femmer objected quite vehemently, saying, "If they want to get me, let them! I have nothing to hide now. I do not require police protection gentlemen!"

La Paz was prepared for this and hastily replied, "Mrs Femmer, you may need to give evidence in court about Billy. You want justice to be served don't you? I know that you are not frightened, but to keep you safe, a police presence would be advisable, Mrs Femmer."

Mrs Femmer relented, and said that she understood. Two officers, one a woman, were organised to remain for the night. Reassuring the detectives that she would be okay, they drove away.

"I don't know about you, but I'm exhausted!" said Marty to La Paz, who was doing the driving.

La Paz agreed wholeheartedly with that statement.

CHAPTER *thirty-six*

On their return to LAPD, no sooner had the detectives entered their room, when Sergeant Clark knocked and came in. He had a glee in his blue grey eyes.

Marty saw this and spoke to Clark, "What's up, pal? You look as though you have won the lottery?"

"Get a load of this. Downstairs, I have a Matilda Rothenburg and a guy called John Eccles. They want to speak to you Boss. They have some facts that you might be interested in." Clark drew a breath and went on in an excited manner, "They both said that they think they can provide some info on a certain star boarder, who lives at the Cavallaro residence. Plus the girl has something she wants to tell you herself. Eccles seems to have persuaded this house maid to come and talk to you. I have put them in Interview Room 4, Boss." Clark was pleased with what he had just revealed to Marty.

"Great, that is just what I had hoped would occur. Leave it to us and we will go and see them shortly, thanks Clark," replied the grateful Marty.

Clark walked out the room. *Things are looking good to arrest a suspect,* thought Clark to himself.

This was the icing on the cake now! What can these two

tell us, I wonder, thought Marty.

"Come on, let's get down there and see what they have to say. I gave my card to this Matilda. I thought she was having a bad time at cash hill with that meddling Peggy Cavallaro. But the other chap is a bonus. He might be the chauffeur who drives the stretch Caddy limo."

Marty and La Paz descended in the lift and upon walking into the room, Marty could sense that Matilda was unsure of herself. John Eccles, on the other hand, got up straight away to introduce Matilda and himself. With some coaxing from Eccles, the quietly spoken and demure Matilda, began to tell Marty and La Paz her circumstances. They listened intently, La Paz taking some notes as the girl opened up.

When Matilda thought that she had completed her rendition of everything, Eccles said with an encouraging voice, "Now tell them about the other business Matilda."

The maid was beginning to stutter a little.

"There is nothing to be afraid of anymore, Matilda," said Marty in a more than usually kind voice. "Just take a deep breath and start from the beginning."

Matilda shook her head, and clearing her throat, told the detectives about the regular visits to a specified meeting place every fourth Tuesday. Matilda had been instructed by Mrs Cavallaro, to go to a set of customer lockers at a small cash and carry store in Brentwood, called Marsdens. Eccles drove the limousine and waited in the parking lot, near the lockers. This particular store aided their clients with storage lockers, mainly for the ladies, to ensure that handbags or other items were secure, whilst they shopped in the store. The lockers were opened by a key card. Matilda had the key card hung around her neck on each visit. The girl had to open the locker numbered 109, and inside would be an envelope. She was to take it with her back to the limousine in a Marsdens carry bag. Eccles would drive her each occasion. This had been going on since Matilda had arrived. Eccles confirmed that since he had worked at the Cavallaro home, which was five years last March, he had been driving someone to this store to collect a package. Previously, another maid had the task, but when her lips could not be trusted, this girl, Lucy Trevenen, had promptly disappeared.

Matilda became very emotional after divulging these details. "I am so sorry, it's just been so difficult living there. I wish I could go and be with Ben. My parents don't understand at all. I am really frightened now. That other man, who lives in the cottage, he is quite evil, that Mr Marsh. I've never really seen him close up like, but he does give me the creeps. Sometimes I have seen him peering through the window when I am cleaning or taking the rubbish outside. Then he just vanishes from sight." Her spine shuddered just mentioning his name.

Marty thanked Matilda for being brave and coming to them. He then turned his attention to Eccles, the chauffeur. "What has Peggy Cavallaro got on you Mr Eccles, to have you as her chauffeur?"

Spreading his wide hands in front of himself, John Eccles explained that a business associate, who had dealings with

Peggy Cavallaro, was foolish enough to tell her about himself. Eccles had been in Las Vegas, working as a financial advisor. He had accumulated some gambling debts. Getting on the wrong side of the people who he owed money to, resulted in his former business associate informing Madam Cavallaro of Eccles's predicament. Mainly in an effort to rescue the blighted Eccles from the heavy weight creditors. Peggy Cavallaro offered to help. Initially, all went well, the funds were repaid to the debtors, and the death threats ceased. Eccles continued to practice as a Financial Advisor. Shortly after, Peggy Cavallaro, announced her intention to reveal Eccles's situation to the Finance Board. Peggy Cavallaro said that she would have Eccles deregistered for malpractice regarding a friend's investment. This would make it impossible for him to work again in the industry. Eccles tried to refute these false claims, but the powers that be worked very swiftly, and Eccles was out of the finance game overnight, courtesy of Madam Cavallaro. Unable to stay in Las Vegas, with no income, the lady who perpetrated his demise, came to the party again, and gave Eccles the job of chauffeur. If he did not take the position, then she was going to blacken his name all over the States, and Eccles would never work in the finance industry again. Eccles took Mrs Cavallaro to task on this, but suffered the consequences. The police had taken him into custody regarding the false investment that had gone belly up. The whole thing had been a set up! It was only the intervention of Peggy Cavallaro, that stopped any further court action and a definite prison sentence; all on trumped up charges. Eccles was caught whichever way he chose to move. Being single, Eccles took up the role of a chauffeur very reluctantly, but he had no choice. The pay was lousy, and he was constantly reminded of the "saving grace" given by Mrs Cavallaro, bringing him "off the streets of sin" from Las Vegas.

Marty then asked Eccles about Enrico Marchetti or Eric Marsh, as he was known. Eccles raised his eyebrows. He gave the detectives a look of deep concern and nodded in the direction of Matilda. They got the meaning and La Paz suggested to Matilda that they had no further questions to ask her. Taking her outside to a lounge area, La Paz returned to hear what John Eccles had to say.

"Sorry about that. But I didn't want Matilda to hear what I have to say. That guy Marsh or Marchetti, as you just called him, is bad news. Can't trust him one iota. One moment he is gardening, then before you know it, he is watching me like a hawk, as I wash and clean the limousine. I know I have seen him at night, all hours sometimes, out in the garden doing a patrol of the grounds. He carries a shot gun with him. No joke, I have seen it! I did see Marsh cleaning it once, that was through the window of the cottage he lives in. He will shoot a bird or a roaming cat, and gut the carcass, and leave it to rot on the ground. Queer bloody chap, I tell ya! Marsh is shifty and totally under the thumb of Mrs Cavallaro. However, I have heard them arguing in the past. I don't know what it was about."

Marty, taking in what Eccles had just said, replied, keeping his eyes fixed on the man opposite, "Capable of murder, do you think?"

"Yeah, for sure. I wouldn't put it past him. Marsh is constantly on the look out for Matilda. The poor girl is almost literally ravished by this guy. Sex starved freak, I reckon. Can't keep his eyes or hands to himself. There have been occasions when a car arrives at night, with some young girl as the passenger. She is taken into the cottage, and the car leaves, returning later to collect the girl. Might be an hour or could be more. But you don't have to be a rocket scientist to know what it is all about."

"How do you know all this?" questioned La Paz, wondering how Eccles knew all this.

"My bedroom overlooks the forecourt area, where cars come in. It is at the back of the house, on the first floor. I can see over to the cottage, with the aid of binoculars. I'm lucky to live inside the place. Although I have to enter the house from the back door. I have my meals in the kitchen, with Matilda and the cook, Jesse Rowlands. I'm not permitted to go anywhere near the dining room, unless summoned by Mrs Cavallaro. I try to keep an eye on Matilda, she is very vulnerable to this Marsh."

Giving each other a knowing look, Marty and La Paz knew they had to ask about the recent killing at Marjorie Femmer's home. As they relayed to Eccles the details concerning the bungled attack at Marjorie Femmer's home, the chauffeur was not overly surprised.

"It was more than likely Marsh. If Peggy Cavallaro wanted this

Mrs Femmer dead, then he would carry out her instructions to the letter. I am amazed that he missed. She is very fortunate to be alive," Eccles said, shaking his balding head. "You have put some police presence there, haven't you? If Mrs Femmer is on her own, there is no telling what this guy could do." Eccles seemed worried, as he starred at both detectives.

"Yes, we have taken that precuation," came La Paz's quiet reply.

Marty's thoughts were piecing this jigsaw together. Perhaps, just perhaps, they could expose Peggy Cavallaro, along with this character, Eric Marsh. He had an idea, that could be the catalyst to expose the truth about the missing Billy Parsons. On impulse, Marty decided to put a plan into place.

With certain arrangements discussed between Matilda and Eccles and the two detectives, the pair left the LAPD and motored back to Harpenden Lodge. What reception would they have on their arrival? The questions would be asked for their late homecoming. Eccles had thought up an excuse which should satisfy Peggy Cavallaro. Would they both be fired? No, probably not. The pair were handy tools, and Matilda did bring in a handsome monthly income!

Today was the fourth Tuesday, that time of the month when the regular collection had taken place. Calling in to the LAPD on the route home was the only way that Eccles could get the scared Matilda into the police confines.

Justice is never done and fate will have its strange twists in life.

CHAPTER *thirty-seven*

Peggy Cavallaro, sitting at Harpenden Lodge, sipping her afternoon cup of tea, brought to her by the trusty steed of Mrs Rowlands, had a smug smile on her dear little pixie face. Her informant had already told her of the visit to the LAPD of Eccles and Matilda.

Well, well. They think that they can outsmart me, do they? We'll see who is the boss around here! Laughing to herself, she picked up a homemade shortbread and began munching away with a satisfied demeanour. *Yes, it was very important to have a finger in the pie, so to speak. I can keep abreast of these bumbling boobie police officers. Sergeant Clark had been paid well to keep me informed of all developments. It was just a damned pity that Marjorie Femmer did not get the bullet, as intended. Never mind, Dirk van Zuutmeyer probably shot his foul smelling mouth off anyway. So at least he is out of the way now. Marjorie can wait!*

Not ten minutes previously, Peggy Cavallaro had just finished a short, but concise phone conversation with the police sergeant. Yes, all was going well for Madam Cavallaro.

The day ended.

***

Marty and La Paz parted for the night, going to their respective places of abode. Or so Marty Hislop thought of his faithful Detective Inspector. A restful night was in the mind of Marty, however Miguel La Paz had some pressing tasks he wanted to complete, before the morning came again.

Doubling back, once he had seen Marty off the police premises, the enthusiastic Detective Inspector wanted to check out this Enrico Marchetti. Perhaps Interpol had some record of this guy. John Eccles and Matilda Rothenburg were also on the list to be scrutinised by La Paz as well. Giving his wife Gloria a phone call to inform her that he would be late, La Paz commenced his work with vigour. Sergeant Clark popped his head around the office door, and said goodnight. La Paz, engrossed in his search on John Eccles, smiled at the Sergeant and reciprocated with a farewell.

Not long before, the plausible Clark had taken a quick mobile photo shot of La Paz's computer screen. The information on John Robert Thomas Eccles was extra food for the ravenous and cunning Peggy Cavallaro. The mobile screen was able to be enlarged considerably, revealing all background details on the luckless Eccles. Marty Hislop and Miguel La Paz were unaware of the listening device that Clark had planted in their office. Hidden under Hislop's untidy desk, sat the device that had allowed Clark to be a step ahead of the two detectives.

Mrs Cavallaro will be really pleased to know what the latest line of enquiry Hislop and La Paz were onto now, thought Clark.

Sending the new information through to Peggy Cavallaro's private email address, Clark put his mobile back into his blazer, and made his way to the lifts. Down on the ground floor, Clark checked up on what contents had been in the pockets of the now deceased Dirk van Zuutmeyer – nothing of any concern or value to Peggy Cavallaro. Clark then left the LAPD. It was a little after 6.30 p.m. The Sergeant walked at a brisk pace to an underground secure parking lot. This was situated two blocks away from the LAPD headquarters building. Taking the lift down to the basement, Clark checked over his shoulder to ensure that no one was following him. The coast was clear. Just a few stragglers, making their way to parked cars. Their thoughts on the journey home and what lay behind front doors. A family, or no one at all. Well, perhaps a cat or a mouse. You never can tell, can you? Clark was very much infatuated with his car. He had purchased the automobile over 10 years ago, and knew how to service it. It had attracted plenty of attention, which Clark liked. He was a man who led a different life away from the rigidity of the police force. Single, but partial to a few flings of doubtful disputation, of the bisexual nature, Clark was always in control of the situation. Giving everyone the assumption that he was "a nice guy". Clark had used this to his great advantage, and success.

A handsome payment from the rich Mrs Cavallaro had

secured Clark a good private income, plus his collusion with the cunning, yet deceitful, Peggy Cavallaro, had enabled her to have first hand information of the case proceedings. A pleasant arrangement all around for both evil parties!

Starting the engine, the car roared into life. The grunt of the V8 engine was music to his ears. Slowly reversing the car out into the exit laneway, Clark made his way out of the parking lot, and into the homeward bound traffic. The red and black 1968 Mercury Cougar purred like a kitten, as the driver manoeuvred the car carefully in the direction of the western suburbs of Los Angeles. A malicious and self-satisfied glow shone in the eyes of Sergeant Robbie Clark.

A plan was about to be hatched.

CHAPTER *thirty-eight*

La Paz continued to research any facts he could on the list of names he wished to check on. Nothing irregular on Matilda Rose Rothenburg. Her parents were wealthy merchant bankers and financiers from New York. The present Wellard Rothenburg the fifth, was a fifth generation descendant of the founding forefather, Wellard Rothenburg in 1861.

Of course there was plenty on John Eccles, but nothing more than what the man had told them already. Enrico Paolo Marchetti, brought some alarm bells from Interpol. Wanted since 1960 in Italy for murder and robbery, he had been a young member of the Mafia gang. Born in Sicily, but moving to Naples later, Marchetti was high on Interpol's list of wanted criminals. He had been unheard of, and there was a note that Marchetti could have been dead.

Well, not so. He is alive and kicking, very much!" La Paz said out loud. He stopped to think more and walked over to the window, to mull over some thoughts.

So, thought La Paz, *here is this fellow Marchetti, hiding reclusively at the Cavallaro residence. How in the hell did he manage to get mixed up with the Cavallaros?*

Then he remembered Anna Serenova's statement, that

Antonio Cavallaro and Marchetti were related. So Cavallaro had obviously arranged for Marchetti to come undercover to the United States, and live a life of relative security up on "cash hill". Hidden away, no one would think twice, since he had changed his name to Eric Marsh, the gardener, at Harpenden Lodge.

Now this Marchetti was possibly responsible for the death of Dirk van Zuutmeyer. *Did he have some involvement with the disappearance of Billy Parsons, and the child's death?* La Paz thought to himself. *Quite likely. .*

Sending an email through to the Australian Federal Police to ascertain if they could find out the blood type of the missing Billy Parsons, La Paz was satisfied with the progress he had achieved. Seeing that the night was getting on, La Paz chose to call it a day, and go home. Turning off his computer, he left his scribbled notes on his well organised desk, ready to tell his boss in the morning. The only item left to be attended to was to telephone Universal Studios and see if they had any record of Billy's blood type. It was probably a long shot after all these years, but worth the try!

One vital piece of the jigsaw had been overlooked by the normally fastidious La Paz.

* * *

A new day had dawned for all our named characters. The night had slipped away and been replaced by a glorious sunrise, like no other that season. The morning sky was dappled with a rich array of vibrant tones of peach and pink, mingled with a soft flush of the purest white. The moon hung in the heavens like a glowing pearl, awaiting to be plucked down and admired by all who gazed upon its magnificence. The breath of life had been granted to each one, yet some were not thankful for this priceless gift. Their thoughts revolved around their own selfish desires, which can only result in the most devastating of finalities. Life is so fragile, and yet we abuse its beauty and privilege with gross disrespect. One particular person had avoided compliance with the law, because they were simply under the law already! You see, they had no obligation or fulfilment to anything's existence because this person had no relation or quality that linked them to anything of any tangible existence.

"Pride cometh before a fall, and a haughty spirit before destruction", as the wise man Solomon wrote.

The black leather clad figure that had emerged from the shadows of the "Garden of Eden", had just obtained some startling ammunition. This could be used to great advantage! The Kawasaki Headliner cruiser carried the smug rider to its destination.

* * *

The morning post was brought in by Matilda, trying hard to appear strong in her duties, yet all the time wondering about her visit to the LAPD of yesterday. Madam Cavallaro, a keen observer of human nature, especially those of a timid and vulnerable disposition, gave the girl a smile of self satisfaction and ambitious resolve.

Yes, I will let her stew in her own juice, for the moment anyway, thought Peggy Cavallaro.

"Here is the mail, Mrs Cavallaro," Matilda said meekly as she handed the silver salver to the ageing monarch of Harpenden Lodge.

"Thank you, Matilda. Did you have a nice afternoon yesterday with Eccles?" replied the woman with an expression of void emotion. Watching the girl's response, Peggy Cavallaro waited for the answer to her question of entrapment.

Matilda gulped, but remained unrattled, replied carefully, "Yes, I got the parcel. I left it on the side table in the Blue Drawing Room, as instructed, Mrs Cavallaro." Keeping her eyes off her crafty employer, Matilda stepped back and dusted down her apron, as though some speck had suddenly lodged itself there.

"Yes, I received the package Matilda. Thank you. You were both late coming back though. Did you go somewhere, child?" Giving a cheese cake smile of utter disrespect to this simple house maid, yet tinged with a decisive taste of venom,

Matilda rallied herself to keep calm, answered with candour, "Oh, I know we were late, Mrs Cavallaro. There was a car accident on the way back, and poor Eccles was stuck in traffic, waiting for the lane to be cleared. Sorry about that, but it was beyond our control."

"Are you quite sure Matilda, that there was not another port of call on the return journey?" Peggy Cavallaro's eyes were blazing now with rage. She despised anyone who blatantly lied to her. This was the height of her composure that was now being tested to its maximum threshold!

"No, we didn't go anywhere else, Mrs Cavallaro." answered the horrified Matilda. Her eyes widening with fear.

Has she found out what we did? Matilda's brain was becoming muddled.

Already Peggy Cavallaro had grilled Eccles on his lateness, and had been given the same excuse.

Either it was true, or both had colluded to make up this story. Peggy Cavallaro knew the answer, before the question was even asked. Becoming annoyed with this foolish girl, standing in front of her, wringing her hands and fiddling with her apron, Mrs Cavallaro had the trump card.

"Where was the accident, dear?"

Feeling light headed and fumbling inwardly for a convincing answer, the door to the study was opened without warning. The cook, Mrs Jesse Rowlands, entered the room and stopped short.

"Oh, I beg ya pardon, Madam. I thought you were alone. I did knock, but perhaps you didn't hear me. I was just coming to discuss the menu for tomorrow Madam, that's all. I can come back later." Looking flustered and apologetic all at once, the 72 year old ruddy faced woman went to leave the room.

"Mrs Rowlands, it's quite alright. Matilda had kindly

brought me the mail." Turning her dyed blue rinse head in the direction of the clearly relieved Matilda, Peggy Cavallaro dismissed the housemaid.

Matilda did not linger, but made her way out of the room with haste, and relief. *Boy, that was close! I had better find Eccles and tell him that the old battleaxe has her suspicions.* Walking with swift steps, Matilda made her way out to the garage to locate Eccles. Eccles was washing the Caddy limousine again.

Seeing the figure of Matilda hurrying towards him, he stopped what he was doing and came across to meet the flustered girl. Placing his fingers over his mouth just before Matilda spoke, the girl got the message and halted her speech. Peering around, they both made sure that Marsh was not within earshot. Bringing Matilda over to a corner of the garage, Matilda whispered to Eccles about Peggy Cavallaro's suggestion that they went elsewhere on the journey home, the day before.

"Don't worry, Mat. Let her think what she likes. But just in case you're asked again, just tell her the accident was on the Northbound exit on Freeway 25 out of LA. That's what I told you to say yesterday, remember? I have told the same story, so don't fret, okay? You look all frazzled and upset. Don't let the woman do this to you. Be strong, look the dame right in that pug dog face, and let her see that you are not intimidated by her." Taking Matilda by the shoulders, Eccles bent down to stare into the terrified eyes of Matilda. She nodded her head, and seemed to relax a little.

Matilda then spoke of the cook, Mrs Rowlands, coming into the room just as Peggy Cavallaro was wanting an answer to their whereabouts yesterday.

"Well, good old Jesse saved the day, didn't she? You had better get back now, Mat. The eyes of Texas are no doubt watching us now!" laughed Eccles.

Matilda was not encouraged by these words of Eccles, and made her way back to the mansion, with a heavy heart. *What if that Marsh bloke saw us talking?* Matilda thought as she made her way back to the house.

Luck had been with Matilda Rothenburg that morning, as she stood in the lavish study of Harpenden Lodge. Far more than she could ever imagine!

CHAPTER *thirty-nine*

With the menu now discussed, Peggy Cavallaro's next task was to tackle the post.

Flipping through the letters deposited on the silver salver, now resting on her lap, Peggy Cavallaro of Harpenden Lodge, perused the letters. Mostly business correspondence, nothing out of the ordinary at all. The bottom envelope however, took her attention. The buff coloured paper looked aged, and the paper was thicker than the envelopes used now. Her name and address had been correctly spelt, yet all the letters had been cut out of a book or magazine or possibly a newspaper. The postmark was Los Angeles Mail Centre, dated yesterday. Turning the envelope over to see if there was a sender's name supplied, there was only some numbers – 82449. Once again, the numbers had come from a magazine or suchlike.

What in earth is this? Curious beyond measure, Peggy Cavallaro picked up her ebony handled letter opener and slit open the envelope. The contents were wrapped in soft pink tissue paper. Yet, the tissue was very delicate. It smelt of a familiar perfume, something she was very aware of, even now. Peggy Cavallaro's face became brittle. The connection had been made!

With some carefulness, the ruthless woman opened the tissue paper. Her eyes became saucers. What she saw was not possible. Inside were photos of the meeting with Eric Marsh and herself that late afternoon. Disturbing evidence that Peggy Cavallaro did not wish anyone to know.

Who has been trespassing on my property? Peggy thought. There was a time specified on the photos. *Matilda would have been in the kitchen with Mrs Rowlands, and I know that Eccles had gone to get gas for the car. He couldn't have taken these photos. Who has been here? Some low-life person wanting to cause trouble. Well trouble they will get!*

Underneath the four photographs, certainly of a startling revelation, was a note. Done with the same cut out letters on pale pink paper; it merely said "I know".

Nothing more was in the envelope. Shoving the photos back into the envelope, the face was one of sinister cruelty.

Could this be the work of Marjorie Femmer? No, she hasn't the brain of a sucking turkey, that woman! Beyond her imagination and capability. Her temper now showing itself, Peggy Cavallaro flung the envelope onto the table in front her. Landing on its back, the number displayed itself again, 82449. Realisation struck a distant and remote cord. Back in the past, a deed of immense spitefulness had reared its ugly head. Yes, she had often wondered. There had been similarities, now it had all fallen into place. This morning's episode had clinched it all!

Not one to let anything upset her plans, Peggy Cavallaro

had to act with adroitness. Pressing a button on her study desk handset, she merely said with gritted teeth, "I need you here now, we have a job to do."

Waiting with calmness, but with every part of her body prepared for its task, Peggy Cavallaro sat down at her desk and waited for the arrival of her puppet on a string. The wood panelling adjacent to the fireplace was silently opened. The jack of all trades had arrived.

"Good, you're here." Talking in a hushed voice, Peggy Cavallaro laid out the plan to her muse. The contents of the envelope were shown to the pawn.

Comprehension was never a poor attribute of the listener. All was prepared, there would be no mistake! Taking her walking stick with her now, the scheming Mother Superior, walked over to the fireplace and pulled a cord. The bell that rang in the capacious kitchen, alerted Mrs Rowlands that Mrs Cavallaro required her presence.

Wiping her hands on a linen hand towel, the cook looked around to see if Matilda was anywhere to be seen. *I wonder what Madam wants,* thought the heavily built Mrs Rowlands. *We have discussed the menu. Just as I was about to put the pastry top onto the apricot pie too! I guess it's me she wants, and not Matilda. Wonder where she is?*

Trudging along the long corridor to the study, Mrs Rowlands knocked on the door and walked into the oversized room.

"Oh, thankyou for coming, Mrs Rowlands. Sorry to disturb you, I know you would be busy now, getting things ready for lunch." Peggy Cavallaro smiled sweetly at Mrs Rowlands. "I am feeling a bit chilly, and wondered if you could get the fire going for me please? I would have asked Matilda, but she has gone with Eccles to collect some registered mail from the post office for me." Peggy Cavallaro clasped her aged hands around her shoulders, the matriarch from hell, gave the impression that she was cold.

Mrs Rowlands raised her bushy eyebrows, and said with a surprise, "Well, yeah, I speks so. It's no good bein cold is it? Outside is quite pleasant really, but I guess bein' indoors like, it's cooler." Jesse Rowlands never had a good education, and her speech was somewhat broad, to say the least.

"Oh, thank you, Mrs Rowlands. That is most kind of you," came the gooey and gushy response. *Illiterate infidel,* thought Peggy Cavallaro.

The woman went over to the fireplace, followed by Mrs Cavallaro. Mrs Rowlands bent down to clear away the fireplace, rummaging around, her head well positioned in the recess.

Perfect! She never saw the heavy iron fire poker that smashed across her back! Once, twice, three times.

A cry of excruciating pain filled the room, then nothing. The room was sound proof, something Tony Cavallaro had arranged when moving into the home many moons ago.

The body slumped forward, limp and lifeless. The spine was fractured in numerous places. Her assailant had a pleased countenance. The dark shadowlike figure appeared from behind a recess in the wall. With dexterity and painstaking attention to detail, the hairy hands worked with accuracy. Any evidence of blood was expertly wiped away. Most of the clothing worn by the hard working woman, had absorbed any blood. Bundling up the lump of Jesse Rowlands into a large black zipper bag, including the weapon, the treacherous fanatic left by way of the secret passage.

Wiping her dear little hands, that were quick to hasten the onslaught of blood, Peggy Cavallaro walked back to her desk. The photos were shredded and now she could get on with the day's events. *I must advertise for a new cook. Matilda has also worn out her stay. She had to be dealt with also. But that could wait.*

There was the sound of cars approaching the house.

Who can this be? I'm not expecting a visitor. Her curiosity getting the better of her, Peggy Cavallaro strolled over to the wide study windows. Two cars had stopped outside the front door. She recognised Detective Chief Inspector Marty Hislop, who was alighting from the first vehicle.

CHAPTER *forty*

Prior to this event, Marty and La Paz had convened at the LAPD that morning to brief the officers that were to accompany them on the proposed visit to 1817 North Beaumont. Having received the sanction of Superintendent Charlie Solomon, although with some reservation on his part, mainly due to the pressure from the Police Commissioner, Marty was keyed up and ready for the planned unexpected visit to Peggy Cavallaro. All the necessary paperwork was in Marty's possession.

La Paz had the information he required from the Australian Federal Police. The blood type of Billy Parsons was O+. This was the same blood type sampled from the trunk of the red '65 Mustang. Rushed work had been completed overnight by the forensic team. A DNA sample from the Mustang had been a match. It was all the police required now to make their move. All was going well. The final breakthrough that they had been waiting for. The bullet extracted from the brain of Dirk van Zuutmeyer was from a high powered assault rifle.

Marty and La Paz armed themselves; they were not taking any risks. The group of police officers departed from the LAPD building at precisely 9.09 a.m. It would take approximately 30 minutes to drive the distance to their destination.

Taking two squad cars into the compound of Harpenden Lodge, another two backup vehicles remained positioned outside on North Beaumont. These latter vehicles contained officers from the specially trained Tactical Response Unit, equipped with bullet proof vests and firearms. They were on alert until the order to move in, came from either Hislop or La Paz. The police vehicles were parked under some street trees, just south of the driveway into Harpenden Lodge. A further three cars, containing 10 officers, were stationed out the back exit of the sprawling property of Harpenden Lodge. Just then, an unmarked police car pulled up very near the entrance of the overdressed mansion. Two figures sat motionless, one now prepared for a final victory. The bait to be offered to Peggy Cavallaro was ready as instructed.

The door bell sounded at Harpenden Lodge.

Peggy Cavallaro sat herself down on the soft velvet blue sofa. *That ratbag has come again, has he? Brought the cavalry with him too. Just wait till I speak to that dimwit Police Commissioner. I'll have his guts for garters! Weak as water, that idiot*! Peggy Cavallaro's body was shaking with fury.

The doorbell sounded again.

Where was that girl? Hasn't she answered the door yet?

Peggy Cavallaro rose from the sofa and scurried over to the study windows again.

She could see two uniformed policemen, standing like sentinels outside the cars, but no Marty Hislop. Looking back to the place of recent lethal activity, Peggy Cavallaro was very satisfied that her visitors would find nothing amiss. Her lacky would be safely back in its den, along with the bag of cooking bones. *That's all she was fit for anyway! Meddling monkey! Luckless sort, thought she could frighten me.* A smile of bitter hatred shadowed the rose pink lips of Peggy Cavallaro.

Some minutes ticked away. Still no sign of anyone entering the house or of that useless Matilda. Again the doorbell rang, but on this occasion, in quick succession.

Absolutely unthinkable! Having to answer my own front door, me, Peggy Cavallaro of Harpenden Lodge. That Matilda will be sorry that she ever put foot in my place.

Striding with purpose out of the study and down the hallway, she began calling in a shrill voice, "Matilda, where are you? The front door has to be answered. Where are you girl? Can't you hear me?"

The house was empty, no one else appeared.

Eccles won't hear, he is in the garage no doubt. Where is that flaming Matilda? She continued calling out for Matilda like a sideshow alley spectator but received no response. *I will have to open this door. Woe betide that man if he has come to cause trouble! I won't tolerate any nonsense from the upstart!*

Checking her appearance in the long French gilt mirror placed on the wall in the foyer, Peggy Cavallaro had no alternative but to serenely walk to the front door and open it.

"Good morning, Mrs Cavallaro. This is Detective Miguel La Paz. I need to ask you some questions, can we come in please?" Pointing to the tall stature of La Paz beside him, Marty could perceive that the woman before him was an inferno. Well, not literally! The face was hardened like steel and the eyes were like flames of fire.

"Detective Chief Inspector, I do not have the time or patience to be constantly quizzed about something that took place years ago, and has nothing whatsoever to do with me. Now, please excuse me, I am very busy."

The door was about to be shut, but the long size 13.5 foot of La Paz came in very handy. He put his shoe through the door opening in time for the small framed woman to be jostled and caught off guard. Trying again to close the door was to no avail.

Peggy Cavallaro stepped back and put her hands on her slim hips and bellowed out, "How dare you try to force yourselves into my home. Get out now, or I shall get the Police Commissioner to personally throw you all out."

Marty began to openly smile, and replied, "Go ahead, phone the Police Commissioner, but he is fully aware of our visit here today, Mrs Cavallaro."

Peggy Cavallaro had her eyes fixed on a person now walking up the driveway.

CHAPTER *forty-one*

The figure was hooded, and wore dark baggy track suit pants. It was difficult to discern whether it was male or female. The gait was slow, yet remained upright and there was an object being carried in the left hand of this person. Once again, it was hard to ascertain what this was.

"Who is this you have dragged in," came the words, spat out with fierceness. Peggy Cavallaro stepped forward a couple of paces.

"Oh, someone you know. They will be here shortly," replied Marty with a matter of fact voice.

La Paz had positioned himself in such a way now, that he was able to get behind the mischief maker from hell, and ensure that Peggy Cavallaro was not able to step back inside the house.

Her attention was now firmly fixed on this approaching figure. *Who was this? Dressed like a conspiratorial archangel,* thought Peggy Cavallaro.

Closer the person moved, until they were within six feet of the two men and the woman who had destroyed so many lives.

"It's been a long time Peggy," came the female voice of the well disguised woman.

Dressed in sloppy dark grey track pants, black hoodie and

black sneakers, it was difficult to determine who the person was. Pulling back the hoodie, there was a gasp from Peggy Cavallaro.

She recovered fairly quickly, and managed to exclaim, "Marjorie! This is a surprise! Have you come for morning tea?"

The last words were said in a tone of mockery. The bitch was playing with emotions and people's feelings once again. But this time, she had met her match. No longer to be ridiculed or spoken down to or deceived any longer, Marjorie Femmer gave a speech of remarkable calmness. Stepping closer to stand almost in front of Peggy Cavallaro, Mrs Femmer's left hand opened up fully to reveal a crumpled off white and green hat. It was obviously a child's hat, and there were some stains on the white fabric showing.

"I thought you would like to be reminded of Billy. The child you killed and had buried. Max came here that evening didn't he? It was you who arranged for Billy to be finished off. He was alive when Max took Billy from our home, and Max came to you for advice. And why was that Peggy? I will tell you why!" Marjorie Femmer was pausing for breath, and continued on, "Because Max was having an affair with you wasn't he? He was under your control. Don't tell me it's not true. I had suspected it long before Max died. You see, I was driving home one day and Max's car was parked inside your grounds. A foolish thing to do, you should have advised Max to have taken more care, so his car would not be seen. Tony must have been out. Oh yes, I knew, but I had no definite proof of the affair. Then just the other day, I had the pleasure of meeting up with Dirk van Zuutmeyer, the day he was mistakenly killed at my home. The bullet was meant for me wasn't it Peggy? Never mind me, but Dirk was innocent and did not deserve to die like that. He told me that he had seen Max and you, in Max's car. This was the year before Billy entered our lives. Laminosa Lane, does that ring any bells Peggy? Dirk had never revealed his knowledge of your dilly dallying with Max, because of his strong friendship with my husband and myself. I found this hat," Marjorie Femmer opened up her hand to show the stained hat. "This was Billy's. His dear mother made it for him. It was in a drawer in Max's studio. I had kept it because it belonged to Billy. The blood stains on it are those of Billy. He was wearing the hat on the day of his accident and disappearance. Max brought it back with him after being at your home didn't he?"

Peggy Cavallaro took the bait very vehemently and interrupted Mrs Femmer, "What absolute lies! Your statement is totally untrue and unfounded. Get off my proprerty you degrading gold digger. Max was too good for the likes of you. He needed love, reassurance and direction in life. And you could give him none of these qualities. Always full of your own ideals, becoming a movie star. You, huh! Drunken vixen, cavorting with any man you could lay your dirty, smelly breasts on. Disgusting behaviour, disrespectful to all and sundry. Wanting a child, what a joke that was! Using that brat of a Billy Parsons as your own offspring. Parading all over Hollywood and beyond, making a spectacle of yourself, and all the time rubbing Max's nose into the ground." Peggy Cavallaro stopped abruptly as the old oak front door slammed closed.

La Paz moved away with stealth from the porch area, and watched with interest what the elderly "Mother Superior" would do now. Matilda had played her instructed part well. Once the door bell was sounded, Matilda moved into her allotted task.

Hiding in the home was not difficult, with so many rooms. Waiting for Peggy Cavallaro to answer the door, Matilda waited her opportunity to close the heavy front door with force, thereby thawting any attempt for her employer to gain entry to her own home. The ornate wooden door was firmly locked from the inside. Marjorie Femmer took a pace closer to the woman who had despised her for so many years.

"Oh, just for the record Peggy. I still have the red '65 Mustang. Max may have told you that it was sold. The bloodstains in the vehicle are those of Billy. The police here have already verified this with the Australian Police."

Peggy Cavallaro's face went ashen, her breaths became more frequent.

CHAPTER *forty-two*

Allowing this information to sink into the scheming mind of Mrs Cavallaro, Marty gave the woman a few seconds to respond. Nothing was forthcoming, however her composure had certainly been broken. A worried expression crossed the face of Peggy Cavallaro.

Marty opened up with, "I have a suspicion that there is more than good soil under those Hydrangea bushes, Mrs Cavallaro. Could you honestly guarantee that we would not find the bones of Billy Parsons, buried under those plants? I for one am certainly prepared to take the gamble and have the plants removed. Would you like to stand and watch, while my men make a search. I have the necessary paperwork." sniggered Marty to the "Grand Duchess", who thought herself beyond reproach or answerable to anyone!

This was the last straw for Peggy Cavallaro, her body language became rigid, her eyes were lethal darts, the fists were clinched, the whites of her knuckles were almost popping through the thin pale skin. Her next move was to turn around and pull on the door handle to re-enter her sanctuary.

Banging on the door like a woman possessed, Peggy Cavallaro called out, "Matilda, open this door at once. Open this door, now! Do as you are instructed!" Rattling the door like a mistress from the back block brothels of seedy LA, Peggy Cavallaro realised that she was caught between a rock and a hard place! And a hard place it certainly was. This scheming brute had began to slide on her backside. Yet more was to dent the haughty pride of Peggy Cavallaro. Realising that the front door was not going to open for her, Peggy Cavallaro wheeled around to face her attacker, Marty Hislop. "You have no right to dig up those Hydrangea bushes. There is nothing under them at all."

A crunch and squeal of tyres could be heard now. The black Cadillac limousine was being driven quickly towards the party of gathered people. The vehicle braked hard and came to a halt.

The driver's door opened like lightning. Out sprang Eccles, who leapt to the back of the car to open the rear passenger door.

Brandishing a revolver, the man called to the damsel in dire distress, "Get in now Mrs Cavallaro. I will take you away from all this. The police have no right to pester you like this!"

Raising her arms into the air, she screamed out, "Good for Eccles. I knew I could count on you. Eccles to the rescue!"

With a belligerent smile on her dial, Peggy Cavallaro was a woman who thought that her saviour had arrived. The desperate woman did not hesitate, and almost ran to the limousine door on the driver's side, and hopped inside. The door was shut in haste.

Eccles continued pointing the weapon at everyone, and shouted, "Keep away, or I will shoot!"

Marjorie Femmer gave a cry of horror. La Paz, Marty and the other policemen, stood their distance and obeyed Eccles's request.

Moving back to the driver's door, he got inside the car and roared the engine. The task that Eccles had been instructed to act out, had so far gone according to plan. However, a slight hitch made things a little sticky for a few moments. Sounding like a true muscle car, the Cadillac reacted violently to the handling of it's driver, Eccles. The car only travelled approximately 50 feet, and Eccles did a magnificent turn of the wheel. The automobile spun up gravel, tyres spinning for grip. The back end of the stretch limousine was jolted. The hapless figure in the rear of the car, was like a jack in a box.

Peggy Cavallaro did not have time to secure a seat belt as Eccles was too quick to engage the car into its racing car status, her body was obviously being flung around like jelly, and what a sight it was for all to see! Eccles drove the car back towards the crowd of police and Mrs Femmer. The car passed the gathered spectators.

Waving her arms around madly, Peggy Cavallaro fell off the rear back seat and onto the floor of the limousine. The car did another spin and came speeding back to its original starting point. Coming to a screeching stop, everyone except Mrs Femmer, was on the driver's side of the Cadillac. With Marjorie Femmer still standing in awe on the other side, the rear passenger door of the limousine began to open. A hand appeared and was endeavouring to brace it's owner, as a leg was placed gingerly on the gravel. Mrs Femmer was the closest to the car door that its owner was attempting to open. She had to think what action to take. Marjorie Femmer manoeuvred her body in such a way that she could push with her backside on the opening door. This tactic was pressing the door against the leg of Peggy Cavallaro. There was a piercing call of pain. Marjorie Femmer continued to hold the door. Peggy Cavallaro managed successfully to retract her trapped leg and retreated into the cabin, and began kicking the door inside the car. Realising that the determined woman inside the Cadillac was gaining strength, Mrs Femmer called out for assistance. Even before the cry for help came from Mrs Femmer, Marty and La Paz could see the situation, and ran around to relieve the efforts of Marjorie Femmer. Just as Marty, who was first to come to Mrs Femmer's aid, arrived, the car door was hit by the feet of the caged Peggy Cavallaro. Marjorie Femmer's reserve crumpled, and the angry lioness emerged. Its hair flopping over the face, the woman was not going to give up without a fight. Pulling a knife from her pleated plaid skirt, Peggy Cavallaro pinned her arm around the scrawny neck of Mrs Femmer. This woman was the dizzy limit!

Holding onto the neck with a vice-like hand, Peggy Cavallaro began to bring the knife closer to the throat of Mrs Femmer. Marty stepped back, just short of grabbing this devious woman.

"Come near me, and I will slit her throat. You hear me,

I will do it! Trying to pin the blame on me. It's this gutter snipe that should be charged with murder. It was her that drove over the child. Left Max to do all the dirty work for her. Well, you will pay for what you have done, you hear me Marjorie Sutherland!" (Sutherland was the maiden surname of Mrs Femmer). This evil woman was raving and ranting like a demonic heathen deity.

Marjorie Femmer's eyes were full of dread. Knowing what this murderous being was capable of, Mrs Femmer was trying vainly to stay calm under enormous strain. Her body was tilting to one side. Peggy Cavallaro, although smaller in height, was a physically stronger woman. Could Mrs Femmer remain upright?

The policemen were acutely aware of the plight of Mrs Femmer. With great effort, Mrs Femmer managed to point down with her right forefinger to the ground. Peggy Cavallaro was attempting to drag Mrs Femmer with her towards the house, but the taller frame of Mrs Femmer was resisting under extreme duress. Fixing her eyes on Marty, Marjorie Femmer lifted her right leg and with as much force as she could muster, Mrs Femmer slammed her jogger clad foot onto the right foot of the struggling crime queen. The effect was extremely successful, and Peggy Cavallaro lost her hold on Mrs Femmer, stumbling backwards, losing her balance and falling onto the gravel. The head hit the ground first, stunning Peggy Cavallaro. La Paz whizzed over to the splayed doll on the ground, grabbing the knife from her hand.

Spitting out insanities that one could never imagine possible from the lips of such a "well to do" lady, La Paz handcuffed Peggy Cavallaro's hands. She rolled around on the gravel, kicking her little legs like a spoilt child that cannot have its own way. Froth dribbling from her mouth like bubbles, La Paz lifted up the frame of Peggy Cavallaro. She continued to kick and speak in "foreign tongues".

Marty guided Mrs Femmer away from the ugly scene and placed her into one of the cars, in the care of a woman officer. Matilda then emerged from the home and walked with pride over to the woman who had made her life such a misery. Carrying a large suitcase, and a shoulder bag on her left arm, Matilda was clearly under no threat to remain any longer at this house of horrors.

"I will be leaving, and I shall tell my parents everything regarding your behaviour. You are a despicable woman! You should be pitied, but you won't get any pity from me."

The once former queen of horrors, was unable to utter any words of sense. Shaking her head like a dog that is fighting the effects of rabies, Peggy Cavallaro had been reduced to a crumpled wreck! Her legs had lost all ability to function, and she fell onto the driveway, howling and gasping for breath. A pitiful scene, especially for someone who always had the situation under her control. Now the opposite had happened, Peggy Cavallaro was feeling the other side of the sceptre.

With that, Matilda spoke a few words to Marty, and then walked over to the car where Marjorie Femmer was, and got inside. Marty had arranged for Matilda to leave as soon as this arrest had taken place.

Eyeing La Paz with the woman who thought she had everyone in her control, Marty walked over to Peggy Cavallaro, and made his arrest. Arrested under the suspicion of the murder of Billy Parsons, and now Jesse Rowlands. Gathering herself together, with the aid of two police officers, supporting her either side, Peggy Cavallaro managed to deny any involvement with these murders. Demanding her lawyer be summoned immediately, Marty had the pleasure of denying the woman's petition.

Justice had been served, but at a price!

CHAPTER *forty-three*

Eric Marsh, or Enrico Marchetti as he is correctly known, was endeavouring to make an escape from the Cavallaro compound in a Ford pickup truck. Using a back exit strategically hid at the rear of the rose encrusted cottage, Marchetti was only a few minutes into his flight, when a police cordon stopped Marchetti. The body of Mrs Jesse Rowlands was found in the back of the Ford pickup truck. Covered over with garden refuse, the black bag was suitably unnoticed by the layman's eyes.

Now, you may ask what has become of our "friend" and faithful informer, Sergeant Robbie Clark? Well, having had first hand information, by way of the listening device installed in the office of Marty and La Paz, Clark had been aware of the course of events that were to unfold that day. He knew that Peggy Cavallaro would spill the beans on him, so why wait around? Clark was not going to be caught easily. He would fight for his freedom, at all cost!

Discreetly leaving the LAPD complex, Clark made his way to collect the Mercury Cougar. Always a step ahead, Clark had a stash of cash, clothes, food and other essentials, and, yes, you guessed it, an automatic assault rifle with silencer, installed in a hidden compartment in the Cougar.

Making his way south on the Freeway, Clark was driving rapidly towards the city of San Diego. After that, the Mexican border. Unbeknown to the police, we know that Clark had been leading another life outside the LAPD. Clark had been instrumental in securing a lucrative contract to supply crystal meth on ice at some selected roadside country stalls. The guise was to sell fruit and vegetables to passing motorists. Mexicans from the drug cartel, under heavy disguise, operated the stalls. Clark was amongst the sellers, and using his police training to identify possible drug users, had worked his magnetic charm to secure continued business. Most of this weekend work, had been in and around the area just north of San Diego. His drug cartel friends over the border had supplied Clark with the necessary "fuel", that Clarks' clients desired. The Mexican boss was reaping a handsome profit, and Clark had acquired some of the spoils. He had done remarkably well, with a list of repeat customers. Influential people, and those in high places were a selection of the purchasers of this delightful delicacy – some we had better not mention here!

Having made a mobile phone call in advance to his drug cartel boss in Juarez, Mexico; Clark was provided with details of his deliverance. Sitting in the car, Clark was furtive and feeling now for the first time, somewhat nervous. Wearing dark sunglasses, a studded black leather jacket, black jeans and black Sendra cowboy boots, Clark smoked incessantly, as he waited for his rescuers to show themselves. The 29-year-old man knew that by now the raid on Harpenden Lodge would have been almost completed. He had a few hours up his sleeve, but time was the essence to foil any attempts at his capture. Clark was desperate.

After what seemed hours, but was only half an hour, Clark could discern the sound of a helicopter coming closer to where the Cougar was parked. Clark had been instructed to drive off the main road and rendezvous at a small, secluded valley surrounded by an outcrop of rocks. This afforded ample protection to Clark and for the helicopter to make its landing. The distinctive colours of the Mercury Cougar were hidden from view. Gradually the machine descended, dust began to spray everywhere.

Breathing a sigh of relief, Clark could see the figures of people in the helicopter as it made a safe landing. The door opened of the rescue vehicle, and two men hurried over. No time to lose now.

One of the men took the car keys of the Cougar and then went and removed the stash from the car, including the rifle. He got out a small object from his black leather jacket. Inflating the bag with instant success, all the contents from the Mercury Cougar were put into this bag. Anyone giving a cursory glance would safely say that this man looked the image of Robbie Clark – same height and build, hairstyle, clothing and cowboy boots. Even down to the dark sunglasses.

Handing over his police badge to the impostor, Clark ran with the other male to the waiting helicopter. They both carried a handle each of the bag containing the "loot" from the Mercury Cougar. Boarding the helicopter, the craft was off like grease lightning and disappeared into the sultry haze. The other accomplice started the Cougar and made his way back onto the main road leading to the border control. Our lookalike Clark, joined the queue of vehicles.

CHAPTER *forty-four*

The Customs boys were busy as always, but our nameless driver had first hand information from Clark. Contact was to be made with a certain Washington Gladden, a native by birth from Montgomery, Alabama. Gladden had settled in San Diego for work reasons, having obtained a position as a Customs Officer. Twenty-seven years of age, he had been employed at the border control for some five years. Having earnt the respect and admiration of his peers, Gladden went from strength to strength. Now in charge of other Customs Officers, Gladden was able to do certain "favours", for the return of a cash incentive, for services rendered. How else was the lad to manage on his paltry income? I ask you!

Robbie Clark had formed a liaison with Gladden some two years ago. Using his influence and coercion, Clark had been able to ensure that each time he came through the customs, Clark encountered no investigation – courtesy of Washington Gladden. The drug supply was expertly concealed anyway, but nevertheless, Clark was taking no chances. The money that Clark was making from his sideline, could easily pay the greedy Gladden to keep his mouth shut.

Steering the Mercury Cougar up to the booth where a female

customs officer was stationed, the driver was required to hand over identification. Gladden, seeing the distinctive car arrive through his glassed in area, made his way with haste to get his friend through the gate.

Our imposter driver, skilled in the art of impersonation, voice likeness, and a host of other attributes, some not to be mentioned here, greeted Gladden with a nod of the head. Gladden was familiar with Clark, his dark sunglasses and same black outfit as the man standing before him. Everything checked out with Gladden, there was no need to seem alarmed with the driver. The lady customs officer had already seen the police badge of Clark, and was satisfied that this was Sergeant Robert aka Robbie Clark from the LAPD. Sunglasses removed, the officer was content that she had sighted suitable documentation, that this was Clark. Gladden spoke a few quiet words to the man.

By now, the lady customs officer, had moved down to the next car. Making his move, the unknown driver, discreetly proferred a packet of cigarettes to the ever indulgent Gladden.

For want of a name, we shall name this chap, "Harry Hoodlum".

Always ready to put his hand out for more, Gladden was eager to try this brand of Colombian smoke. He had not seen the packet before, and being a keen smoker was waiting for his break to have a puff. With skilful dexterity, Gladden took the packet and put it in his right hip pocket. The exchange went unnoticed. A packet of smokes for a "no hassle" exit to freedom. Getting back into the Mercury Cougar, our slippery fiend, Harry Hoodlum, gave a wave and headed off into Mexico. The vehicle was travelling to the drug haven of Juarez. A smug smile of satisfaction and expectancy was plastered across the face of Harry Hoodlum. The 1968 red and black Mercury Cougar drove off into new territory, much to be admired by all who cast their eyes upon it.

We never did find out what became of Sergeant Robbie Clark. Perhaps he assumed a new identity, one can only speculate. He certainly became a much wanted man!

Gladden, looking at his watch, decided that it was time for a smoko. A tall, lumbering man, who was overweight at a hefty 17 stone, from too many late night TV takeaways and 6 packs of beer, Gladden was eager to try the cigarettes he had just taken possession of. Sauntering outside to the rear of the customs complex, Gladden opened the packet of cigarettes. The brand name was "Speziality", containing 25 cigarettes for "the discerning smoker". He smelt the aroma of the tobacco. *Nice stuff this. I will get a kick out of this for sure*, thought the self important Gladden.

Authority had given Gladden a feeling of control and autonomy. He was his own boss now.

Lighting the cigarette and drawing on it, smoke curled up into the air. *This was real good!* The flame of the cigarette was ignited more by the sucking mouth of Gladden. With the intent of removing the cigarette to exhale smoke, Gladden was unable to do so. The cigarette was literally stuck to his fat lips.

His lips were sealed. A thin veneer of sealant over the cigarette had ensured that contact with any surface would produce this effect. Vainly trying to get the burning cigarette from his lips, Gladden couldn't even shout. He was only able to make deep grunting noises, waving his arms in the air, and still the flame burned. Smoke was still wafting up into the air, and causing a choking feeling to the gargantuan Gladden. No one saw the man was in distress. A sudden flash came without warning, as the lethal lollipop exploded with a roaring sound. Gladden was now a headless horror!

Clark knew that Gladden had to be removed from the scene, in case the customs officer came under surveillance, and grassed on him. Knowing that Gladden was familiar with Clark's get up, the "unlicensed to kill" assailant, was able to convince Gladden that he was Clark.

The plot had worked amazingly well.

CHAPTER *forty-five*

Back at police headquarters in Los Angeles, Enrico Marchetti was given the choice of being deported back to Italy to face criminal charges into the deaths of no less than 26 individuals from Sicily and Italy. This was over a period of years from 1956 to 1960. Marchetti had been quite an active lad in his younger days!

The other option was to tell all, regarding the deaths of Jesse Rowlands, Olga Serenova, Vladimir Nijinski, Dirk van Zuutmeyer and Billy Parsons. Fearing the worst from the former offer, Marchetti indicated via way of interpretation, that he would come clean and make a confession. Marchetti had come to the realisation that life in a jail in the United States was far better than being extradited back to an over crowded cell in Italy.

Marchetti's English was vile to understand coherently, so a police interpreter had been assigned to assist. Amazingly, to the minds of Marty Hislop and Miguel La Paz, Marchetti stated quite defensively, that he had nothing to do with the death of Dirk van Zuutmeyer. It was ascertained that Marchetti had never owned or driven a red and black Mercury Cougar – but Sergeant Robbie Clark did. The penny still had not dropped!

The graveyard outside the bow window of Harpenden Lodge finally gave up its dark secret. A child's skeleton was found. The skull had been smashed in, this had caused death. The left leg was badly crushed, bones broken, but not enough to inflict death. Peggy Cavallaro's precious collection of diaries was combed through with painstaking care. No comment was overlooked. Very thorough and precise in her record keeping, the diaries sounded the death knell for this woman who knew no mercy or compassion. Never envisaging that the pages of the diaries were to ever be read by anyone else, the graphic description of the hours just prior to the untimely death of Billy Parsons, made gruesome reading.

Under the date of July 24, 1965, this is the extract, written by the neat and flambouyant hand of this beast, known as Peggy Cavallaro. The opening sentences did refer to the red '65 Mustang "belting up" North Beaumont, but that was in the morning of July 24,1965. This was obviously Marjorie Femmer on her way to the Brentwood Amateur Dramatic Society meeting. Peggy Cavallaro had cleverly deceived Detective Chief Inspector Marty Hislop when showing him the diary, the day he first called to interview her regarding Billy's disappearance. Using her hand to cover over the portion that she did not want Marty to see, Peggy Cavallaro had succeeded in deflecting suspicion off herself.

And so the record states for the afternoon of July 24,1965:

"This nuisance of a child, Billy Parsons, was put out of his misery, and mine too, today. Max came here with him in that racing red Mustang. The child was wailing and moaning like a spoilt brat. Rolling around on the ground, blood oozing from his legs, making a mess of my Aubusson carpet. All he needed was a clip behind the ear hole. And I gave him one too! Did not want the cool pop that dear Max took the trouble to go and buy. Getting dark for Max to be out! Thankless child! Marjorie is a complete scatterbrain, reversing over the little runt. You would think she could have done a better job of it! Ha ha!! Max is beside himself, but I took the matter into my hands. He was not strong enough to deal with this. No hospital would look at this little monster. Too many questions, that can't be answered! We took the screaming child to the garage, placing him on the bench. More outbursts of temper. He had to be silenced. Enrico held the thankless child down. Max was a cot case, pleading with me to withhold justice. But it had to be carried out. Took a long and heavy hammer from the wall, and belted it down into his skull. Two blows were enough to end the uproar from this chatterbox. At last, peace! Perfect peace. Enrico dug a hole outside the blue drawing room, and put the body into a calico bag. I will have some of those new perfumed Hydrangea plants put there. Enrico will like that. Tony is away again!! But Enrico is always there for me. I think once I have got rid of Max to go back to that slut Marjorie, we will have a spot of funtime together. Hehe!"

The diary entry for August 24, 1949 made heartless reading also. Deliberately allowing her own daughters to be the scapegoats for the nanny's decision to visit her aunt and daughter, the twin girls' deaths were so meaningless and brutal.

Further reading of the diaries covering other people's lives were sickening to say the least! This included having Marchetti deal with Olga Serenova and Vladimir Nijinski. They had threatened to expose Peggy Cavallaro, regarding the photos of Billy Parsons. Short on cash flow, the pair thought that they could take matters into their own flimsy hands, and play a deal with Peggy Cavallaro. This was not a hand to play when it came to Peggy Cavallaro. She always held the trump card!

So, Marchetti went to work. Knowing the route that the pair would take that night, to supposedly meet with Peggy Cavallaro at a motel, Marchetti used the high beam of his pick up truck to blind the driver, Olga Serenova. Well, we know the rest, don't we?

Marty ordered that the grounds of Harpenden Lodge be searched painstakingly for any other bodies. A recent burial was found, containing the body of the last maid, Lucy Trevenen, who had disappeared quite conveniently, one evening. Lucy asked too many questions and had been seen snooping about Peggy Cavallaro's desk. Her demise was strangulation with cat gut at the hands of Peggy Cavallaro. Marchetti confirmed this. He only buried the corpse, cleaning up the mess, so to speak!

A man by the name of Steven Bateman, had come forward voluntarily to the police. He said he was the cousin of Jesse Rowlands. Having called Jesse on her mobile phone, and obtaining no response, Stephen Bateman was certain that something was amiss. With the police presence at Harpenden Lodge, Bateman approached the police regarding his cousin. It was he who had taken the revealing photos of Enrico Marchetti and Peggy Cavallaro, having a fling in the rose covered cottage.

Why was this all necessary, you may ask? Well, it just so happens, that Mrs Jesse Rowlands, was the daughter of the nanny who had worked at Harpenden Lodge, when the Cavallaro twins had tragically drowned. The nanny, an Elsie Chandler, was distraught when finding the bodies of Ruth and Ada Cavallaro in the ornamental pond. Apparently, from a diary kept by Elsie Chandler, she was punished for leaving the two girls in the care of their own mother, Peggy Cavallaro, the day she went to go and see an elderly sick aunt, who was caring for her daughter, none other than Jesse Rowlands. Peggy Cavallaro was annoyed to be left with the girls, and in a fit of malice beyond the comprehension of any mother, allowed the girls to stray down to the pond and drown. The nanny, Elsie Chandler, was blamed for the incident, and sacked from her position. Not prepared to stay and look after the girls, her divided loyalty was paid a terrible sacrifice. Apparently Elsie loved the girls dearly, but her heartstrings were still attached to her only daughter, Jesse. The twin girls were wearing pale pink dresses the day they drowned.

Elsie Chandler's name was blackened by Peggy Cavallaro, and Mrs Chandler found it difficult to obtain work. No references, no work. That was the stark reality! Trying to raise her daughter on her own, after the death of the aunt, was more than Elsie Chandler could bear. The death of the Cavallaro twins had blighted her mind, she turned to drink and eventually shot herself. Jesse Rowlands found her mother's body slumped in the bedroom, of the two rooms they rented in Wichita, Kansas. Jesse was a mere 10 years old.

Stephen Bateman, a cousin and professional photographer based in Los Angeles, was approached by Jesse Rowlands, to take the photos. Jesse Rowlands had everything well organised as to when Stephen should come to Harpenden Lodge and take the discreet photos. It was Stephen who had mailed the package containing the photos. The envelope had already been prepared in advance by Jesse. He was aware that the numbers on the reverse of the envelope, placed there by Jesse, was the date the twins drowned. Jesse Rowlands wanted Peggy Cavallaro to be answerable to the death of her mother and the circumstances surrounding the deaths of the two girls Sending the photographs to Peggy Cavallaro, was to let her see that others knew of her daliance with Marchetti. Unfortunately, the hand of Jesse Rowlands was overplayed, and she paid the ultimate price, by way of death. Jesse Rowlands was quite similar in looks to her deceased mother, Elsie. It was this likeness that had alerted Peggy Cavallaro to the link between her former nanny and the current cook, Mrs Rowlands. The final straw had been the sudden entry of Jesse Rowlands into the room, the day Peggy Cavallaro was grilling meek Matilda. It was possible that Jesse Rowlands had overheard the conversation. The lady of Harpenden Lodge had taken swift action. Jesse Rowland's revenge had been bittersweet!

CHAPTER *forty-six*

Marty and La Paz had an eventful day. Back at LAPD Headquarters, Marty informed La Paz that they would deal with Madam Cavallaro in the morning.

Foolishly, the Police Commissioner had given strict instructions that Peggy Cavallaro be allowed to remain in her own attire and footwear. Her lawyer was contacted, who wore a grave expression, when informed of the charges against Peggy Cavallaro. In private, the gentleman spoke plainly and firmly to his client. The mounting evidence was going against Peggy Cavallaro ever securing her freedom again.

Harpenden Lodge had been crawling with forensics and other police, removing all the evidence they could, to nail this vicious woman. Superintendent Charlie Solomon was extremely supportive to the two men, who had brought closure to this case after a remarkable and disturbing string of events. The Police Commissioner had been questioned by Peggy Cavallaro's lawyer regarding her arrest. Remaining firm, no possible release on bail was imminent for his client. This information was relayed back to the lady sitting with a cheery smile on her "throne" of self importance, namely a police cell chair.

The mental state of our most interesting and detestable characters, had sunk into a permanent state of non-admittance. Peggy Cavallaro had no remorse. In her limited and clouded vision, the actions carried out over many years, were needful and necessary. The innermost depth of this lady's soul was still justified. However, knowing that redemption was not a possibility, her fate was sealed. Do what she must!

Marchetti's confession had also sealed Peggy Cavallaro's outcome. The diaries that Peggy Cavallaro had kept, were her downfall. Her own pride and conceit had been the fruit of her demise. Yes, indeed, a demise it really was for Peggy Clothilde Cavallaro. The sensible walking shoes that she often chose to wear, were equipped with a deadly potion. Sliding open the right heel of the shoe, Peggy extracted the vial containing the substance.

That night, in her dark cell, Peggy Cavallaro, clutching her gold crucifix, took a dose of cyanide.

She was dead in moments.

CHAPTER *forty-seven*

Finally, closure could be brought to Billy Parsons's family in Australia. His ageing and sick parents, were briefly told of the finding by the Californian police. Shortly after the knowledge that Billy's body had been discovered, Mr Parsons died.

Anna Serenova was duly informed of the events surrounding her mother's death. La Paz chose to be the one to visit the woman who had never known love or true sincerity.

Four months after the remains of Billy Parsons had been flown back to Australia for proper burial, Detective Chief Inspector Marty Hislop went to see Marjorie Femmer.

The autumn leaves were like jewels of gold, falling from the trees, as Marty drove into the Hollywood Hills. Marty was relieved that this case was finalised. The bitter realisation that Sergeant Robbie Clark had been an accomplice in this case, was something that Marty had found hard to come to terms with. You never know someone, and in this instance, a trusted work colleague La Paz had been resourceful to track down the movements of Clark on the day that Dirk van Zuutmeyer was shot. However, Clark had been a cunning and cagey man. Knowing that eventually the police would try to trace the Mercury Cougar's owner, he had bargained with Peggy Cavallaro to have the car registered in one of her company's name. This would protect Clark from exposure. After all, Peggy Cavallaro was being fed the information she wanted. So a deal was struck between the two villains.

A lot had happened, and the grizzly outcome had been somewhat of a let down. The main perpetrator had escaped the law, once again in control of circumstances. However, Peggy Cavallaro did not live to enjoy any further retribution on the lives of innocent people.

As Marty drove the squad car into North Beaumont, he contemplated the awful truth that had been recorded in the diaries of this vindictive and vicious woman, Peggy Cavallaro.

Shortly after the brutal murder of Billy Parsons, Max Femmer began to question the need for the helpless boy to be done away with. An entry for April 8, 1966, refers to Max Femmer's "dislike" for the events that had taken place the prior year. Then again on June 30, 1966, a similar remark is made in the diary: "Max will have to come to terms with it. There was no other way! He is becoming a proverbial pest and pain. Damn the child ever setting foot on my property."

By the beginning of August, 1966, the comments had become stronger and alluded to possible quietening of Max Femmer. Knowing that Max Femmer had a poor heart, and had a fondness for brandy, the plot was hatched that would silence him for good! Regular trysts with Peggy Cavallaro, gave her ample opportunity to slip a narcotic into his brandy.

Mixed with the heart and blood pressure tablets, Max Femmer was already taking, this all became a deadly cocktail to give a fatal heart attack. Max Femmer's doctor could not detect any problem with his patient, and declared the man quite healthy for his age. Without warning, on September 14, 1966, Max Femmer suffered a massive heart attack, whilst at work. He was pronounced dead before arriving at the hospital. Exit Max Femmer. The horrific secret was safe!

Could Marty inform Mrs Femmer these details now? *No, I can't do it,* he thought. *The woman has gone through enough, without the knowledge that her Max was murdered by his lover. Better to leave things be, give Mrs Femmer her peace she deserved.*

Parking the car in the driveway of Marjorie Femmer's home, Marty could see that the garden was looking pristine. New stone fencing around the beds and a selection of varied cacti enhanced the overall appearance of the garden. Koi carp gracefully played with each other in the pond, bobbing up to view their onlooker. Fresh white wooden window shutters had been placed around the timber framed windows, giving the viewer a sense that someone really cared for the home. The tiled roof had been steam cleaned, giving the home a smart upmarket look. The stone feature wall at the front porch had also been cleaned, and the grouting had been expertly repaired.

As Marty went to press the buzzer, he could see that the front door had been repainted a vivid shade of blue, the panels had been highlighted in gloss white paint. *Very impressive,* thought Marty.

Marjorie Femmer opened the door, with a huge smile. Already expecting Marty's visit, as he had phoned in advance to arrange the time, Mrs Femmer leant forward and gave Marty a kiss on his cheek. Not accustomed to this, except from his own Mom, Marty blushed.

"Come in, lovely to see you, Chief Inspector." said Mrs Femmer.

"Call me Marty, please." replied the bashful man.

"Very well, Marty it is." Mrs Femmer had a radiance about her that Marty could never imagine her possessing. Her eyes were like dancing starlets, and she seemed stronger mentally and physically too.

Entering the once drab lounge room, Marty admired the complete change the room had taken on.

Marty remarked, "Gee, this has had a facelift. I like it!"

The tired carpet had been removed and replaced with a plush beige carpet. The furniture had also been altered. Instead of the lumpy chairs, a dark brown leather suite enhanced the bright room.

Striking orange and white cushions were placed on the suite. Mrs Femmer's signature colours of brown and orange tonings had been utilised to great effect. The drapes had been changed to a soft biscuit shade, with pinch pleat pelmuts, speckled with an orange fleck. The walls had been repainted a brilliant white gloss, giving the room a fresh and vibrant finish.

Over a delicious lunch, Mrs Femmer said she was relieved that the ordeal was over. She could now get on with her life.

The endless worry about the blackmail was all behind her. The watchful eyes were gone and most importantly, Billy had been laid to rest. The sense of abiding guilt that had constantly hung over Mrs Femmer, had been lifted.

After lunch in the dining room, which Marty told Mrs Femmer was fabulous, she said for them to come into the lounge for a drink.

"Pour us a drink Marty, please. You can have one too. I know you are on duty, but a small drink wouldn't hurt." said Mrs Femmer.

"I will pour a drink for you. I will stick to orange juice Mrs Femmer," replied Marty.

Marty went over to the drinks cabinet, and opened the lid. There was nothing there, the whole area was empty. Marty looked over to the waiting eyes of Mrs Femmer.

"It's empty, Mrs Femmer!"

She continued to look serenely at him, but with a face of confidence that her past had been conquered.

"I stopped drinking the day you found Billy, Marty. I have not had a drop since! I feel wonderful, I really do!" said a joyful Mrs Femmer.

"Well, I am pleased Mrs Femmer. You are really enjoying life now. Get back into doing those things you used to do. Do some bowling, and meet up with those old friends again." Marty stressed to Mrs Femmer.

"Yes, I have done just that. But, I have something that I want to show you. Now come with me, Marty."

Leading the way out the front door, Mrs Femmer lead the way around to the door of the garage.

A new remote garage door had been installed, white with blue panels. A semi circular arched window was placed at the top of the door.

"Here, press that red button Marty, to open the door please," said the expectant Mrs Femmer, handing the remote control to him. "There is something inside that I want to show you," beamed the happy lady.

Marty was wondering what was inside the garage that Mrs Femmer wanted him to see. Pressing the button, the door began to rise up. Making its way up, Marty could eventually see that a vehicle was facing them. Marty could not believe his eyes. It was the red '65 Mustang. The car had been returned to Mrs Femmer, after forensics had concluded their investigations. Now it was positively glowing! The duco had been resprayed. New tires, with the white wall edging. Marty grinned from ear to ear.

"Wow, this is fabulous! You had the Mustang done up, did you Mrs Femmer?"

"Yes, I decided to keep the Mustang. I had so many memories of joyful days with Billy, in this car. I couldn't part with it, not now. Plus the fact that dear Max had bought the car for me. So I engaged a man to do the restoration for me. Mind you, he was gob smacked when he came to quote me on it. He said that he had never seen one in such original condition! The money wasn't an issue, so I got the engine reconditioned and new leads. There is a new exhaust, with twin extractors, all chrome. The bumpers were rechromed. Surprisingly there was no rust after all those years! Of course the car had been covered all that time. The paint job he did was superb.

It is just like a new car again. And, guess what?' said Mrs Femmer, with a question mark in her voice.

"No, what, Mrs Femmer?" asked a curious Marty.

"I have renewed my driver's licence. Now come on, let me take you for a spin in this fun machine!"

A few weeks later, Marty was on a flight to Vermont to visit his family.

EPILOGUE

As we conclude our reading of this story, we can look back and realise how thankful life can be.

If we use our skills to the benefit of each other, and not to cause harm of the direst sense to our fellows, how satisfied we are that life is indeed, good.

Marjorie Femmer is a prime example of a life that was almost non existent, but through inner strength and fortitude, she overcame these odds to triumph gloriously. Life had been restored, where once only shame and fear were attempted to be drowned in sorrow. Her example had played a major part in allowing Marty to perceive that our thoughts are governed by our actions, and the events of everyday life.

Detective Chief Inspector Marty Hislop was certainly a changed man. No longer the man who trod on other's feelings without regard, he had now learnt what it was to love, and still love, in spite of losing those dearest to them. Mrs Femmer had taught Marty a great deal.

It is so easy to manipulate and extinguish the one aspect in life that fires all our emotions, love.

As the wise words of Somerset Maugham say, "The great tragedy of life is not that men perish, but that they cease to love."

the RED '65

ISBN 9781925367157			Qty
	RRP	AU$24.99	.....
Postage within Australia		AU$5.00	.....
		TOTAL* $_____	
		* All prices include GST	

Name:...

Address: ....

....

Phone:...

Email: ....

Payment: ❏ Money Order ❏ Cheque ❏ MasterCard ❏ Visa

Cardholder's Name:...

Credit Card Number: ....

Signature:..

Expiry Date: ....

Allow 7 days for delivery.

Payment to: Marzocco Consultancy (ABN 14 067 257 390)
      PO Box 12544
      A'Beckett Street, Melbourne, 8006
      Victoria, Australia
      admin@brolgapublishing.com.au

Be Published

Publish through a successful publisher.
Brolga Publishing is represented through:
• **National** book trade distribution, including sales,
marketing & distribution through **Macmillan Australia.**
• **International** book trade distribution to
    • The United Kingdom
    • North America
    • Sales representation in South East Asia
• **Worldwide e-Book distribution**

For details and inquiries, contact:
Brolga Publishing Pty Ltd
PO Box 12544
A'Beckett St VIC 8006

Phone: 0414 608 494
markzocchi@brolgapublishing.com.au
ABN: 46 063 962 443
(Email for a catalogue request)